ALONE

Book 4
of
'The Band'

Also in this series:

Book 1 Alison

Book 2 'king Rock

Book 3 New Direction

First published on Kindle 2024
Published in paperback 2025
Revision 1

Cliff Bond asserts the moral right
to be identified as the author of this work

TABLE OF CONTENTS

CHAPTER 1

Alone

Alison's Story

Could it be that long? It seemed as if the desk calendar was forcing her to acknowledge the date.

Eighteen months that were the most distressing of her life.

At fifty-three she felt young and looked, so everyone said, in her late thirties. Content, happily married, she and Chris had made love in this very room, she protesting that it was silly and taking the pleasure for granted.

It was silly and fun and friendly and loving then two months later he had died.

Had died; it all came flooding back, washing away relentlessly the belief that she was over it. Over her suicidal worst perhaps, over the near clinical depression where she was alone in a deep dark pit that almost engulfed her; a pit escaped through the loving effort of family and friends.

The bitterness, the sense of unfairness and the loss of purpose remained. His last letter had helped and hindered her recovery. Its message of love and pragmatic encouragement to move on had uplifted her and accentuated her loss.

Her crazy venture back into music had lasted a few months, its distractions enabling a suspension of common sense and activities that made the memory humiliating.

How could she have committed to a relationship with Tony of all people? She was flattered by his interest just as she had been by his pursuit of her younger self but his objective was unchanged, his aim the vicarious thrill of relieving her of her 'nice girl' reputation.

She dropped her head into her arms folded on the desk and began to cry; silently at first, then as the emotions released, noisily and helplessly; sobs that were lost in an empty house where there was no one to hear or care.

The good time could not return any more than youth could return.

Was it such a good time she asked herself. It was hard work mitigated by excitement hope and love but there had been ugly events that had upset and shocked her before youthful resilience carried her forward and the incident became a forgotten part of yesterday.

As a band they had been fortunate to sign with Mr Morris.

Dave's father had spoken to a fellow lawyer with some knowledge of the business who had recommended him. He had acted on their behalf and obtained a deal that was the best any beginners could expect.

Maurice Morris was hard but honest by the standards of his business. His 'honesty' had provided a reasonable share of their earnings, had promoted them and given them tough but rewarding engagements.

The hardness had been exhibited when the band broke up.

She had told him of her wish to form a new band; he had listened, stared at her and walked around his desk while she shrank into the chair afraid that her future was disappearing.

'A new band? A new start is that what you want?'

'She nodded.'

'I look after my artists you realise??'

'Yes Mr Morris.'

'Synergy is tired and unfashionable and its music is no longer saleable. There will be no more recordings and no promotion but

the name is still known and I could place them on a club circuit.'
'I will be honest with you; you were fortunate to achieve your small successes and now you are telling me you want a second chance.'
'I hoped...I need to try.'
'A new start? Touring with a new band? You have a band?'
'I think so.'
'Is Terrance on board?'
'He is finishing Synergy's contract but...yes, and I think Terry.'
'I'll be in touch.'
I was dismissed; I rose to leave.
'Do you have a name.'
I had tried to think of a good name. 'Cat's Whiskers'?
'Hmm. Is it available?'
'I don't know.'
'Find out!!'

Mr Morris could also be unexpectedly kind, warning her when she was a naïve star-struck teenager that she would encounter people who would try to use her.
'Understand this luv, charm and kindness are not always good friends. There are people who will flatter you, rubbish your boyfriend and promise you what you think you want.' He had backed off a little. 'It's your life darlin, you make your own way but' he paused for emphasis 'it does no harm to know that there are unscrupulous people out there. Let's be straight luv, people who would prostitute you if it made money for them.'
He had smiled his humourless smile. 'Tell me to mind my business. I tell you because you are a good girl and your boyfriend does not have the wisdom to protect you.'
Red with embarrassment she had recovered sufficiently to ask what she should do.
He screwed his mouth sideways and thought for a second. 'Trust no-one and most important' he looked me in the eye, 'never be afraid to run away.'
She had listened, nodded and remembered his advice.

His advice was only words until linked events had demonstrated their truth.

The first happened at the beginning of Synergy's final tour.

I was relaxing in the lounge of our guest house when a pretty girl of my age came in. I looked up and smiled and she smiled back. Our exchanged hellos began a conversation and we were soon chatting amiably.

I didn't meet many girls of my age and opened up to her more than I normally would. I suppose friendliness invites intimacy and she told me she was moving from modelling for camera clubs in her home town to what she hoped was a big break in a major magazine. I didn't know much about modelling (nothing at all) and as she told me of her situation I could see parallels with my own career but in a different direction.

She had left school at sixteen and taken a hotel management course.

On her first assignment working as a receptionist, she had caught the eye of a professional photographer who asked if she would sit for him.

Modest studio sessions produced publicity photos and these generated requests from camera clubs and individuals which provided a little extra money. When asked to do bikini shots, there had been objections from her boyfriend but an assurance that her activities were no threat to the relationship was accepted.

The photographer who had now added her to his portfolio of models eased her from bikini to topless and semi-nudes until she was making enough to turn professional.

Naïve me began to feel slightly uncomfortable when I realised that she did nudes.

I was shy about nudity, had already learned that few girls need to encourage interest.

My new friend was called Anne; she was easy to talk with and when I told her about our band she was interested saying or claiming that she had heard of us.

The boys had been setting up the equipment for our evening gig; I heard the car return and when they came into the lounge I introduced them.

Chris was instantly smitten, was charming and when joined by Sol the two took over the conversation, spoiling my new friendship and my afternoon. Irritation became annoyance when on their parting both kissed her, Sol embracing her as if she was a girlfriend.

'What a lovely girl,' Chris said afterwards, 'I told her to be careful because there are people who pretend interest and promise everything but are clever manipulators.

I was cross because they had spoiled my afternoon and said 'I'm looking at one!'

It was a couple of years later that a second event emphasised the value of Mr Morris' advice.

Tony produced what he would have called a glamour magazine though it was vile, not glamorous at all. There on the page was my transient friend, over made-up and scarcely recognisable as the pretty girl we had met.

I recoiled after a glance at what should have been an intimate scene, my retreat followed by an offensive suggestion.

Tony's remark was typical but even he never resorted to the subtle bullying that led my passing friend to the activity shown on the page.

Making love is personal; it is thrilling but also about love and caring.

Exploitation makes it ugly and as my horrible husband pointed out, seen dispassionately, the actual act is either ridiculous or comical.

She felt alone; she was alone, everyone was alone.

On their honeymoon, leaning on the rail of the night ferry as it left the harbour, comfortable and blissfully happy she had expressed a wish to take in the scene, to enjoy the moment.

Chris had remarked that 'Moments are momentary. I wonder' he added 'how we humans cope with continuous change, never having a "now". I suppose change is life, it powers the universe.' 'Sorry darling, God enables us to cope.'
A cuddle had warmed her and brought her back to a contented present; the incident was forgotten.

With his death the comfort of continuity had gone and now the hope of renewal had gone with it. Nice reliable Andy, the subject of guilt for a past unkindness, when let back into her life was not the Andy she remembered.
He was still kind, but the 'nice' boy was now a middle-aged man; stolid, unwilling to have fun, wanting to be with her but only in safe boring situations. He was possessive in a negative way and at a friend's birthday party had been grumpy, had no wish to dance and scowled when she did.
Irritated by his childish behaviour she had asked the band if she could do a song. She had performed like the professional singer she was, surprised the band, enjoyed the applause and annoyed Andy further.

When she and Chris were young and intensely in love, each had been anxious about the other and both were forced to deal with possessiveness. They had recognised and discussed the problem; had learned how to trust and to give the other space. It was difficult in a situation where praise, admiration and hidden agendas were abundant. They had invented the sacred 'Precious Promise' and trust had grown.

The crisis had come early in her friendship with Andy. She had been ambivalent about sex (doubly so after her recent humiliation) unsure of her commitment and uncertain about his intentions.
It was after a cinema visit; they had returned to his house and were sitting together, their talk desultory. A kiss followed by a hug and an innocent enquiry as to where the relationship was going had elicited a veiled comment about her reputation.

Aware of his sensitivity she had suppressed a denial recalling her happy marriage. The happy marriage he conceded, 'but it happened' she was reminded, 'after they had lived together, a pregnancy and other relationships.'

She wasn't having that; they had never 'lived together', were soul-mates in a stressful working situation, marriage was always intended. The conversation had become a little heated and her relationship with Gary, a brief but essential support, had been mentioned. 'And,' he had added, 'you once told me about the price you paid Bruce Kay to get into 'king Rock'.

It came to her suddenly that she had always been there in Andy's mind; the girl who had hurt him many years before had been a shadowy figure in his marriage, may even have contributed to its end.

Heather, his ex-wife had told her before they were married that 'Alison' from the youth club was still on his mind and she had contrived a story that made herself look cheap in the hope of breaking the link.

Instead, her fabrication had become the source of further hurt, diminishing the perfect girl who existed only in his mind.

He was in a purely cerebral way a stalker; harmless in that he would never intentionally hurt her or anyone else and would be mortified by the suggestion. Nonetheless, obsession was discernible in his inquisitive letters and in the phone calls that seemed to check on her activities.

It was normal in a youngster in love but with age should come wisdom and the ability to give space to others.

There was a chasm between the girl he imagined her to be and the person she was; she had already experienced mild pressure to be someone she never was, and disappointment when she failed to meet his expectations.

Their small flare up had lasted only a few minutes but she knew intuitively that the relationship was over and was wise enough to ease away from it gently.

'I'm sorry Andy,' she told him, 'I think it would be better not to continue this conversation or I will get cross.' She stood up to leave. 'I'll see you on Tuesday.' They kissed and she was gone.

Driving home, her mind worked overtime as fragments of half incidents grew into a pile of broken hopes.

For the second time since Chris' death she realised how often she used him as a sounding board when a problem arose. He would listen, think and throw back a question; her answer often helped towards her decision.

Presented with the problem of Andy she could imagine his response 'You seem to be ok dating but would you be happy living with him?'

She was comfortable with him but a moment of intimacy had provoked the half joking comment 'I guess a lot of men have told you that you have a great body.'

'No, I was married for thirty years.' Her reply was relaxed and matter of fact but there was an edge to his comment that made it offensive. The woman he was holding wasn't the seventeen-year-old innocent he had loved.

She asked and answered her own question; a continued friendship perhaps but anything more would be a mistake.

Any doubts that this was a spat were gone, the relationship was over.

Following their Tuesday date, a friendly lunch at a pub near to his work a week passed before they spoke again. She raised the subject of their relationship in the public space of a local cafe suggesting that it wasn't working too well. She felt that perhaps they should cool things for a while.

He had blanked, was shocked. 'We are friends,' she had repeated encouragingly 'but I am still unsettled and I need more time to sort myself out.'

There had been a phone call and a letter which disturbed her. She was determined not to be worried; Andy was essentially a kind and decent person but he was struggling with an obsession. There was a second letter and a distressing phone call. She had finally told him not to ring, to let it go.

When she had discussed the situation, her daughter had been worried. 'He could turn nasty mum; you mustn't be alone.'

In the end her mother had phoned him, had explained kindly that he was unintentionally causing upset that could spoil their friendship. 'Wait for a month then send an apology, she won't feel threatened.' He had understood, the calls had stopped and she hoped it was over.

Dave, still a close friend of her mother had been told of the problem and had visited her. 'If he phones, writes or visits I could threaten to rearrange his face.' He told her.
'Don't be silly. You wouldn't, would you?'
'I could phone and tell him to let it go for a while but it might make things worse. If things got bad I could give him a scare.'
'You are a treasure but there is no need.' he was told firmly.
The letter had come, passionate, anxious, accusing and affectionate but it was written to a girl who never existed.
She had replied with a gentle honesty, had appealed to the 'nice man' who had confused the girl she had been with the middle-aged woman she now was.
There was no-one in her life, her present was family, friends, her business and her church activities. Our close relationship is over but I hope our friendship remains. I blame myself for imagining that the older damaged person that I now am could replace the girl that I never was.
His reply was painful to read, an apology, he understood, hoped they might meet from time to time. The 'nice' boy appeared to have triumphed over the obsessive but she was alone again.

CHAPTER 2

Panic

Christmas came, its joy and happiness bypassing her once again, only the excitement of her grandchildren had been uplifting after the emptiness of the previous year.

It was a Monday in early January and Edie, her adored two-year-old grandchild had been dropped off by Lisa. It was a weekly event that was a duty and a pleasure.
She was collecting a box of building bricks when the house phone rang. A glance at the phone showed that it was her younger sister and depositing the box on the kitchen table she picked it up.
'Hi Rachel.'
'Alison, I'm so glad I've caught you.'
Her sister sounded worried and the worry communicated itself.
'What is it?'
'It's Mum,' the worry became anxiety 'she was taken into hospital.' Panic!
'What is it?' She picked up Edie and hugged her; the presence of the unconcerned child giving comfort.
'I don't know the whole story but there was a break-in at one of the ground floor flats and when she arrived home there was a police car outside and she wasn't allowed in. She was shaken up and felt ill so she went to her friend in the flat next door and her neighbour called an ambulance.'

'Where is she?'

'She's in the BRI, I'm there now, she's in intensive care, in the heart ward. She seems ok apart from pains but she's very unsettled...I mean they thought it might be a heart attack but they aren't sure. It's not like Chris, darling, it's not. She has chest pains but not severe and she seems ok.'

Anxiety gripped tightening her mentally and physically.

'I'll come straight down, now. Promise to stay with her, I must get Ann to look after Edie until Lisa gets home...no, I'll take her straight to the factory.'

'Yes, I'll stay, until you get here.' 'Alison...'

'What? What?'

'Don't rush, hurry but don't rush I couldn't cope if you had an accident.'

'No, of course not, I'll be with you as soon as I can.'

Fear was rising but with effort she stayed calm enough not to frighten her granddaughter.

'We must go and see mummy. Let's get our coats.'

She hurried o the door her actions automatic, phone, money an extra jumper, keys, a coat.

Damn, damn, her Polo was being serviced and she would need to use the old Vitara, their jack of all trades. Damn. Damn, no child seat. She bundled her grandchild into the car, 'Sit her for a minute darling, granny will get your seat.'

Where was the other child seat? Think, think.

It was in the barn.

She raced to fetch it, banging the worst of the dust off it as she returned to the car. She wove the straps through the fittings and settled her granddaughter into it.

'Is that comfy darling?'

'It smells.'

'I'll open a window.' She rushed to the driver's door, jumped in blessing the fact that she kept both keys on the same ring. She turned the key and the engine started; another blessing, it hadn't been used for several weeks. Engaging a gear she drove cautiously out of the gate and headed to the factory.

There, with the briefest of explanations that minimised the situation she deposited her grandchild and leaving Lisa trailing in a flurry of words dashed back to the car and hurried towards the junction of the M5.

Forty-five minutes later she parked in a convenient multi-story and walked rapidly to the hospital.

A word at reception, a lengthy walk down corridors, a lift up six floors, a further walk and there was Rachel waiting.

She ran the last few steps, pent up emotions releasing, and fell into the waiting arms. The sisters hugged one another.

She was led into the ward, fearful of what she would find, remembering the shell that had once been her husband.

Her mother was sitting up looking as she always did.

'Darling, it's good of you to come.'

'Oh mum, I've been... how are you feeling? You look ok, what happened.'

'I feel ok except for the pain, it isn't bad but it is uncomfortable. They are monitoring me to find the trouble.'

They were still talking when a doctor arrived on her rounds, looked at the notes, frowned and spoke to her mother. She checked the medication, nodded, turned and looked towards her.

'My daughter.'

The doctor turned back. 'Can you undo your nightie.'

Diane complied, pulling at the bow at the neck and undoing a button.

The doctor ran the stethoscope over her chest and back, listening carefully at each stop. Alison watched carefully, anxiously, distracted then uncomfortable, looked away.

'Good.' The doctor consulted the notes again and frowned before turning back.

'We are not sure what the problem is, it isn't typical of a heart attack; we will need to do more tests. I am trying to arrange for an MRI scan. I have spoken to a consultant and he has suggested what the problem may be but we need to check.

After a long conversation and a series of hugs, Alison reassured by the visit returned home. Tomorrow she would come back to her mother's neat new apartment and remain there until she was discharged.

She phoned the following morning and receiving no reply contacted her sister.

'I rang before I came to work. She was...what time is it...she's probably having her scan this morning, there was a cancellation and they put her on the list.'

'I'll come down at once. Are you staying at the apartment?'

'Yes, I wanted to be near in case I was needed.'

'I will do the same.'

She packed a bag, phoned Lisa and Vickie, locked the house and set off for the hospital.

Her mother was sitting up in bed looking relaxed, her glasses perched on her nose.

'Darling!' She put down the book she was reading.

'Mum.' She crossed the room kissed her, releasing all her tension with a second 'Oh mum' kissed her again and slumped onto a chair. She reached out and gripped her mother's hand.

'How are you?'

'I think I'm ok.'

'What is the matter, do you know.'

'Not for sure, they need to confirm, but I had a scan at 9.30 this morning and I asked the doctor when she did her rounds. She said they aren't sure but they think it is...I must get this right... Takotsubo Cardiomyopathy.'

'Oh mum! Is it...'

'It can be serious but treated promptly I will make a full recovery in a few months.'

'When you say full...'

'Yes, a full recovery probably with no damage. It isn't one of those situations where you survive but have problems or end up on long term medication.'

'That is good news.' Relief flowed, a warm silent giggle. 'A full

recovery in months' settled at the back of her mind. 'What is it?'
'They used to call it broken heart syndrome; if you get a shock
it actually affects your heart and if it is bad enough it causes
an enlargement that feels like a heart attack. With proper
treatment, rest and a course of tablets I will soon be back to
normal'.

Diane received a tearful hug and was told that her daughter
would collect some clothes and come and stay indefinitely. 'No
arguments, if I can't look after you, you will need to look after
me.'

'Thank-you darling, a week or so would be lovely but not too
long, I do have a life you know.'

CHAPTER 3

A Meeting

Alison's Story

It was one of those summer mornings in early May that make life seem worthwhile.

It was nearly two years since Chris left me; I was beginning to re-engage with life and small pleasures were becoming more frequent.

My return to music had lasted for only three months and I had then renewed my friendship with Andrew. At twenty he was a considerate and trustworthy companion and I had hoped that he would provide stability and friendship.

Both decisions proved to be flawed; how could anything replace youth and shared memories?

The church was bright with late spring sunshine and the floor and pews were patterned with colour from the stained glass in some of the south facing windows.

From the choir vestry I made my way to the back of the church where coffee was served. I was intercepted by Ruth who ran the social committee and reminded me that I was in charge of what was euphemistically called 'Support Lunches'.

These were provided at low cost and great effort primarily for two dozen pensioners most of them churchgoers who took the amenity for granted and often complained about content, quality and quantity of the food. Sometimes the complaints were justified and I would add some extras out of my own pocket.

I was only responsible for providing the lunch every third month but as organiser I often had to help in the kitchen.

I spotted V standing near the tower talking to a man who had recently joined the congregation. I approached, hovered and waiting for an introduction or a break in their conversation.

I waited. Vickie was in full flow, smiling and being charming.

'Can I have a quick word V.' I eased in during a momentary silence.

'Yes of course. What is it?' V was a little abrupt.

I explained about the food for the lunches. 'Yes, I know, I'll buy the ingredients when I'm next in Thornbury.' She waited for me to leave then frowned and reluctantly introduced me. 'Have you met Phillip?'

The name gave a small shock. 'No. How do you do Phillip?'

'I'm good.' He nodded.

'This is Alison.' V seemed to wish it wasn't, and the penny dropped. She was establishing a friendship and didn't want any competition.

'Hello Alison, I'm pleased to meet you.' He is formal but has an attractive smile.

'I'll come round tomorrow and we can discuss what we need then.' Vickie's statement dismissed me.

'Thank-you Vick.' I turn back to her friend. 'Bye Phillip, I expect I'll see you again.' I feel a small shock as I say the name.

'Yes, I expect so.'

He has kind eyes, is probably in his late fifties.

I was walking back through the village after our Tuesday meeting and decided to call in at the Village Café.

I had bought my latte, resisted a 'brownie' and seated myself at an empty table when I met Phillip Christopher Barnes for the second time.

He entered, recognised me and said 'Good morning, Alison isn't it?'

'Yes, I'm still Alison.' My mind leapt backwards to my first meeting with Chris when I had made the same facetious joke. I felt a slight blush colour me.

He was looking at me.

'Sorry, I was remembering something.'

'You don't need to apologise for remembering things.'

'No. It was…never mind. Do you, are you…' I was stuttering.

'Might I join you? I hoped your friend Victoria might be here, I know few people in the village.'

'Yes of course, can I get you a coffee?'

'Thank-you. Shall I get my own this time?'

He went to the counter to order and I sat wondering why I was being so silly.

I didn't want to admit the answer. He was nice looking, pleasant and seemed to be intelligent.

He returned and gave me a look that said 'OK?

I nodded, he sat down and a stilted conversation began.

With strangers the first few minutes are cautious, inconsequential generalities followed perhaps by a few details about ourselves. I was telling him about Chris and that I was coming to terms with the loss when Vickie arrived, saw us, gave me disapproving look, smiled at Phillip, said 'Hi Phil' and joined us.

It put an end to our conversation and Phillip turned his attention to her.

I discovered that he had already been asked to dinner and was expected again on Sunday. Gwyneth, a widow in her mid-sixties would not be coming this time but Clive's elderly parents would be joining them. Did he mind?

Conversations from the previous dinner were revisited and I was excluded.

It was clear that V was keen on Phillip, how keen I couldn't judge. There were no known incidents of unfaithfulness in her marriage; we had shared some naughty moments but they were fun not destructive.

Isolated by my exclusion from the conversation I wondered if it was her age; she had admitted that she envied my new found freedom. (Freedom?? Loneliness broken by moments of misery or happiness.) Perhaps she just wanted some reassurance that she was attractive? We all need that. Whatever the cause, my best friend was unsubtly excluding me from Phillip and I felt slightly miffed.

'Alison was telling me that you play in band together.' Phillip spoke and I was included again.

'Yes, we do,' V answered 'we've played together for years but only' she turned to me 'about a dozen gigs a year,'

'Yes, about that.'

'I'm impressed, my experience of girls in bands doesn't equate with...' he stumbled and for the first time revealed a hint of reticence, '...nice ladies like you.'

Vickie was straight in. 'Al was a bit of a wild child in her youth.'

Phillip raised his eyebrows 'She still is in a more elderly way.'

V will tease but she isn't bitchy; this was serious.

'You must tell me more Alison.' Phillip was half smiling.

'There isn't that much to tell if you mean the wildness.' I smiled back. 'How do you know so much about rock chicks?'

'I played in a semi-pro band for about fifteen years; we were a good cover band and occasionally we supported professional outfits' he raised his eyes 'the sort who had a couple of hits in the sixties and were still touring in the nineties.' 'Some of the girls we met were great, talented and friendly but a few were less appealing' he paused 'profoundly unpleasant is a better...' He seemed about to explain further then went silent.

'What did you play?'

'Covers and crowd pleasers. Oh, I see what you mean. I was a guitarist.'

'Alison was in 'king Rock, do you remember them?' Vickie cut in, damning me by association.

"king Rock? That's my era.' he looked at me with surprise 'You played with them? They were big, becoming very big. They were a wild band.'

'Not all of them. Chris my husband was a guitarist with the band, I was a backing singer who was allowed to play guitar sometimes.'

'Really?' He frowned then light dawned. 'Chris? Chris Phillips was your husband?' He smiled but the smile was uncertain. I am now an aging 'rock chick' associated with the rough amoral organisation that was 'king Rock.

'I am impressed, that isn't patronising, I really am impressed, they were big time.'

It was a kind thing to say but my reputation was blown. I was about to speak when V interrupted and the conversation returned to Sunday and lunch.

'I'd better go.' I stood up. 'Nice to meet you again Phillip, bye V.'

'Bye Al.' She frowns, wrinkles her nose. 'Bye, I'll see you.' She pats my arm like my best friend.

'Bye Alison.' Phillip raises his hand and smiles. He is rather nice.

I saw him sooner than expected.

Our egg packing business had moved to more convenient premises on the other side of the village. The lorry drivers had never liked backing from the lane into our narrow drive and we had made the decision to move to the smallest of the three industrial units on the new trading estate.

Lisa, my youngest after an expensive and educationally wasted period at university had followed it by 'travelling' and had then charmed her way into the Bristol offices of a large financial organisation. She had taken an unexpected liking for the office and accountancy, passed her examinations and astounded us by her *marriage* to a boyfriend that I had liked from our first meeting.

She then presented me with a grandchild after which she decided that money and more flexible employment was needed. Mum, being a soft touch had taken her on as a book-keeper explaining that the business was tiny and we all had help with the grading and packing. I did not expect her to stay for long and was confounded.

The new Lisa had proved reliable and happy working with Ellie from the village and the two Poles who recommended and were replaced by two others at regular intervals.

It took about eighteen months for Lisa to suggest that she should be groomed to take over from me. 'After all mum, you aren't getting any younger.'

My darling is charming but seldom tactful.

I had taken her on as assistant manager which enabled me to keep a watching brief and run my little empire working two and a half days a week.

It was a good decision; after Chris' death I had been unable to function effectively. Lisa had stepped into the role and had kept the business running efficiently for a year.

I was collecting eggs when Phillip arrived at the house.

'Victoria tells me that you sell free range eggs.' He spoke like a customer that I had never met.

'Yes, I still keep a few hens and the eggs are for friends and family.'

'Do you sell them?'

'I will sell them, how many do you want?'

'A half dozen will be fine. I don't use many since Mary and I parted.' He paused and I looked away. 'We got on well but our jobs made things difficult. She was a nurse working all sorts of shifts and I was away a lot. After the children went to University we drifted apart then she left.' He suddenly gave a big smile and looked young and attractive.

'Oh dear, sorry. Do I get a discount for telling my secrets?'

'No, I charge for listening. Would you like a cup of tea, perhaps we can finish our earlier conversation.'

I picked up the egg basket and headed for the kitchen; I was making huge assumptions about someone I scarcely knew; I was treating him like a friend.

We were comfortably ensconced in the kitchen the sun was

shining through the end windows and that summery feeling was returning.

I placed the china teapot and the matching cups and saucers on the table, discretely slid a milk jug from the back of the cupboard, filled it from a bottle and placed it next to the cups.

It was a contrast to my normal tea ceremony when the bag floated at the top of the mug until fished out with the handle of the spoon.

I sat on a stool on the opposite side of the table. 'Biscuit?'

'No. Thank-you.' He bit his lip. 'I'm here under false pretences, I was enjoying our chat this morning and when we were interrupted it felt as if something was unfinished. I am not sure if I called to continue our conversation or apologise for being side-tracked. I do need the eggs but could have gone to the shop.'

'I see.' I hoped I understood him. I too had felt the frustration of an unfinished conversation.

'I don't get too many visitors, friends pop in and I see the family regularly but you are welcome to get your eggs here.'

We began to chat and the talk was comfortable. No striving, no attempt to impress. He told me about his wife, their situation friendly but their lives fragmented. She had suggested that they should separate, that the marriage was little more than companionship anyway and they could stay friends.

He straightened up. 'I hadn't realised how much I took for granted and it upset me badly. It was later I discovered that there was a relationship with a surgeon. He had gained an appointment in Scotland and wanted her to join him.'

The comfortable feeling began to evaporate. A stranger was telling me details of his life.

'Damn!' It was as if he had woken up. 'I am sorry, I normally keep things to myself.' He frowned. 'You are too easy to talk to.'

'When you are with a band you meet all sorts of people, I guess conversing becomes a life skill.' I relaxed again. 'If you become annoying, I am old enough to tell you to shut up.'

'Ok. In future I promise to stick to village gossip and pop music from the eighties.'

'I don't mind what you talk about but perhaps village gossip would be wiser. Can I balance the confessions by putting you straight on my time with 'kR.'

'I would be interested.'

'I met all sorts of people when I was part of that band; most were ok but there is always a dodgy element amongst the hangers on; you know, dealers and people with something to sell.

Chris was part of the band and when I joined we looked after each other.

It wasn't easy to stay grounded because it was a tough gig. Chris was under a lot of pressure and could get very edgy but mostly he was tolerant and easy going. I expect you would have liked him.'

'Vickie thought he was wonderful and couldn't do enough for him.' (One all!)

I stood up to refill the teapot and as I passed I patted his shoulder. 'Talk about anything, I hear enough gossip from the village ladies.'

'Thanks, I'm not sure what's the matter with me today, talking too much followed by teenage shyness isn't the normal me.'

I switched the kettle on and as it began to boil the door opened and Vickie entered.

'Hi Al, I just wanted.... Oh! Hello Phil.' V was not pleased.

'I came for some eggs and Alison kindly invited me in for a cup of tea.'

'Yes, I'm sure she did.' I felt her response as a small blow in the back. 'Well, if you've company, I won't stay.'

'Don't be silly V, you aren't interrupting anything.' I suppose.

V joined us but the conversation was slow and stilted and Phillip after a suitable period said that he needed to get back. He thanked me for the tea and headed for the door. 'I'll see you on Sunday.'

'Yes.' We spoke together.

'Oh, how much for the eggs?'

I didn't know. 'The first six are free after that they are the same

as the village shop.'
'Fine.'

After he had shut the door V looked up at me.
'So?'
'Not 'So', he came for eggs and I can see why you like him.'
'Me? I'm happily married.' She frowned 'Oh alright cow, he is rather nice isn't he?'
'Yes, but I'm not sure why I took to him.'
'Aren't you?'
'No. He's quiet and seems straightforward but I'm not looking for a man and even if I was there's nothing special about Phillip.'
'Oh no, of course not.' Heavily sarcastic,
'What do you mean?'
'Well, it may be superficial but in some ways he reminds me of Chris.'

We met again in church on Sunday. I decided to keep contact to a minimum because I didn't want him or Vickie to think I was keen. 'Good morning Phillip.'
'Hello Alison.' He glanced around. 'Can I have a word? I'd like to ask...'
I interrupted him. 'I'm sorry Phillip, I'm in a rush this morning.' Too abrupt. I softened and added over my shoulder as I passed him. 'I may see you in the café. Sorry, must rush.'
'Yes.'
I left the church and hurried home kicking myself (if you can kick yourself when walking). Why was I so rude? Unless I went down to the tennis club I had no activities until dinner at Sarah's in the evening.
I suppose I was avoiding entering into any kind of friendship before I knew a little more about him.

Perhaps I did make a little effort on Tuesday. The first words of my darling daughter when I called into the factory were. 'Morning Mum.' followed by 'You are looking very smart, are you meeting someone?'

'Don't be silly.'

He didn't go to the café. Of course not, he was the injured party in a broken marriage; now I had publicly snubbed him.

These things happen and he was only an acquaintance but I was sorry if I had caused upset.

Perhaps I should contact him and apologise but didn't know where he lived or his phone number. V would know; I would tell her I had been a little abrupt and I didn't want him to think I was rude.

I waited until the evening before calling at their house. Clive met me with 'Hello Al, have you come to see me?' followed by a kiss on the cheek.

'Vickie!' he called up the stairs 'It's Al for you.'

'Coming down.'

Fifteen minutes had passed and I was into a second sherry before I mentioned the reason for my visit.

'On Sunday, I had a long chat with Ruth about this month's lunches and as I was leaving Phillip spoke to me. I was in a hurry and afterwards I felt I might have been a little abrupt....'

'It was all round the church after you left. Margaret told me you choked him off and everyone thought you were very rude. He happened to be coming to lunch that day...'

'Happened??' Clive's voice from the next room 'He seems to come every bloody week.'

Vickie raised her eyes shrugged and continued 'He and Clive get on very well don't you?'

'Just as well!'

'He was subdued over lunch and I wondered if it was because you had upset him. I said that you could be abrupt with people (I'm not!) and that he shouldn't worry about it. I explained that you had a difficult time when Chris died. We all thought it was much too soon for you to join a band and that you were running away from your grief so it was understandable that you fell into a bad relationship.'

'What!'

'We didn't actually say that.' Clive from the next room.

'No, of course not, just that you are cautious with strangers.'

I suppose a best friend might think that a knife in the back is a cure for heartburn.

'I'd like to apologise to him, do you have his phone number?'

'No, I don't think....'

'Yes we do,' Clive from the next room, 'I've got it on my phone, I'll text it to you. He lives five doors down on our left, number 5, it's the last one in the new terrace.'

'Thanks Clive darling.' No sex for you tonight. I smile at my own thought.

'What are you laughing at?'

'Nothing. You were going to tell me about Erin's new job.'

I phoned the next day suffering from nerves generated by a scenario that was only in my head. I had handled far more difficult situations but when he answered I began with a stutter and followed it with a rush of words which included an apology for being abrupt.'

'That's ok, you said you were in a hurry.'

'I was afraid I might have sounded rude; it wasn't intended.'

There was a pause.

'I was surprised. You seemed so relaxed when we met that I assumed that was how you always were.'

'I am most of the time, you will find out if we get to know each other better.' That was better, positive but meaningless.

'I hope so.'

'I was in the Café on Tuesday but I didn't see you there.'

'I had an appointment in Thornbury; I didn't have a chance to tell you on Sunday. I will probably be there tomorrow, around eleven if you are passing.'

'I will call in if my meeting has finished.'

Damn! I'll have to cancel the hairdresser.

'See you then.'

'Bye.'

I felt ridiculously pleased; a potential friendship was back on track.

CHAPTER 4

A New Friend

Vickie's Story.

Phil Barnes is new to our village but he has already caused a stir amongst some of the unmarried ladies.

I was on welcoming duty in church when I noticed that he was alone so I took him under my wing. He seemed to be civilised and made no effort to impress.

He told me that he worked in Thornbury most of the week and from home the rest of the time. 'Working from home can be isolating' he told me 'but if I feel lonely sometimes I go to the village café for a break.'

I use the café after Pilates to top up their caffeine level and because of our Sunday conversation I felt I should go in case Phil was on his own.

I was settled with a latte when he arrived. He looked at me, offered a nervous smile, told me that he knew few people in the village and asked if he could join me.

I said 'Of course you can' and 'I'm pleased you remembered our conversation.'

He made a flattering remark about 'Kind ladies'.

Sometimes you meet a man and you wonder why any women would be interested, but Phillip was intelligent and treated me as a person without any suggestion that he was checking my availability. I felt a slight regret that I was unavailable.

Our conversation was probably mundane but it seemed interesting and it established a friendship. My first impressions were comfortable, straightforward and safe to be with so I asked him to Sunday lunch. Clive questioned my motives because we tended to ask widows or the elderly but he took to Phil straight away and over the next few weeks they became friends.

The friendship gave me a small problem with Alison. Despite her denials some men are instantly attracted and I wanted to establish my friendship with Phil before he met her.

He came to lunch a second time on the following Sunday and we arranged to meet in the café on Tuesday. I was a little cross when I entered the café to find that A had already commandeered him and was more annoyed when I visited that afternoon to find him sitting comfortably in her kitchen. I decided that I needed to push myself forward a little because I didn't want Alison taking over my friendship.

I didn't push too hard but I did invite him to join me for my weekly shop in Thornbury. We met for coffee and a sandwich then went on to Tesco where we each ran through our shopping lists.

The meeting was repeated within the limits of discretion demanded by the village and on our third outing I felt I could dress attractively; nothing outrageous, just a hit of cleavage and my smart work trousers.

It was a nice day and we went for a walk by the river before shopping. The river has a large embankment to prevent flooding and as it was low tide we were able to walk on the river side of the embankment.

When we climbed up the bank at the end of the path-way he took my hand to help and we walked for a short distance holding hands. He was obviously enjoying it and behaved as if it was fun. When he released my hand I asked if he was embarrassed.

'Not at all.' We turned to walk back and after a moment he slipped an arm around my waist.

'Is this ok? I've avoided being too friendly because I respect marriage and I try to behave circumspectly but I'm just a normal man. I hope you forgive me.'

'I can forgive you for being a little naughty.'

'Thanks.' He reached for my hand and we walked back to the car.

In the car he thanked me again, said he had enjoyed our walk, looked into my eyes and warned me not to look so good next time. It led to a friendly kiss which led to a friendlier cuddle.

I was thinking this is nice when he said 'You can slap me or tell me off' and slid a hand into my top. 'Very nice lovely V' he said.

He is assured but gentle and I might have allowed further exploration but after a breast had been appreciated, he pulled himself together, looked anxious and said 'Sorry Victoria, are we still friends?'

'Yes.' I very gently tapped his face. 'If we weren't you would have had a proper slap.'

I was true; I should have been offended but in fact I enjoyed the interest.

On the drive back I mentioned music and asked if he would like to play a session with me and with Alison. He told me that he hadn't played for 30 years and probably wouldn't know our songs.

I was sure that he would know some of our music and said so.

He thought about it and said 'Ok, if you are serious. I still have my guitar and an old bass but I don't have a bass amplifier.'

'Al will find something, Chris had a big rig he used when he played bass and I think he had a practice amp.'

'I wasn't much of a bass player,' he said 'I can play a melodic support line but I would need a lot of practice if I'm going to try the 'kR stuff.'

'Don't worry I have a file of our songs, I could bring them to your house and we could play some music together at the weekend. If it works well I will arrange something with Al.'

CHAPTER 5

Getting to know Phillip

Alisons Story

Our meeting in the café was nothing special, just two people chatting over a cup of coffee but it was the beginning of a new friendship.

I could tell from his looks and his conversation that he was sizing me up, assessing my character.

Was I honest or devious seemed the main thrust of his investigation; it wasn't a problem because I am honest and straight-forward. Sometimes I am cautious, not entirely candid but seldom devious and never unkind.

There was a plus side; his assessment of my character suggested that physically I had already passed the test.

Well Mr Barnes, if we are to become friends you need my seal of approval and that will only happen if wysiwyg.

We didn't meet again until the following Sunday; I was on coffee duty and was able to speak briefly to him after the service. V saved him from feeling neglected for the next twenty-five minutes and returned their empty cups just as I finished the washing up. She then asked me to lunch and we walked back from church together.

I enjoyed lunch, enjoyed Clive's "Hi favourite girl, looking lovely as always" and stifled a giggle when he said "What's happened Vick, has Phil broken a leg?"

I hope she isn't getting too interested, I don't want to fall out with my best friend. I think she is just being competitive and to tell the truth I am rather enjoying it.

Life isn't all about social engagements. My weekly meeting with Lisa at the factory had raised the thorny subject of expansion and the purchase of an additional egg grading machine.

It was a standard business problem; an opportunity for new business, insufficient capacity to handle it and the need for capital investment on new machinery which would work at half capacity and barely pay for itself.

I would need to put up our field as a guarantee against a loan, and if things went wrong the field would go.

In business I was more suspicious of motives than in normal life; I had had offers for the field which had development potential and if it became part of a loan guarantee who was to say what devious activities might result.

Maybe I was over suspicious but as farmland rented to Geoff its value was low, as development land it was worth a great deal.

The loan is used to buy equipment the initial returns are low, a developer mentions it to his bank official friend over a round of golf; the bank panics and calls in the loan when I can't repay; the field is forfeit and sold at farming prices.

Maybe not, but it does happen.

Lisa was keen to expand but it was my money that was at risk.

An alternative solution seemed to be to take out a mortgage or release equity from the house. If things went wrong business would survive but I would need to downsize.

There was another possibility; the videos of 'kR on tour and in concert had been re-transmitted and generated a renewal of interest in the band. It wasn't a rebirth, only three of the band were still alive but it had made a difference to the cheque that covered airplay and use of material. I had received a call asking if I was interested in auctioning Chris' 335 which had appeared on the video.

I said 'No' then reluctantly 'I'll think about it'. It was a really nice Gibbo that would cost nearly £4k new but with provenance?? I was reluctant but the suggested auction price was significantly greater. We decided that the best bet would be to release equity on the tiny cottage that had come with the house.

Sad because it was simple, plain and solid like its original tenant. It had cost us a fortune to renovate but if the promised contract failed to materialise I could stand the loss.

Returning from the meeting I swept into the kitchen with a loud 'Sorry I'm late' to find Mum deep in conversation with Phil.

He greeted me, smiled, finished his tea, said 'A pleasure to meet you Diane', kissed in the region of her cheek said 'Must rush sorry to miss you Alison, Bye.' and left.

I should have guessed that Mum would pick up the vibes and charm him.

'Goodness, he is nice isn't he?'

'Is he?'

'Oh-ho! Are you that keen?'

'Don't be silly, I only met him a month ago, I hardly know him.'

'Nonsense, the look on your face when you came in told me that you like him and if you want to know him better you had better push yourself.'

'I will not!'

'Every eligible woman between fifty and seventy-five will be interested. He mentioned Victoria and from the way he spoke he likes her.'

'She's happily, well mostly happily married. Don't give me that look, I'm not seventeen.'

'He's nervous about you, he was told you had a wild youth. I told him that it wasn't true, you were always a good girl, a very good girl considering that sometimes you found yourself in difficult circumstances.'

'You didn't!! Really, I can manage my own affairs.'

Mum is a kind person but she looked sideways and muttered 'Tony' in a singsong way.

'And you.' I said blushing.

'I meant that if you like him find out if you can tolerate the annoying things then ease into his life. After that you can take it slowly. I know these days the media encourages us to believe that relationships start with sex and if it's satisfactory you decide whether to make it permanent. It's nonsense, once men are getting their pleasure why should they commit to a supportive relationship, even nice men, and to be honest darling even nice men tend to prefer girls who...'

'Who what?'

'Who are reliable and trustworthy. It's isn't about 'you know', I mean if you are married for forty years you've probably ....' she hesitated 'been more active than someone who is...' she hesitated again 'available but if you are a nice person men seem to appreciate it.'

'Sorry mum, I do know what you mean but it doesn't always work, I've been condemned by association several times.'

'Have you? I know mums are prejudiced but to me you are obviously a good person. I was listening to a so-called discussion program on the TV the other day' she continued before I could speak 'and one sensible woman broke ranks and told the truth.'

"Ninety nine per-cent of the time you spend with a man is about talking, shopping if you are lucky and being with friends and family, ordinary things. Twenty minutes of pleasure is no compensation if he is self-centred, narcissistic, un-co-operative and unreliable the rest of the time."

'There was the usual chiming of "ninety minutes of pleasure! why not with a woman? I suggest you change your man ho ho!" from the others. So desperate to maintain their falsehoods; one suffers from prolonged bouts of depression poor soul, and another is over sixty and was never much of a catch.'

I'd never known mum to be so explicit.

'You are speaking from experience I assume.'

'Yes. No, don't be rude, Granny knows best.' She broke into giggles and set me off.

I had followed her advice from childhood except for my teenage rebellion period. Even then I had cherry picked, ignoring the things that didn't suit and reluctantly going along with the advice that made sense.

Despite a natural interest and strong feelings I had never treated sex as a throwaway thrill, had always been cautious, seeking love, confidence then fun and thrills.

Sorting myself out and giving my life direction was my current priority and I didn't want the restrictions imposed by trying to keep a man happy. If the right one came along I wouldn't run away but I don't think it is likely.

'I have some tickets for a play in Bath.' mum was continuing, 'Malcom was given them at work, he can't go but I wondered if you would like to take Phil'.

Phil? Mum has only just met him and they are Phil and Diana. I was distracted by Malcom and his tickets, who was he? Mum is now in her seventies and since Dads death has attracted several men-friends; I didn't like one of them but Colin is very nice. Malcom was new.

'Who is Malcom.'

'Just a friend,' mum shook her head, 'what about the tickets.'

'Yes, thank-you. Who is Malcom?'

'A friend, he's a little younger than me, a widower. He still works part time.'

'How much younger?'

'Really dear you are getting worse, he is about seven years younger.'

'What does Colin think?' Mum fixed me with her 'behave' look.

'Colin has had to go to Canada. His ex-wife is living there with her daughter and she is very ill. They parted on fairly good terms and he has gone out to help. Is that enough information?'

'As long as you don't spoil your friendship with Colin; honestly Mum, even at that age there can be jealousy especially if you are...'

'I am what?'

My turn to blush. 'Well…' I became defensive 'too friendly.'

Mum fixes me with a disapproving gaze and I turn fourteen.

'You mean if we are intimate. Darling, things are different when you are past seventy.'

'No! I meant…whatever. Oh don't take me seriously then. Colin is nice and you wouldn't want to spoil your friendship.'

'I think we'll leave this conversation. So, do you want the tickets?'

'Yes.'

'I'll post them unless I see you.'

'Thankyou.'

I love mum, forget she has a life. Even so, surely she doesn't do things at her age. From what she has said her new friend Malcom is only five years older than Tony who was energetic to say the least.

The memory makes me squirm then blush and Mum shakes her head. She looked youthful even into her sixties and though she no longer looks young she is well preserved and is attractive in an older way.

Clive said a few years ago that he couldn't believe she was in her sixties; the auburn hair was greying in places and was tinted to give a sort of reddish hi-lites. Chris had put an arm around her and said 'Looking great Di treasure, I may have to entice you into the orchard.'

Mum had smacked his arm but her smile implied that she wouldn't mind.

Oh damn damn damn! If only I could go back, I wouldn't mind!

It was later that evening that I wondered how Phil managed to get so much time off.

CHAPTER 6

A Dinner Party

(Alison's Story)

Clive sounded apologetic when he rang and asked if I would like to come to dinner. The reason soon became clear; Iris from the choir had cancelled at the last minute; would I do him a favour, make up the numbers and make his evening. 'Phil Barnes is coming, is that OK?'

It certainly was. 'I would love to join you Clive darling.'

C and V are very kind and often invite me to dinner but if Phil was coming, I suspected that I was V's last choice.

I looked forward to the evening.

The dinner was excellent and afterwards we settled down in the lounge, V manoeuvring to sit on the settee next to Phil.

I had avoided the wine but now found myself nursing a large brandy.

The conversation, which had been about the state of the choir drifted around to my life as a singer. It didn't actually drift, V eased it into the conversation. She likes being friends with an ex-minor (very) celebrity and despite my effort to correct her, she still imagines that I have colourful if not wicked past.

'We know you were in several rock bands darling; why don't you tell us the whole story I'm sure Phil would be interested.'

'I suppose I could give Phil a brief synopsis of my career if he doesn't mind.' I looked at him and he shook his head. 'It's mostly mundane and it isn't very exciting.'

'I would be interested,' Phil said, 'if you are happy to talk about it.'

'Oh she won't mind,' V grinned at me, 'most of it came out in a biography and she'll keep quiet about the sordid bits.'

'After a comment like that, Phillip could suffer the embarrassment of watching two respectable middle-aged women wrestling on the floor.' I flashed my eyes.

Clive pursed his lips. 'Wow, seconds out.'

'I'll start by saying that most of a performer's life is the same as everyone else. Some of the venues and occasionally the circumstances were shabby but I was given the moral guidance that helped me to avoid most of the pitfalls.'

'I won't pretend it was always easy; there were stressful situations and sometimes I had to avoid' I looked at Phillip and blushed slightly 'situations that might have compromised my marriage.'

'A very happy marriage' I added looking at V 'and my few failings were minor! So there!'

'Round 2' announced Clive.

'Shut up Clive.' I smiled at him. 'Sorry Phil, do you really want to hear?'

He frowned. 'In the last few weeks I have formed a positive impression of Alison Phillips.' He paused. 'Are you prepared to spoil my illusions?'

'If they are illusions there is nothing to spoil.'

'Spoil away.'

'Ok, but stop me when I become a bore.'

'I met Chris when I was still at school, fell in love and decided he was everything I wanted. It sounds pathetic but it is absolutely true.'

'I joined his band after taking A-levels; I was just eighteen, in love, playing music regularly in folk clubs and life was just heavenly. Looking back, I get a sense of total happiness and endless sunshine.'

'We played a big festival in Wales and were spotted by an agent who thought we had potential; after a lot of heart searching, we turned professional.'

'I expected life to be the same as before but more glamorous.

It wasn't. We had three months living in squalid conditions with scarcely enough money for food and none for clothes and luxuries. Life was miserable; Chris had one decent pair of shoes and his normal pair had holes in the sole with rubber patches stuck over them.

To make it worse we had to practice our music endlessly until we got it absolutely perfect and I began to hate every song.'

'After a while we started to play illicit gigs in pubs and clubs which gave us some money but the whole thing was an awful shock for a schoolgirl and some of the venues were scary. I was sitting at the bar in one of the clubs while the boys were setting up and a man asked me if I was available, he assumed I was a prostitute.' 'Are you sure you want to hear?'

Phil nodded and smiled his understanding smile.

'When the management considered we were good enough we started touring which was tiring but we began to earn some steady money, enough to feed and clothe us and buy better equipment.

After that we did a summer season in a theatre on the east coast; it was rather shabby but it was exciting, there was no travelling; and life became wonderful again. We released a record that squeezed into the charts and began to make some extra money.'

'I was in love and' I looked at Phil 'silly me became pregnant. Chris didn't mind, he wanted to get married but I wanted my freedom and took it for granted that mum would look after the baby. I didn't understand anything.'

'Six months later Dave, who was our closest friend, left the band and Sue joined. She and I got on well and it was wonderful to have girlfriend when we were touring but letting her join was a mistake.'

I stopped for a moment recalling the highs and the lows.

'Emotionally I was all over the place, sometimes totally happy at others behaving like a prima donna; I started seeing Chris' faults rather than his support and I took his love for granted. Then Sue became pregnant and in a moment of temper I spoiled my life.'

'You are getting upset Al darling. I'm sorry I got you started, don't say any more.' V patted my arm.

'I am alright V. I cannot believe that after thirty-five years it still gets to me. I might as well finish.' I took a deep breath. 'Chris married Sue.'

I saw Phil's look of surprise. Was it compassion? Oh, the darling, he has guessed how I feel.

I wondered if I could make a potentially harmful admission and stupidly decided that I could.

'After his marriage I had a fling with someone who wanted to manage me.' I immediately wished I had said nothing, blushed slightly and hurried on.

'The band broke up and I started my own; it was a good band but it only lasted for a year because I was the singer, guitarist and manager and the stress was too much for me. I was still angry with Chris but I began to understand the problems he had trying to perform and manage the band.'

I went quiet, there was silence.

'Then Sue was killed in an accident, I felt awful because...' I felt that same rush of shame 'because sometimes I had wished she was dead. Not really but....'

The room was silent.

I took a deep breath and continued.

'Mum brought Chris and I together, our friendship revived, the magic was coming back and then 'kR happened.'

'KR?' Phil spoke.

'king Rock, I told you in the cafe; Chris was asked to replace one of the guitarists. A few months later I was brought in as a backing singer and life became wonderful again. When 'kR collapsed we restarted Synergy and it ran for several years.'

I sat back. 'That is my early life in a nutshell; it was mostly good but I had a year that wore me out physically and emotionally.'

'That was the drugs darling.'

'Shut up V, I never indulged, except perhaps just a puff on someone else's ciggie.'

'Isn't 'Just a puff' what everyone says?' V giggled.

'Stop it V!' I was getting irritated 'A few times in a career and believe me, at different times all sorts of things were available. I didn't indulge unlike your idol Phillips.'

Phil looked up sharply.

'V was a very big admirer of my husband weren't you darling?' I turned to Phil. 'She would do anything for him.'

'We were friends, like you and Clive.'

V's look said, "That's enough!".

'Al is my dream-girl.' said Clive.

'The only time we lived the high life was with 'kR and it was so busy that our main priority was sleeping to avoid exhaustion. Your hero,' I turned to V, 'was on uppers for three months, not counting the pot and the drinking.'

'Alison! That's so disloyal.'

'It's true! He didn't smoke so a puff on the weed was a release not a habit and he drank to keep in with the boys.'

'I meant it was disloyal to say about him taking drugs.'

'Well, he did! He had to take bennys to keep going. When we finished the tour and the pressure came off he made a big effort and stopped using them. You wouldn't have admired Mr Grumpy if you had seen him when he was Mr Snappy Ratty.'

'How about you Alison, how did you cope with the situation?' Phil spoke.

'Moderation I suppose. I did drink a little, but you had to be careful because there were idiots around who might spike your drink. Mine was spiked once and...'

'What?'

'I don't know but Dave said that I went silly.'

'What happened?'

'I don't remember anything happening.'

'What did Dave say?'

'He probably made it up.' There was a silence that held a question. 'He said I became aggressive and started to take my clothes off but luckily he was there to stop me.'

For the second time I wished I had said nothing.

'That sounds like Alison the entertainer.'

'No, it's totally unlike me. I wouldn't do that even if I was stoned.'

'If you can't remember, how do you know?'

'I know because a band is like a village, everyone knows everything. If I had done anything embarrassing Chris would have known next day; he was edgy at the time and would have given me hell. He never said anything and nor did anyone else so it must have been very modest.'

Vickie looked at me with an expression that said, 'I understand darling, you don't want to say too much in front of Phillip.' The evening was becoming competitive.

'I don't suppose Phillip is at all interested in my small embarrassments. I can recall a time when Sextet did their tour and a certain person behaved as if she was a teenager.'

Vickie went red. 'We all enjoyed ourselves, I don't think any of us behaved badly.'

'No. It must be my memory playing up again.'

I turned to Phil. 'I always tried to behave in a practical and sensible way; running my own band was hard work and my satisfaction came from the performance. I could never do the free and easy lifestyle and on tour if you met someone interesting they would be gone next day.

My only close friends were the band, there were no romances and my high life was a brandy and a couple of cigarettes after the show. I must have been the only rock chick who followed her mum's advice.'

'You became a happily married rock-chick. I feel envious sometimes, not about being happily married Clive darling, about never having been a rock chick.'

I offered a quizzical look. She had made up for it on Sextet's sole tour.

'Never mind,' said Clive, 'Sextet allows you to be a rock hen.'

The gathering laughed.

I stood and walked to the dining room where I picked up the bread roll from her side plate and returned. 'Rock hen roll' I said. Clive frowned and V looked puzzled. I was a Chris type joke.
'Too clever Alison.' Phil spoke. Perhaps engineers all have the same sense of humour.

I have known Phil for a month and after an initial flood of information the flow has reduced. I like him, his faults seem to be minor ones, fussy about food without being obsessive, no colour coordination and several lady friends. I suppose it's unavoidable, he looks quite young is good-looking and personable but if he thinks I will be jealous he is mistaken.
His main fault as far as I am concerned is that he isn't Chris but I must not think like that; it is good to have a new friend.
As a friend I wonder if I should warn him about Maureen Sparks. Vickie tells me he has been seen out with her in Gloucester and though it isn't my business she was notorious in the Village as a man chaser even before she separated from Dennis.

'Are you alright Al, you seemed miles away?'
'Yes, fine, I was thinking.'
Phil is looking at me and my face feels a little hot.
'Were you born in Bristol?' Clive asks him.
'No, Torquay. I came to Bristol to go to Uni, did some placements in the vacations and ended getting a job there.'
'Is that where you met...' V stopped.
'Yes. It was at a New Year's Eve gig, there was a group of nurses and we got talking to them in the interval.' He spoke in a rather constrained manner and V took the hint.
'Was your band based in Bristol?' I asked. 'I started singing with our folk band at the end of the seventies and we might have met.'
'No, I was a late starter. I played in a band at Uni but I didn't play seriously until after I was married.
We were living in Yate and I met a drummer at a Cricket club who knew a singer who was looking for a guitarist. You know the process.'

'We might have met without knowing.'
I don't think so, our band was small time and we didn't start until the early eighties. I think you were in the big league before we started.'
It didn't feel like the big league.
'That was when our first band broke up; I wasn't having a happy time.'
If chance had caused us to meet...supposing!
Phil was continuing. 'We were a decent semi-pro outfit and started to get good gigs by our standards, country clubs, working men's clubs, that kind of venue.'
'That's good, if you can crack those you can play anywhere.' I offered an admiring smile and he returned a sideways look as if unsure whether I was pulling his leg.
'I mean it.'
He raised his eyebrows. We understand one another. I colour slightly... again.
Why! What am I thinking, why am I reacting like a teenager.
I glanced at my watch, 'I mustn't be too late this evening I am looking after the packing plant tomorrow.'
The gathering generally agreed that we all had work to do and ten minutes later, after a kiss from V and a hug from Clive I found myself walking in silence with Phil towards his gate. It took barely a minute.
'Goodnight Phil, that was...'
'Can I walk you home?'
'There's no need, yes if you want.'
We walked towards the junction where the road ran past the end of our lane. I wondered if V was watching, the lights ended just after Phil's house.

We walked on in silence, I was unsure how to react to the situation. Was a new friend walking a friend home, was he going to kiss me or what? How was I going to respond? Was Phil thinking the same? I hadn't been in this situation for forty years.
'That was a nice evening.'

'I hope I didn't bore you with my life story.'
'No.' He paused. 'Alison, I don't want to make assumptions,' he sounded anxious, 'I think I like you.'
'You think? Don't you know?'
'I like the person I know but I don't know you very well.'

There was silence as we turned into our lane. The light from the streetlamps on the main road petered out and the next lighting was on the corner of my house a hundred metres away.
'I wanted to say that I think I like you a lot.'
I didn't know what to say and said too much.
'It's the same for me, I don't know howe to behave in new situations.'
I paused. 'It wasn't a problem when I was married, if someone showed interest it didn't matter, but since Chris died I have needed to relearn how to behave. I'm an old woman and I am totally out of practice with relationships. When he died I was suicidal, nothing seemed to matter. I am much better, almost normal but I still get misery moments.'
We were at the darkest part of the lane and my gabble was followed by silence.
'It's hard to explain why someone is likeable' Phil spoke 'I guess you have a lot of admirers but I hope you might have room for another.'

I was certainly not going to commit. I liked Phillip, he was becoming a friend and we had reached the house so I felt I should say something.
'Life has been a struggle since Chris left me so I am cautious. There is no-one in my life at present, except for Chris there never was.'
We stopped at the gate. I had not been in that situation for forty years and had a moment of panic; it was followed by inspiration.
'Shall we take things slowly and see how it goes?'
'Alison, can I?' He held my shoulders, hugged me and kissed my cheek. 'Thank-you.' He released me and half turned away. 'Ok?'

I nodded.

'You've just added five years to my life.'

'Silly! See you soon. Bye.'

He began to walk away, turning momentarily with a small wave.

I floated to the door and let myself in. Life was getting better.

CHAPTER 7

A Problem Solved

Alisons Story

It was part of life's progression. I had passed my fifty-fifth birthday, my bad moments were getting fewer and I was beginning to enjoy small pleasures.

The business was running well and Lisa's management skills were a revelation; she had inherited Chris' determination and sense of fun and my common sense and exuberance. At Uni this was demonstrated by having exuberant fun but now common sense and determination were surfacing.

She enjoyed gaining and retaining contracts using her charm and looks and had recently asked me to join her when entertaining an important middle-aged client.

'Glam up darling.' she told me 'He was a fan of yours.'

My 'fan' had seen Synergy in concert over thirty years ago and had fallen in love with young Alison. He was charming and told me I had hardly changed; the lunch was a success and Lisa retained her contract.

I told V the story a few nights later. I had returned a borrowed casserole dish and stayed for drinks. She laughed when I mentioned the important client and said 'So now it's prostitution.'

I shrugged 'I saw a little of the reality when we were working the clubs, it wasn't particularly attractive.'

Clive asked what the girls were like.

'The few I met were...' What was the description? There wasn't one. 'mostly ordinary, some were very professional, checking out the possibilities, acting interested but no real engagement. After all, it's just business.'

I was getting in too deep. 'Sorry, I really know very little about it but there wasn't a 'type'. One I remember was more like a shared wife with a number of 'boyfriends', some were ordinary girls who earned a little extra and others were professionals either working for themselves or being used by a pimp.'

'The band were there to provide music but sometimes we saw a little of what you might call other activities linked to the club. When I was acting I met some actors who between jobs might find employment as 'escorts' though more often it was casual work.'

I smiled 'I had a little experience of that side of it.'

There was a shocked silence.

'How much entertainment did you offer darling?'

'Don't be silly. Sometimes, at formal parties it was suggested that we talk to and show an interest in influential people. It was useful because you make contacts and get to know people. They used to call it 'working the room', these days they call it networking.'

'Was it difficult?'

'No, it was fun and it could be useful though sometimes I had to smile and not listen. I only got it wrong once.'

'It was a small party to do with the film and I was paid a fee to act as a hostess.'

'I dressed smart, glam almost but as soon as I arrived I knew I had made a mistake; apart from one other actress the girls were 'models' in the broadest sense of the word.'

'After some introductions I was paired up with an older man and I realised that I had been set up as his partner for the night.'

'I could have walked out but he was civilised and pleasant so when I had the opportunity I explained that I had been misled as to my role. He said that it was no problem but I could see he was annoyed.

I said 'I really am sorry, it isn't your fault; I am annoyed with myself for being naive.' It made it impersonal and used the moment to get my coat and sneak away. I never told Chris.'

'Another incident where your virtue saved you darling.'

'Saved me from what?' I fixed Vickie with a look 'I simply avoided a situation that could have had repercussions. You sometimes take clients to lunch, does that mean you go to bed with them afterwards?' I was getting cross.

'You are just being silly now.'

'No, I'm saying we have both entertained clients. Anyway, you started the subject.'

'Sorry Al.'

'I don't know why you think that I spent my early life going to wild parties. I was a singer with a band that was all. There were some awkward situations and I dealt with them. Honestly, Vick I expect your score is much higher than mine!'

'Al!' That's a wicked thing to say.' She blushed.

I noticed Clive look at her suddenly.

'Sorry, I didn't mean it but sometimes you talk as if you have a low opinion of me.'

I changed tack. 'To be honest I was always a bit nervous with boys and even now I find it difficult to get close to someone new; I don't understand how pro...professionals manage.'

'I suppose if you enjoy doing it, being paid is a bonus.' Clive looked up again and Vickie wished she had kept quiet. 'I mean, if it's your choice....'

'Let's leave it, it isn't a subject that we know much about, I don't know how we got on to it.'

'Lisa.' V was relieved that her past wasn't going to be explored.

'Yes of course.'

I do ramble when I am writing up my diary and all this preamble is about the nail in the road that punctured the stability that I was regaining.

Our girly (at fifty plus?) band still played occasional gigs and the 'girlies' still received a small amount of reassuring interest.

The venture had come to a halt when Chris fell ill and was forgotten during my foolish and disastrous return to the professional stage.

It took a while to overcome the humiliation and only when my life was beginning to settle down did I consider reviving the band.

I phoned Bob our latest drummer to see if he was available and was told that he was happy to play provided it didn't clash with his other gigs.

The girls met in a Bristol café to decide if we wanted to restart the band; the vote was unanimous and we contacted our agent to see what transpired.

What transpired was some intense practice and we were rolling again; rolling slowly it is true, a gig a month except for one weekend when we found ourselves booked for two gigs on the same day.

We settled down quickly and confidence was returning when Liz dropped a bombshell; her husband had an eighteen-month contract in Saudi and she would be available only for the next six weeks.

Finding a new bass player wasn't a problem, finding one that was prepared to play in a middle-aged girly band that gigged monthly was a different matter.

Age and sex was a problem; there were some good female bass players but none that might play with us. The boys would laugh in my face. 'Play with a lot of grannies? You must be ...' the comment would be unprintable unless the woman was a star. Chrissie would get the seal of approval but there were few others.

Vickie suggested Phil whom, she had discovered, played bass.

'Good looking, experienced and fun, he's a godsend, literally.' She laughed at her joke.

'And which of us is he going to enjoy after the gig?'

I don't know where the remark came from, I don't say things like that.

'Alison. Really, that is disgusting. I'll pretend you didn't say it.'

'Don't be silly V it was just a wind up. Phil might be a solution but we don't want to spoil friendships by inviting him to practice and then tell him he is no good.'

'Why don't we ask him to join us for a fun session and if he is useless or he doesn't fit we don't ask him again.'

'That makes more sense. When he next calls for eggs I could work the conversation around to music and ask him.'

'Yes ok' she paused 'I'm seeing him on Friday, I could ask him then.'

'Are you?'

'Yes.' Silence. 'He's doing a weekly shop in Thornbury.'

'Oh yes?'

'Well? I have to shop as well.' Her voice rose slightly.

Liz' rang me on the Wednesday to tell me that the situation had changed, her husband would be managing the contract from his office and would only be required to make occasional visits. I stopped listening, had heard all that mattered. We had no need for a new bass player.

CHAPTER 8

First Date

Alisons Story

Nothing is free. My first date, if you could call an arranged meeting a date' caused a degree of gossip.

Vickie visited the same afternoon ostensibly to buy some eggs and as usual she stayed for coffee and a chat and if the comments she passed on to me had been edited then what was really being said was slanderous.

Her first question before even the kettle had boiled was 'How did your date go?'

I explained that our meeting could hardly be classed as a date; I was in Thornbury shopping and we met for lunch.

The chat became more general but my lunchtime meeting was clearly the object of her visit and my best friend was slightly displeased.

I was reminded (again!) that I had always had everything, good looks, an exciting husband, meeting stars (one, and I once saw a Rolling Stone at a party... I think) and I had my own business.

She was still my best friend but where Phil was concerned there was resentment.

I explained that it was only lunch and a chat, that she had done the same and that she was married.

I hurriedly followed it up with 'He likes you a lot, he said so, not directly but if our situations were reversed I wouldn't get a look in.'

It helped but not much.

'That's all very well but it's nice to have a friend who sees you as a person, someone who makes you feel you're attractive and wanted. You had an adorable husband now you've grabbed the only man who is worth knowing. It just isn't fair.'

I decided not to mention that a proper date, if there is such a thing when you are over fifty, had been arranged over lunch.

Mum had given me some free theatre tickets and we would go together.

I was looking forward to it.

I understood V's annoyance, Phil is interested and interesting. During lunch the subject of my husband had arisen and I felt comfortable enough to describe our relationship.

'I loved Chris, we were soulmates but he had his flaws, mostly he was caring and considerate but he certainly wasn't the paragon Vickie sometimes implies.'

I then fell into one of his most annoying flaws and gave an analogy.

'Sometimes the papers report a 'tragic incident' where a teenager gets beaten up. There was an incident recently and a local press campaign turned the victim into a martyr. One of the national papers did a little digging, the victim was a minor criminal, theft and drugs and he had cheated a villain who arranged the beating."

Phil was looking at me with an amused expression.

'Well,' I ended lamely, 'all I'm saying is that Chris was mostly lovely but Vickie didn't have to live with him and sometimes I could have strangled him.'

We laughed together.

The theatre visit was a disaster.

I took an age deciding whether I should dress young, smart middle aged or comfortable.

I retired undecided from the chaos of blouses and skirts, long dresses and tights, short dresses and woolly tights for an extended shower and got chilled standing half naked in front of the mirror overdoing the make-up. I then proceeded to dress and made a pig's ear of it.

I gazed at myself in the mirror, realised I had got it wrong, The shortish, high neck dress with long sleeves and black tights was ok but with the make-up, miss-matched mutton stared back at me. I was about to start again when a bell rang, the one on the front door that is never used.

I threw a long cardigan over the dress, struggled into high heels and rushed down to greet Phillip.

On the second step from the bottom I tripped, twisted my ankle, caught my dress on the handrail and bruised my thigh. I dragged myself upright and hobbled to the door.

'Good evening Alison.' Phillip looks very tidy in smart casuals.

'Come in.' I squeak.

He enters and smiles. 'You look…' he hesitates 'very glamorous.'

'Thank-you. I'm only just ready.'

'I brought a small thank-you present.' He brings a small packaged orchid in a pot from behind his back and presents it to me.

'Thank-you. It's…' no one has given me anything for ages 'lovely.' I lean forward to peck his cheek, stumble on the heels and we clash heads.'

He steps back rubbing his forehead.

'Are you from Glasgow?'

I rub my head, it hurts and tears start. This is awful, farcical. He runs his finger gently over my bump. 'Are you alright?'

'Yes. Thank-you for the present.' I wipe my eyes 'Shall we go.'

He looks at me again. 'You still look very nice.'

I reach for a short coat, it may get chilly.

He opens the car door and I get in. We are leaving the drive when I realise that the dress, a modest handspan above the knee has ridden up and is now a handspan below my knicks. A ladder is visible below the hole in my tights. A thread has pulled on the dress. The cardigan hangs below the hem of the coat.

The play by a respected author was awful. One of those unsubtle intellectual exercises in publicly exorcising the author's demons. I had seen a previous offering by the same author, ninety minutes of rambling which flogged to death the premise that God (in its most infantile definition) doesn't exist. It was brilliant because the two actors playing the main characters were brilliant. Even the two actors in question couldn't have saved this one.

As soon as we left the theatre I apologised 'Sorry, that wasn't very good, shall we have an inquest.'

'I think a gin and tonic would be better.'

We drove to a pub five miles from home, parked in the long narrow car park and trekked to the door. Once we had our drinks we retired to a table in the corner, the only free one; the place was busy.

'I'm sorry it was such a bad play.'

'It wasn't bad, just rather dull and it had the benefit of showing we have similar tastes.'

'I saw one by the same author about ten years ago and it was very good, very well done.'

'I think I saw the same one. It is strange that the doyens of the left get lionised for writing small ideas in big letters. I think' he added 'the author was connected or associated with the theatre of the absurd so it pursued the theme that life is absurd when you analyse it. We get buried in what is and don't see the pointlessness of it.'

I was reminded of the line that Chris often repeated. 'Doctor, when I do this my head hurts.' 'Well don't do it.'

'It is strange' Phil continued 'that we are bombarded with boredom when there is some wonderful stuff out there.'

'I know, I saw Arcadia, do you know it? I thought it was so clever. I suppose it's easier to find a simple theme and write it with a half brick.'

'I didn't know you were so passionate about things Alison.'

'I'm not, all authority needs bashing occasionally but not constantly by professional moaners. Sorry Phil, I'm sounding like my husband.'

I remembered sitting in this same pub with Chris pontificating and me saying 'Oh do shut up darling.' I instantly wished he was there to be told off, flushed and felt the tears coming.

Phil looked concerned then eased up next to me and put an arm around my shoulders. I reached up and held his hand.

We sat for a few minutes and I smiled at him.

'I had a sad moment.'

He removed his arm. 'I have them too. Not the same as yours, small upsets.'

It seemed a good time to tell him about my past.

'Phil, we are becoming friends and if we are going to become better friends then I had better tell you about my failings.'

'If you want.' He frowned and held my hand like a schoolboy. 'I thought it was more usual to offer an expurgated idealised version of your past.'

'Most of it is good but I have always been as anxious about my failings as I have happy about my successes. Is it a problem?'

'No. I am curious about your life and a little worried that you won't be the impossibly lovely person that I imagine.'

'I won't. I hope you were being ironic.'

'Not really.'

'Chris my husband was my first love. He might have been my only one except that we went through a very bad patch and he married Sue who was very pretty and pregnant.'

'You told me.'

'Was it when we had dinner with Vickie and Clive?'

'Yes, you told us a little but kept saying you didn't want to bore us.'

'I'll stop if I see your eyes glazing over. The truth is that I took up with our road manager. He wasn't my type, unsuitable really but he was there and keen. I had to get back at Chris and I needed someone.'

My mind went back to that unhappy period, the unique (for me) situation where I was having sex with someone I hardly knew and deliberately causing pain to someone I loved.

'The relationship only lasted a couple of months and when it ended started my own band. We were called 'Cats Whiskers.''

'I saw you!!' Phil interrupts. 'You played a club outside Bristol.'

I could remember the gig. Mum and Dad had been there with cousin Phil and his wife; it was one of the happy gigs when I was praised and hugged by people I loved.

Phillip was still talking. 'I can't remember much of the evening but I do remember one song and I thought the singer was fantastic.'

He is looking at me admiringly. 'You haven't changed much.'

'Huh, if only.' I dismiss the remark but inside I am delighted.'

'The band was on its second tour when Chris' wife died'

'Running the band was exhausting and there had been a nasty incident that undermined my confidence. I was still angry with Chris and sometimes I wished that Sue was dead then she was killed in a riding accident.'

'It was a terrible shock and not long afterwards I had a nervous breakdown.'

'Now you know how lovely I am.'

Phil squeezed my hand. 'Being angry is natural if you have been hurt, being ashamed of your anger' he looked at me and smiled 'adds sensitive to lovely'.

'I enjoy flattery but I only believe so much. Do you want to hear the rest of how unlovely I am?'

'If it is really appalling, I will look disgusted and walk out... no, I will look disgusted, drive you home and never contact you again.'

'I recovered from the breakdown but was very fragile. Mum was in touch with Chris and sometimes she visited with our daughter.'

'One day she phoned from his house and I spoke to him. It was a difficult conversation but few weeks later mum took me to visit. Within a few minutes of meeting all the good feelings started to return. We were both in a bad place but I think we knew we were meant to be together and eighteen months later we got married, happily ever after.'

'You weren't tempted to look elsewhere?'

'Not really. It isn't difficult for a reasonably attractive girl to find a partner, but it is almost impossible to find someone worthwhile when you are travelling around performing with a band. You meet a lot of people but you can't make a valid judgement on a brief acquaintance.

Some girls can do the rock chick thing, but with me it is all or nothing and nothing was easier.'

'So your mothers description was true.'

'More or less.' He raised his eyebrows. 'Yes, more or less.' I said firmly.

'It doesn't seem a very good score for a gorgeous rock chick.'

I poked him in the ribs. 'It isn't Mr Barnes. I was lucky enough to find my soulmate when I was still innocent and free of baggage.' My feelings were bouncing, I didn't know if I was cross or happy.

'How about you then.'

'Oh, I'm Mr Purity.'

I pouted, 'I'll bet, come on, your turn for admissions.'

'Seriously?'

'Yes.'

'An incident when I was at uni; to my shame it was with a rather nice lady cleaner at the halls of residence; then there was a relationship in my final year. A year later I met Mary and nothing except ...' he stopped.

'And?' Sorry, don't say if you don't want to, I am prying.'

'It's ok, not painful, just embarrassing, a brief fling not long after Mary left. I suppose I was convincing myself I was still attractive.'

'Your fans at the church should convince you.'

He leaned over and kissed my cheek. 'Thanks Al.'

It was the first time he had called me Al.

We drove back to my house and after a moment hesitation he turned into the drive and stopped.
There was a brief silence which I broke with a gabbled. 'Thankyou for a nice evening, despite the play.'
'I enjoyed it.' 'Alison...'
Oh dear, here it comes. I am aware that I am old.
'...is it alright to kiss you?'
I tighten. 'Yes.'
Phil turns, holds my hand and kisses me. I reach, hold his face and return the kiss. I feel a moment of nervous excitement.
'I don't need to tell you that you are lovely.'
'Thankyou.' I squeak. I want to be hugged, loved and looked after but I am tense and resistant. I spent my life with Chris taking such things for granted. Why was I running away from it?
'I'll take a risk.' Phil holds me gently, kisses me again and I respond.
A couple of cars pass and our comfortable cuddle continues then we kiss again and he releases me. As he does so his hand brushes over my breast. I assume it was deliberate.
'Yes it was.'
'What? Oh you horror, how can I be friends with someone who knows my thoughts.
'It was a guess.'
I open the door. 'I did enjoy the evening, honestly.' 'He slides out of the car, walks around to my side and holds the door open.
'The best I can remember.' He reaches to help me out, the seat is low.
I struggle out reaching for his hand. The dress has rucked to my thighs; I tug at it uselessly drawing attention to the ladder which now runs from my knee to comfy nicks visible through the tights. For once I am happy that our drive is poorly lit.
I stand up and tug my skirt down to a sensible length.
'Next time I will wear something more suitable.'
'First dates are always fraught and there have been a few

hiccups but how you look isn't one of them. Please don't change anything.' This time he puts his arms around me.

'I'm not blind, I did notice you have great legs,' he kisses me, 'and that they go up a long way.' The kiss is extended, it lasts half a minute; another car passes. He releases me, pats my bottom in a way that says he feels comfortable with me. I feel happy, almost elated.

'Shall I ring you about another date?'

'Yes, please.'

'Goodnight Alis…what should I call you?'

'Al is fine, Alison if you want to be formal, A if you are cross.'

'Goodnight Al.'

'Night Phil, see you soon.'

I wait outside the kitchen door until he pulls out of the drive. I wave and enter the kitchen still feeling content but somewhere a tiny unconscious part of me wants Chris to be with me.

I lie awake for half an hour reliving the evening. I was right; he is kind, a little shy and nice to be with. I have met all types and learned to make judgements. I reckon that Phil is a good guy.'

I woke next morning and lay in my warm bed happily reliving the previous night. I had a new friend, a male friend, we had talked and kissed. The warm feeling cooled, why had I told him about Gary? I hardly knew him and my brief affair was now public. Think, think, did I say anything else? One large g and t and I had gabbled. A dozen years in show business and I had never shaken off the retro-cringe, I could control it but only with a lot of mental effort and diversionary techniques.

I slipped out of bed, took off my pyjamas, stood momentarily in front of the mirror and decided I looked pretty good except for the large bruise on my thigh and a faint red mark on my forehead. I turned away and headed for the bathroom.

I was in the shower singing happily to myself when the phone rang. I let it ring, changed my mind, turned off the shower and reached for a light bath robe hanging on the door. I slipped it on and wrapped a towel around my head. The ringing stopped.

Sun was streaming though the small paned window in the bathroom, it was going to be a warm day for the time of the year. I walked out of the bathroom into the passage that runs the length of the house to my bedroom; the sun was reflecting green from the hedgerow opposite, the sky was blue with fluffy clouds and I felt light, young and full of life. I skipped to the bedroom, put on slippers and decided not to dress, throwing off the bath robe and draping it over my shoulder my nakedness in tune with my feelings and the day.

I stretched and took a deep breath, wished Chris could come in and hug me, felt sad but not crushed.

It was nine o clock when I went down to breakfast. I was now half dressed in chinos and slippers, the top half covered by a shirt and dressing gown. Kettle on, too happy for toast, don't fancy cereal, I decide I would like a fresh roll with bacon; there was no bacon but I remember that I bought some frozen croissants. I switched on the oven, searched the freezer and found them, only just out of date.

The kettle boiled and I made tea. I had just put the rolls in the oven when the phone rang.

'Hello?'

'Phil. Hi Al...ison.'

'Hi Phil...lip.'

'Just a quick call to say thank-you for last night, I really enjoyed it.'

'Me too.' A pause.

'Will I see you soon?'

'Yes. On Sunday I expect.'

'I meant...'

'I know, I shouldn't be facetious, it's a defence mechanism. I assume you were reminding an elderly friend that she agreed to arrange a date.'

'I don't know what to say to that unless you are referring to some other friend. Yes, I was asking when we could next meet; there is no hurry but...well not too long.'

'I am busy with work and family next week; you can call in for coffee if you are passing and we can arrange another night out.
'Great. That will be good.' Long pause. 'Alison, I really wanted to say I enjoyed being with you.'
'Yes. I enjoyed it too.' It is too soon to say any more.
'Ok. Good-Bye…friend.'
'Bye you. Phillip, did you ring earlier, about half an hour ago?'
'No. I thought nine was early enough.'
'It is, I'm not an early riser. Bye again.'

The phone rang as I was taking the croissants from the oven. I let it ring, put them on a plate and collected the marmalade and butter. Both? No, yes. I changed my mind several times, poured myself another cup of tea and sat down.
I was licking marmalade and flaked of croissant from my fingers when the phone rang again. Has the world gone mad? I picked it up and returned to my chair.
'Hello. Alison Phillips speaking.'
'It's me.'
'Hi Vickie, is anything wrong, you don't normally ring this early.'
'Nothing wrong with me. I thought you might like to tell me about last night. What happened?'
'We went to the theatre. I told you; neither of us enjoyed the play, it wasn't very interesting.'
'Not that, afterwards, did you…Faith said…'
'Faith?'
'Faith at the store. I needed a loaf for toast this morning and she said you were getting very intimate outside your house at nearly midnight.'
I was speechless. Were people spying on me? 'How on earth…?'
'Faith's sister was coming home late and saw you but never mind that, what happened afterwards.'
The shock brought on a moment of anger 'I invited him in of course, he's still here, would you like to speak to him?'
V was momentarily silenced.
'Can you come to the phone Phil, Vickie wants to know what we

got up to in bed last night.' I said to the empty room.

'No I don't.' V went quiet. Good, I had shocked her.

'Are you sure? Phil, come and tell Vickie how much we enjoyed last night.'

'Don't be horrid Al.'

'Me?? Nobody is here! Phil went home straight after your spies saw us having a very brief and modest kiss. Is that permitted? Perhaps the grapevine would like a second-by-second account?'

'Don't be objectionable, I thought you might want to talk.'

'I might, but not at nine in the morning when the whole village has already decided that I'm having an affair. I had an innocent evening out with a friend and my so-called best friend is interrogating me.' I felt sorry for myself, 'It's really mean and insensitive.'

'I was just concerned, I thought you might want to chat, I didn't mean to upset you.'

'Well, you have!' I backed off. 'The evening was a series of disasters but despite that we enjoyed it. If you are desperate, I'll come over later and disappoint you with the details of a pleasant but unexciting evening.'

'Yes, if you want. Come over for coffee at eleven or better still meet me in the cafe.'

'OK. CU at eleven.'

I was a little early at the café and went to the counter to order a latte. Christine, a friend from tennis was on duty.

'How are thing Christine?'

'Much better Al, Susan got the job she applied for.'

'That is good news.'

'Yes, she is so excited though it means a move to Exeter so I don't know what Ellis will say.'

'Difficult isn't it, they have been together for a while. Still, it is really good news about the job.'

'Yes it is.' She steamed the milk. 'I hear you have been dating Phil Barnes. He's nice isn't he.'

MY GOD!!! It's like living in a glass house. The whole village knows.

'Not dating exactly, we had an evening together at the theatre.'

'That's nice.' Her smile says 'Oh yes?'

'Hi Al!' Vickie has arrived.

'Hi V, what would you like?'

'The usual.' The usual is an Americano with a splash of milk. I sometimes have the same after our aerobics but V is very keen to keep her weight down and thinks drinking something she doesn't enjoy will help.

I find a table and she joins me. We talk around the subject before I tell her the essentials of my evening with Phil.

'Enjoyable but very ordinary.'

'Ordinary by your standards. She frowns. 'I would love an ordinary evening like that. It makes me jealous.'

'There's nothing to be jealous about, the high spot of the evening was a brief kiss and I couldn't decide whether I was a teenager on her first date or an old woman being silly.

'That is why I'm envious, you have had so many highs in your life that your reaction to a cuddle is more memorable than the cuddle itself.'

'It isn't! I was thinking about some of the special moments a few days ago and they were all personal; when Chris kissed me the first time, when we got engaged and when we first met after the break up.

The last one was tearful, uncertain and utter happiness but probably the emotional high spot in my life was with 'kR.'

'You mean when you were with the band?'

'Yes. It happened at the end of the US tour; the management wanted us to do a tribute to the US that said a big thank you to the audience. There were several suggestions but since we were in California and Chris suggested 'California girls.'

Bruce wasn't keen because it wasn't our style and Vince said 'F that' but the management liked it. They had the parts sorted out in a day and Bruce said to Chris 'Your suggestion, you can effin sing it.'

Vince had to be threatened with the sack before he would play and he absolutely refused to sing so they brought the backing singers up front to do the harmonies and I asked if I could play the rhythm guitar part on Chris' acoustic. Bruce said yes but if I didn't do it well he would spank me.

We had some intense practice and learned it in about three hours but we needed to rehearse between shows to polish it and we performed it on the last show when I was standing in.

Bruce thanked the audience and handed over to Chris who said 'Our tribute to the fabulous Beach Boys'.

I was wound up; I knew I could do it but I hadn't played guitar since 'Cats Whiskers'.

Bruce played the intro and Chris started to sing. I was just strumming my rhythm until we came in with the harmonies and something magical happened. Sarah and I were sharing a mic on Bruce's left and he looked across with this big smile on his face as if he had totally relaxed and from then on the song just got better and better.

We did an extended version where we repeated the verses and chorus and by half-way through the audience had bought into it. It was fantastic, like taking the best drug and having sex with your dream man at the same time...but better.

At the end we got an ovation, a real ovation and I felt so high it was unbelievable. When we went off stage there was a buzz and a lot of talk about repeating it but it wasn't 'kR, just a party piece that worked fabulously in the right place and time.'

It never was repeated but we had the video of the concert. I watched it recently to remind me what it was like, it was very good but it wasn't the same; I needed to be twenty-four, in love and there, part of a team playing live, creating the magic.

It felt huge at the time especially after Synergy and Cats Whiskers. It was huge, 'kR was on a rise; the songs and the performances felt fantastic and we generated excitement but whether it could have been sustained, whether it had that edge we will never know.

Tony once said to me 'When we make it the dead wood will go.'
I asked him what he meant and he said 'Bep's lost it and our Bass player is only temporary.'

I waggled three fingers at him because his hand was still damaged.

'Works better than Chrispy's five. I might ensure one of our singers is kept on if she I nice to me.'

He wasn't joking but when Bruce died the band died with him.

CHAPTER 9

Phillip

Phillip Christopher Barnes was the second son of Jack and Iris and was followed by his sister Sheena.

I suppose I had an easy life. Being born in Torquay in the nineteen fifties was a good deal; getting a place at the Grammar school a better one.

My first mistake was to pursue a course in civil engineering. There is nothing wrong with engineering, it's a good profession, but from a status viewpoint I should have followed my contemporaries into law, politics, medicine or art.

Engineers like farmers are presented by the media as a yokels with dirty hands yet without them the above mentioned would be discussing the abstract in their caves.

Design engineers are muti disciplined, highly creative artists of products that can be beautiful and useful.

They do sometimes appear in sitcoms where they draw a couple of lines and sneak off to play golf; more often they are confused with stylist who provide us with teapots that leak, cups that are hard to hold and slippery mobile phones that leap out of your hand to destruction.

Sometimes they become embittered.

At eighteen I went to university in Bristol to study my subject.

In the seventies it was still a busy city with docks, aircraft and engines, paper, tobacco, printing and packaging machinery factories which, together with the trading and industrial activities at Avonmouth created the wealth that supported the social and service industries. Sadly, as the demands for social services increased the wealth creating industry slowly disappeared. Worse, as the city struggled to meet the expectations of its population the migrants who had come seeking a better life found themselves facing an increasingly uncertain future.

But that came later. As soon as I finished my degree and was settled into a career I became engaged to Mary and a year later we married. It was a good marriage, there was attraction, affection, we got on well and our children grew and prospered with no more than the normal glitches and worries.

There were negatives; the nature of our jobs kept us apart and when Mary's job demanded night duty our family life and our social life became disjointed.

The relationship was comfortable and as is often the case with 'satisfactory' couples, and when our second child left home (for the second time) Mary gently told me she was leaving me.

It seemed that a friendship of several years standing had turned to love and when it was convenient, she would be following her new man to Scotland where he had a surgical post.

It wasn't the devastating news that it would have been early in the marriage but it was upsetting and unsettling.

Marriage break-ups are not unusual, the process is a feature of modern life, but at fifty-three, the anxieties, the stress, the upset and sense of ill-use left me unsociable, grumpy and with a serious loss of confidence.

Compared to many my ordeal was modest, the separation a surprise but emotionally no worse than the loss of a good friend, the divorce reasonably fair and amicable.

When I had recovered from the initial shock I began to construct a future; I would take my time, become an eligible bachelor and enjoy a few innocent or less innocent dates with ladies of a suitable age. When the traumas of the divorce had diminished and I felt able to pick up the threads of normal life I would began to socialise.

My difficulty was that I needed to relearn the rules that governed the actions of a single man in middle age.

I was helped by a caring sister who offered words of advice concerning potential encounters with single females.

'They will all have baggage', 'some will be sensitive or fragile or both', 'there are some gold-diggers out to take what they can', 'some are deceitful and some' she added 'are total liars. Never commit yourself.'

There were many more helpful warnings and after several dates with ladies that I knew moderately well I began to understand her concerns.

None of the ladies was unpleasing but at the time I had no wish for more than a friendship.

The first had no designs on me except as a social support, a listening ear, a handyman and a provider of self-worth, these were received in abundance and repaid with tea in heroic quantities and affection in homeopathic doses. She was a friend but had nothing to offer.

The second was met whilst I was living in temporary accommodation and still unsettled. I fell or more accurately was dragged into a relationship with a lady who worked on my caring instincts.

As soon as our friendship was established she 'needed' a little affection, 'just a hug' which developed in the following weeks and became sex.

I didn't dislike her, far from it, she was ten years my junior, attractive, kind and well-intentioned but maintaining a friendship was difficult when affection was replaced by lust. An edginess crept in and the blow up came when a well-meaning but ill-chosen phrase was misinterpreted, and I found myself less welcome than chopped liver at a Vegan party.

The divorce though fair had brought the inevitable financial problems. We had been living in a large house in Thornbury but the need to share our assets required me to downsize and it was a while before I found a newish small semi in a nearby village and was able to pick up the threads of my life. I was pleased to distance myself if only by a few miles from my erstwhile relationships.

As a partner in the firm work kept me busy, there were deadlines and copious electronic paperwork but provided these were completed I had a degree of flexibility in my lifestyle.

I joined the local tennis club and the local church community to meet new people though I intended to keep my distance from unattached females.

I wasn't very successful; on my first Sunday at church I met a charming lady who was welcoming, friendly, attractive and safely married. In the following weeks I got to know her better discovering that she was sensible, kind and fun. She was mildly flirtatious and since she was safely married I felt that I could respond in a similar manner.

Like most men I appreciate kindness, enjoy friendships and over the ensuing months we became a little more friendly than was wise.

She knew that I liked her and could be a little mischievous. I accepted the small flaw in a character that was otherwise very likable.

We had shared a couple of shopping trips and on one occasion had walked by the Severn. It was an enjoyable and friendly walk and she had been playful. When we sat together on a bench her cheekiness had driven me to say 'If you continue to tease me <u>Mrs</u> Mason I will be forced to kiss you.' She put her head on one side, closed her eyes and pushed out her lips.

'Serves you right.' I said and kissed her. A hug was added to the kiss and since no-one was around my hand began to explore.

'Phillip!' She clasped my hand, held it for a few moments then slowly removed it. 'Sorry, I must stop you, don't be cross.'

'Of course not, I shouldn't have taken the liberty.'

'Affection is appreciated but when it becomes enjoyable it might get out of hand ...you know.'

I did know and a feeling of guilt set back my burgeoning social renewal.

By the time we had walked back to the car and settled in our seats, friendship seemed to be restored, then out of the blue.

'Could you give me another hug to show we are friends again? Just a hug.'

It was a little more than a hug.

Then I met her friend. Totally unsuitable, adorable, everything that was right and wrong for me.

Alison's personality, questionable background and unquestionable good looks immediately gained a nervous admirer and in the following weeks my admiration grew in a more positive way.

Liking her wasn't a problem it was good to make another friend but when our conversation touched on her bereavement she said 'I'm over it really, but sometimes...' forced a smile and looked so vulnerable that I wanted to hug her. I reached out for her hand.

'I'm alright. Thank-you.' She acknowledged my automatic gesture and suddenly I wanted her.

It required a lot of mental chastisement for me to suppress my interest.

I suppose our real friendship began after an evening dinner with Victoria and Clive.

They were a decent couple and I was ashamed of my mix of feelings for Victoria. I genuinely appreciated the married lady who was welcoming and kind but another part of me gently lusted after the attractive woman.

After the meal Alison was encouraged to tell me about her life as a singer or 'rock-chick' as Victoria called her and it gave me a chance to study her. She was Victoria's age, good looking and possessed of an indefinable charm. When recounting her life she was bubbly, sometimes shy and always careful with what she said.

At the end of the evening I walked home with her and in the companionable situation forgot my caution and common sense confessed my liking and told her that I hoped we would become friends.

She said she hoped so too then kissed my cheek and I fell in love. All my wise intention to take it slowly, to find out about her faults and past misdemeanours evaporated.

I hugged her and felt wonderful but as soon as we parted the warm glow disappeared.

I was unsettled by feelings that were unrelated to our friendship.

We were little more than acquaintances and I knew that a youngish widow with looks, personality and presumably money would have many admirers. She had been kind to me but when it came down to it, what had I to offer a woman who knew all the angles.

The thought depressed me; perhaps I should back off and stop kidding myself that I was anything special. I realised that since our first meeting I had installed her into a corner of my life.

My common sense was pushed aside and any wisdom I had gained over the decades was ignored, despite my worries I had to pursue her.

She was recently bereaved, living alone in a farmhouse where she kept a dozen hens. She ran a business on the other side of the village with the support of a daughter who lived half a mile away and she had a second daughter who lived in Thornbury. She also had the support of a number of established friends, several of whom were male.

On my second visit to her house I met her mother who must have been in her late seventies; nearing sixty myself I conceded that she was pretty fair for an older woman.

She was friendly and talkative and I took to her immediately. The conversation went in many directions and I concluded that she was assessing me and checking my suitability for her daughter.

I asked if she was living with her daughter and she stopped talking for a moment, gave me a frowning look and said 'The idea has never occurred to us. It would make sense but I would lose my independence.'

She looked me in the eye 'You are a surprise.'

I didn't know what she meant.

'Can I tell you something about my daughter?'

'I can't answer a question like that.'

'It isn't anything bad, it is simply that some people get a wrong impression of her because she was in rock band and has been an actress. Has she told you about that part of her life?'

'Her friend Victoria told me about the band but not the acting.'

'Oh, Vickie. She's very kind, a little indiscreet sometimes but she has been a wonderful support for Alison since darling Chris died.'

She paused. 'Alison was in a film, not a very good one but it was seen and she was offered a part in a series on TV, after that she had a few small roles.' She looked up. 'She admitted that she was limited in the roles she could tackle but she was very good in them and for a while it took her away from home and the family.'

'I see.'

'I just wanted to say that Alison has made a few mistakes, who hasn't, but she is a very decent and moral person. We all have our moments of silliness even me (I could believe it) but in a difficult profession she coped well because she had standards and she loved her husband.'

At that moment the paragon entered and the conversation ended.

Alison looked young for her age; close there were lines and blemishes but she was well preserved and from a short distance could have passed for a girl in her late thirties.

She looked tidy whatever she was wearing and normally displayed a quiet mixture of self-assurance and liveliness. When I knew her better I would discover there was another side to her;

a sudden loss of confidence when she would withdraw and try to conceal her unhappiness. It happened on our first serious date and my offer of sympathy was foolish because I hardly knew her and had no idea of her real feelings.

Our first 'date' was scarcely a date at all; my tentative suggestion that we might meet for lunch was accepted after a long pause and a scrutiny that seemed to assess my intentions.

The lunch was modest, little more than a snack in a café in Thornbury. I had a meeting with a client that morning and Alison had agreed to join me for lunch at one.

She was on time, looking young and slightly glam with her sparkly scarf and matching bag. As she approached the table I reminded myself that she was a middle-aged woman, not a girl. I rose to greet her and she kissed air; our cheeks barely touched but I felt a mix of nervousness and excitement.

I remember little about the meeting, was happy to be with her and I enjoyed my time with someone who slowly became alive and created a longing for a closer relationship.

Our conversation was mundane, mostly about friends and family, the farm and my job but she made it fun. There was a sexual element but her attraction was mostly about authenticity, character and a sort of niceness without a pretence of perfection.

For the second time I realised I was falling in love. Worrying!

I suppose the longing was mitigated slightly when I asked if we could meet again.

'Yes I think so,' she said, 'ring me.'

It is the nature of village politics that my friendship became known and the situation such as it was caused a noticeable cooling in an innocent friendship with one of the church ladies and with Victoria who was quite abrupt when we next met in the village café.

My discomfort must have shown because after a curt 'Oh, hello Phillip' she said, 'Still talking to your old friends?'

'Of course I am, I thought we were good friends, you have been a wonderful support since I came to the village.'

'Thankyou' she said then after a long pause 'sorry Phil, I supposed that there was liking as well as friendship. I am probably a tiny bit disappointed because you now have a proper lady friend.' Then she squeezed my arm.

'One light lunch does not make Alison a lady friend in the serious sense, just a friend who' I hesitated and chose my words carefully 'who might become as good a friend as you.'

It's a pity that their situations aren't reversed, Vickie is uncomplicated attractive and easy to get on with but she is married; A is a widow, is hard to know and keeps her distance; I don't think it is contrived, she isn't playing 'hard to get', it is how she is and it makes her special.

A few days later I phoned Alison, enquired about a date and was asked if I would go with her to the theatre. Her mother had given her tickets for a play by a well-known doyen of the left; I wasn't discouraged, had seen excellent radical productions by small companies and I drove to her house more concerned about the date than the promised entertainment.

The date was not as expected; unsurprising since I didn't know what to expect.

All experience affects us and as my sister warned me, 'the more baggage the bigger the problem'. Despite her mother's eulogy, there was probably some truth in Victoria's comments about a wild youth.

My knowledge of the 'wild child' was confined to the newspapers. Reading between the lines I concluded that re-branded survivors buried incidents that were more sordid than they cared to admit.

I rang the bell on the front door and waited...and waited. I rang a second time and heard a clatter and 'Damn!' There was a scuffing of several bolts a loud click and the door flew open.

'We don't use this door! Come in.'

She was wearing a dark green dress that suited her perfectly with an unsuitable brown cardigan over it. Her heels brought her to within a few inches of my height.

'Come in.' she repeated and I followed her into the small hall that ran from the front to the back of the house.

'Good evening' I said formally 'It's nice to see you.'

'Yes.' She was tense. 'Yes' she repeated 'you look very smart.'

She looked good except for the cardigan; modest thirty-five met attractive middle age and a tingle of lust unsettled me.

'I've brought a small present.' I offered a potted orchid.

'For me? Thank-you, I haven't had a present for ages.'

She stepped forward, tottered on her heels and we clashed heads. She staggered and clutched her forehead; the knock was painful but I was more anxious for her and held her shoulder to steady her.

'Oh god.' she said, there were tears and I didn't know what to do. I went back to the door, turned and rang the bell for a second time.

'Good evening, can I come in?'

She dabbed her eyes and frowned. 'What?'

'I'm looking forward to this evening and may I say' I have to think quickly 'you look lovely.'

The frown intensified. 'Don't be silly, I'm a mess!' 'Do you still want to go?'

'I would be silly if I didn't, I've been looking forward to our date all week.'

'Have you? Alright then, let's go before things get worse.' She found a bag, collected a coat and after locking the door followed me to the car. I opened the door and with a 'thanks,' she slid in.

I had noticed that the dress was shortish and as she sat down it rode up to the top of her legs. She dragged at it ineffectually drawing attention to a hole in her tights then gave up and tucked her cardigan around her.

The play was ok, an intellectual exercise in making a lot out of little but it was well acted and produced. We discussed it later when we stopped at a pub on the way home. As before our conversation was easy and it was inevitable that we began to talk about our lives.

I was charmed by the bubbly woman who could become a vulnerable girl at the turn of a memory; nothing in our short acquaintance had spoiled my first impression.

She was 'nice' meaning considerate, outgoing and straightforward; add interesting and attractive and I began to worry that no-one could replace her. I relaxed, her friend Vickie was attractive and easier to know; Alison wasn't unique.

She was surprisingly candid when giving me a brief history of the ups and downs of her relationship with her husband who was clearly the biggest obstacle to any future intimacy. The history mentioned a relationship that had happened when she had broken with her soul-mate.

Her description of her 'soulmate' made me feel inadequate and the admission of the long-ago affair with someone 'totally unsuitable' provoked a mild irrational jealousy.

To be honest I wasn't ready to hear everything she told me but her précis of her time with the band was interesting and her animation when recalling an amusing incident was enchanting. Then, suddenly she was silent. 'All so long ago' she said sadly.

It was a good evening; in its way the best since I had separated because despite her flaws Alison was a joy to be with. When we arrived at her house I parked in the drive and waited for her to get out or perhaps to ask me in. When neither happened, after some preamble I asked if I could kiss her.

She nodded and I kissed her properly for the first time with my arm loosely around her shoulders, cursing the headrest; after a while I hugged her and felt her tightening up.

'Are you ok?'

'Yes. I'm not used to this and I don't know you very well.'

'No.'

'I think I'm ok with you?'

'I think so too. First dates should be about getting to know people but if you like someone you want to show some interest.'

'When I was young I learned to keep people at a distance. I was just out of school knew nothing about people and I relied on Chris and the boys to look after me. There wasn't a problem with dates because Chris and I were an item but there were parties where you met all sorts; most were ok but some were predatory.' She patted my arm then kissed my cheek.

I gave her a squeeze and released her, as I did so I brushed a breast. She jumped.

'Yes it was deliberate.'

'Pig' she said 'how can I be friends with a mind reader?'

'Just a guess.' I got out, walked round the car and opened the door. I enjoyed the sight of the ladder now running from her knee to thigh and a glimpse of nicks. She noticed and tugged feebly at the hem of her dress, made a cross noise and said, 'Chinos next time.'

'I'm glad there will be a next time.'

'Oh!' She is anxious again. 'I shouldn't assume that you would want to spend another evening with a clumsy women who talks too much.'

'I can't imagine why you would enjoy an evening with a dull man. You look great and I'm beginning to think you are the impossibly lovely person I suspected.'

'Of course I'm not!'

My remark was dismissed then with that sudden change of direction that made her loveable. 'That was a very kind thing to say; nonsense but appreciated.'

'A last kiss?'

'If you...yes.'

We kiss for about a minute, I am holding her, her arms rest on my shoulders then she relaxes and pats my back. I feel very alive. A car passes and I release her.

'Can we arrange a date?'

'I think so, yes. Ring me.'

'I will.' I need to touch her to maintain contact.

'I do try' she said 'I always have but it isn't possible.'

I don't know what she is talking about.

'Try to what?'

'Be the person you thought I might be.'

I knew what I wanted to say. 'It is being her all the time that is impossible.'

She is looking at me, uncertain, then she smiles; it is a happy, uncertain smile and a tear explores the corner of her eye.

'Silly.'

The evening hadn't been a great success, but the minor crises were overcome and there was a sense of burgeoning friendship.

I am conscious of the world around me the sky the stars and Alison. I haven't felt like this for over thirty years. It must be love.

I was up rather late next day and could not resist a temptation to call her to reassure myself that our friendship is real. When she answered I felt foolish, but we exchanged a few words and the day brightened.

Friendliness was less marked when I walked to the café at lunch time. My friend Victoria was there.'

'Good morning Victoria.'

'Oh. Hello Phillip' she offered me a cool look. '

'Can I join you?'

'Yes of course; I'm afraid you missed your new girlfriend by ten minutes.'

My guess is confirmed. 'You knew that Alison and I were going to the theatre.'

'It's not my business if you are dating my best friend.'

'I think you are teasing and pretending you are jealous.' I instantly wished I hadn't used the word jealous even if it was qualified by 'pretend'.

'I'm not!' She looked up at me sharply; she could look very pretty but she could also look severe. She shrugged. 'Certainly not!'

'We are the same friends we were yesterday I hope.'

'I am, I don't know if you are.' She lowered her voice and pretended disappointment. 'My only man friend is dating another woman.'

'My best lady friend is happily married.'

'I'll let you into a secret Mr Barnes, few women are happily married at fifty, content, comfortable, satisfied maybe but happy I'm not sure.'

'Your friend was or so it seems.'

'Well, of course Mrs Perfect would be. Mrs Perfect had an exciting life with her soulmate and who knows how many other mates as well.'

I decided I had better shut up, Victoria was sounding bitchy and I was no longer sure that she was teasing.

The last thing I wanted was to come between her and her friend; I might lose two friendships.

'I seem to be spoiling your friendship with Alison,' I didn't want to say it but 'Perhaps it would be better to stay away from her.'

'Don't be stuffy. I'm not cross just a bit disappointed. I may be married but our friendship' she lowered her voice 'adds a tiny bit of excitement to my life.'

'And to mine.'

She smiled for the first time. 'Does it?'

'Of course it does. Having a very attractive lady' I whispered 'showing a little interest does a lot for my self-esteem.'

'Is that all?'

I lowered my voice further. 'Victoria, I'm a normal man, you know very well that in different circumstances we would be more than friends.'

'Would we? What circumstances are those?'

She was now pretending that she was offended and I suddenly was tired of the game.

'Circumstance' I whispered 'where when I was teased I could put you over my knee and smack your rear.'

I had never hit a woman in my life and never would, especially someone I was fond of but I had been feeling great and it was spoiled.

'I wouldn't if I were you.' She means it.

I stood up. 'Stop it V! You know I wasn't serious.'

'Oh, don't go, sit down. Please Phil.'

She was my friend again. I sat. 'I don't know what the matter with me is today.'

'I do. You've got it badly.'

'I don't think so, I am too old to be taken in by first impressions.'

'Alison doesn't push herself, she doesn't need to, all she ever needs to do is to look unhappy and men rush to help. The only time it didn't work was when she chose the wrong man.'

I must have registered annoyance because she quickly said 'I'm not putting her down, she is a darling but she has an appeal that sometimes makes me envious.'

I wondered later if Vickie was exaggerating Alison's talent for attracting men to suggest she had many affairs and relationships. That wasn't my impression but the attraction was there and the consequences were possible.

The lightness of feeling that had engulfed me since the previous evening evaporated.

CHAPTER 10

Sextet

Alisons Story

If Liz had left to join her husband abroad the band would have needed a new bass player. I knew that Phil played bass but his possible recruitment needed careful handling; I didn't want to lose a friend or employ a useless bass player.

The situation had been upsetting and adding to the misery was a phone call from a club outside Bristol informing me that due to electrical problems they would need to cancel our Saturday gig.
It was trivial, a small setback but it would have been Liz's last gig before she left and my reaction to the cancellation was disproportionate to its importance.
It was a huge relief when Liz rang to tell me that they would not be moving and she was available.

I wasn't short of activities and I had a number of good friends; my business provided interest, work and sometimes stress. Christianity gave me spiritual and practical guidance and my personal relationship with 'God' as 'father figure' or 'power behind the working of the universe' remained strong and gave substance to my life. My Church activities were supplemented by the band and my volunteer work for my favourite charity. If that wasn't enough there were plenty of daytime clubs offering everything from Art to Zoroastrian study to keep me busy.

As a child my parents gave the comfort I needed and as an adult praise from Chris, from Mr Morris and other friends gave a good feeling and a sense of worth.

That was the trouble, I needed the world's approval.

I couldn't lean on my children and all my close friends were married or had new partners.

Maggie had a new man-friend who in my opinion was a waste of space; one of those elderly teenagers who had drifted through jobs, relationships and life.

I couldn't understand how my sensible schoolfriend was willing to take on someone else's reject. If the current partners of both Margaret and Heather were typical examples, then both would have done better to stick with their husbands.

The negative wave began to rise again and erode the substance that allowed me to function; friends seemed remote, God was diminished and I felt isolated from my family.

Misery seeped unbidden from the shadows in the corners of the room, drifted from the darkness under the furniture and floated unseen in the empty rooms of a home that was too big for me.

I had sufficient money to manage but I was alone without a close companion; under pressure I became poor in spirit and my beliefs bent under a modest stress.

What was my life, what had it been? A singer gaining nightly approval, an actress gaining plaudits out of proportion to her skills because I fell into a character part that was made for me.

Had I started at the bottom I would have soon failed or struggled on to minimal success whilst my personal life fell apart.

What was I now? A small-businesswoman, successful only if success was measured in longevity rather than profit.

I had been smug in my attitude to others once telling Sarah how important it was to maintain moral standards.

She said rather sarcastically 'I wish I had known it was so easy; my experience is that you get nothing for nothing.'

I had pushed myself a little, had traded on my looks, had manoeuvred to be in the right place, had kept my ears opened and chased possibilities but I had never sold myself and had assumed my small success was a reward for effort. Later I realised that many others with greater ability had achieved less; I had been lucky.

Tears began, self-pity seeped in and I cried. When I had cried myself out and silence filled the empty room I lay looking at the warm embers of the fire.

I had a fire, a fire in a warm house; I had friends and family who cared. There was no lack of food, warmth or clothing and money if not plentiful was sufficient for my needs. I had all that mattered.

Jesus died and his disciples coped. If I was unhappy it was because my expectations were too high.

I was able to see the setback for what it was a small hiccup in a corner of my life. It was an important corner; Sextet was my link with the past, singing songs that I had sung with Chrissie, playing riffs he had taught me, performing.

Sextet:-

The girly band had started over twenty years ago and become a long-lasting source of enjoyment.

It started as a piece of fun between Vickie and myself.

KR was gigging regularly, mostly medium sized venues with a few big gigs each year; Vickie had helped backstage at one of these and thoroughly enjoyed her role.

We met the following day and in the ensuing discussion she told me that she could play a simple version of our keyboardist's part. I said she must come to the house and show me so we arranged a session.

Her performance was stilted with a few stumbles but not bad for an amateur and after a second session the concept of a fun band began to form. I spoke to Liz who thought it was a great idea and after a word with KR's drummer, some practice and a little deceit we planned a gig. When we were performance ready we would surprise the boys.

It was a trawl through Chris' diaries after his death that reminded that me of our beginnings.

Chris' Diary:

I should have realised that something was going on, had arrived home early one Friday and could hear the sound of music in the barn and crossed the yard to investigate.

Al looked startled but quickly recovered, Vickie, standing a little behind her playing our keyboard. She looked a little uncomfortable.

'Hi Chris you're early, Vickie came over and we thought we would try a little music.'

'I heard. What are you playing?'

'Things we both like.'

'Vickie was now smiling sweetly but still red faced.'

'Let's hear you then.' I had caught a stilted version of one of the simpler Pretenders songs.

'Go away darling, this is girl's fun. Go and make some coffee, two, white, no sugar.'

I hesitated.

'Go on, you are spoiling things.'

As I left I could hear giggles.

An hour later I had a pleasant moment (though I paid for it).

I had gone upstairs wanting a word with Al; I pushed the half open bedroom door to discover Al wearing a sparkly white top and pants standing in front of the mirror. 'What do you think?' she said.

Vick was facing me wearing a similar skirt and lifting a sparkly top over her head.

'Hi Vick' I said. She squeaked, and covered herself with her hands. Al turned to face me wearing the expression that can melt glass.

'Get out!!' She said.

'Shall I fetch a camera?'

'Go!' Ouutt!!

It was a couple of months later that Clive asked me what was going on and why was Vickie being secretive.

'What's going on about what?'

'Vickie's being a pain and all she'll say is ask Chris.'

'Why me? I mean ask me about what?'

Clive looked suspicious. We were good mates but he knew I liked Vick as much as he admired Al. 'I don't know but she's started playing the piano a lot and it's not the classical stuff she used to play and I caught her hiding some clothes away, not the sort she usually wears.'

'I always thought Vick was straightforward.'

'She is. What's going on?'

'I've no idea, but if she said 'ask Chris' it must mean that Al is involved. I'll ask her in a roundabout way and see what I can find out. Let's go for a jar tonight and I'll let you know.'

'...she did that bloody, 'that's for me to know and you to find out' routine. Told me nothing, but I reckon it's a girly's secret between her and Vickie and someone else. She was a bit smug but in a happy way as if she were pregnant but was waiting for confirmation.'

'If she is,' Clive grinned at me, 'it wasn't me...sadly.'

'Bastard. If she is, I'll tell Vick you assured me it wasn't yours.'

'Don't you bloody dare, Vick isn't so confident as Al, or so tolerant...from what you've told me.'

It was another week before the secret was revealed. Al told me that she was 'going out with the girls' on Friday.

'Fine,' I said, 'my parents are having the children for the weekend so I can go out too.'

We enjoyed an early dinner then retired to smarten ourselves ready for our respective evenings out. Al was a long time in the bathroom and I was obliged to shower and shave in the tiny en-suite. By the time she appeared wrapped in several towels I was dressed.

'I won't be long.'

I had heard that before and went down to the office where I gazed at the weeks correspondence and wondered if there was time to finish before she appeared. I stared at the pile, decided to leave it and was sitting in the lounge watching TV when she came downstairs looking really glam.

'Wow. You look terrific, can I come with you.'

'Yes.' She offered an excited smile.

'Thanks, but Clive and I are meeting so...'

'Clive is joining us.' 'Do I look OK?'

'Like a dishy twenty-two. I love the sparkly top but I thought short skirts were out.'

'Not necessarily.'

'I suppose I had better tell you.' She said as we entered the car park of the large and slightly rough pub.

'Perhaps you had; obviously something is going on.'

'Something is.' She parked near the entrance, slid out, walked to the rear of the car and opened the tailgate.

'Give me a hand. will you?' Her eyes sparkled and she stood to one side with a happy smile on her face.

'You've arranged a gig? I guess I'll manage.'

She looked even more delighted.

'Not you darling, it's *my* new band. This is our first gig. You will be supportive. won't you?'

'I always am; will I be jealous?'

'There is no reason to be jealous, I hope you will be impressed.'

'Ok, let's go.'

She picked up the 8-channel mixer amp and headed for the main entrance. I hefted up the first of the large speakers, passing her as she returned for a bag containing our microphones. Successively we collected the remaining speaker, the small foldback, her two guitars, the mic and speaker stands, a bag of leads and her Marshall combo and my effects pedals. Already on the small stage were the drums and I could see Gerry adjusting them. He waved and gave me a grin. Our keyboard and an unknown Carlsbro combo stood stage left.'

'So? What's going on, you've taken over the band?'

'Don't be silly.' She pecked at my cheek.

'Chris.' Can you give me a hand?' It was Liz accompanied by Brian who was struggling with her Peavy combo. 'Can you fetch the extension cab, I've got the guitar.' She kissed my cheek and gave me her car keys. Her skirt was short like Al's.'

Reluctantly I returned to the park and collected the heavy 2x10 that supplemented her combo.

We had just finished setting up and I was wondering about the special occasion when Clive appeared with Vickie. She looked nervous and when we kissed she gripped me for a second. She was wearing the skirt and the sparkly top that I had seen before; belatedly the penny dropped.

'He's so slow sometimes.' Al kissed Vickie and looked at me.

'So that's it you conniving lot." What are you calling yourselves?'

'Sextet' she muttered.

It seemed rather rude for Al; was it I wondered a coded message. When I asked later I was told 'Only a man would think like that.'

'Isn't that the point?'

They looked attractive; an adjective not always applicable to girl bands. They also played very well. There was a lot of leg on display but the only flash of nicks was accidental when Vick coming forward to bow, caught the hem of her skirt on the keyboard and it lifted to reveal her briefs. Red faced she disentangled herself accompanied by whistles and catcalls.

Sextet was good; with three ex-professionals and good songs that were well played they were much better than the average pub band.

Vick's keyboard playing was stiff but good for a first gig and Al was bubbling with a kind of loose happiness that always gave me a good feeling. It's called love.

I was also impressed by their singing. Al's excellent and Liz' good (otherwise she wouldn't have joined KR). Vickie, though clearly nervous, added low harmonies in a breathy contralto which were more than satisfactory.

Gerry gave excellent professional support but was unnoticed by most of the audience.

Their beloveds had to enjoy their own and Gerry's company when afterwards the girls received admiration from some 'fans'; the three at the bar surrounded by half a dozen noisy blokes one drunk one keen, and a couple fancying their chances.

Clive was unsure 'Should we rescue them? One bloke has got his arm round Vickie.'

'She deserves it; she did well for a first gig.'

'He's being over friendly.'

'Let it go, Al can deal with it, don't start a fight unless we have to.'

'What? You mean there could be a fight.'

'I doubt it, they look keen not nasty.'

'I'm not having that.' Clive was getting annoyed. 'The guy put his hand under her skirt.'

'She gave him a slap.'

'She didn't mean it, she smiled.'

'Sorry boys, it's been just lovely to meet you'...Al raised her voice...'but we need to get away, tired after all that singing.'

There were a few comments, I could guess what. Al smiled, 'Yes, we'd love to come again' she said and shepherded Vick away.

They joined us to enjoy further appreciation.

Alison's Story cont'd.

Gigging was part of my life, a part that could have ended with Liz departure.

We had been playing together on and off since V and I got together for our fun afternoon. Drummers had come and gone, pregnancies had interfered but we had reformed and maintained continuity.

We had quickly established ourselves on the local scene but it took eighteen months or more to establish a reputation as a '*good* band' and to overcome the '*Girl* band' label with it's belittling implications.

We were employed because we played what the customers wanted and did it well.

We practiced regularly and our act developed and improved. We gigged irregularly, about once a month because KR came first but I enjoyed the whole scene from our first gig.

Three women together sharing admiration in stressful circumstances is not a recipe for good feeling; but the inevitable conflicts never became acrimonious and the nearest thing to a blow up was unrelated to our performance.

It was six months after we had established ourselves as a good reliable band that fate threw us a curly one.

Mr Morris rang and told me that we had been noticed and asked if we would like to tour as the support act for a band that was charting.

It was an amazing offer, tempting but totally impractical.

We had played several big gigs but the band we were to support was way out of our league.

We could do a good show and had a great set that included some Synergy, Cats Whiskers and 'kR originals but a tour would cause a huge disruption to our lives and the burden of organisation would fall on me.

I was cynical enough to suspect that our attraction was not 'Good Band' but 'Girl Band', maybe even after show entertainment for the main attraction.

It was unlikely, we were in our early thirties and had young families (not Liz at the time).

The logistics could be sorted but V wasn't up to professional standard and had no experience of the hard work involved. Added to that we would need to find and pay a full-time professional drummer.

I gave it a lot of thought; Liz was up for it and V was very keen ('I'll never get another chance, we must take it, please Al, it is important to me.') but I wasn't happy.

On this occasion when I wanted Chris to be contrary and difficult he was helpful saying 'I managed when you were working with glamorous actors, I don't think it is likely that you will be seduced by the charms of a thick rocker.'

'I was!' I said but he ignored me.

'Sextet is a good band; V isn't pro-standard but she will be ok. You look great without being tarty and musically you are damned good, much better than many girl bands.'

'Your problem' he added 'is to find someone to look after Lisa. I can work and look after the others but I can't manage a baby as well.'

I had already discussed it with mum; Sarah and Simon were settled at school and though mum was seeking secretarial work she was happy to put it off for a few weeks.

Perhaps I worried too much about the problems when I should have been positive and found the challenge stimulating but despite Chris' support I decided to turn it down.

I knew it was for the best, knew the difficulties far better than Vickie, but the decision left her upset, in tears and so angry it nearly ended our friendship.

Then Ollie our drummer phoned and said he would be glad to support us and the gig became possible.

I took the positive line; instead of worrying about the difficulties I changed my mind and decided to meet the challenge.

Chris had given me his assessment of the band we were supporting. The guitarist was an ok guy and a good musician, the drummer the same, a drinker but a friendly drinker and the singer had a great voice and a talent for promotion.

The keyboard and bass players he dismissed, the former as a one talent thicko and the latter as 'a mate of the singer'.

'If you take the gig don't undersell yourself, 'kR was big so don't let them pretend they are doing you a favour.'

'Moneywise I'd suggest...' He named a price.

I told him that I was thinking about half the amount and he said

'Maurice knows why they want you and how much they will pay.'
'Remind him,' he added, 'they are buying a band, not after show comforts.'
I said I would speak to Mr Morris.
He told me to ignore my husband who was a fool (he's never forgiven him for retiring) then indirectly said that his advice was about right.

It was a six week intensive tour, more than twenty fairly big gigs. Clive was not keen on letting Vickie loose but she was determined and with Chris being helpful when I needed him to say 'NO!' Clive had no option.
I went ahead and agreed to do the gig subject to a decent deal.
Mr Morris got us a good deal; less than Chris had suggested but he had negotiated an up-front payment that would cover our initial costs, the balance would be paid to him at the end of the tour. He said that he knew the other management 'They ain't what I would call 'top drawer' but unlike some their finances are sound. It's' just a matter of extracting the mazuma darling.'

So we did it; strange and scary it was also exciting like 'kR but without Chris.
V was shaking with nerves on her first night but she did the business to the best of her ability and we were pretty good, getting a lot of applause from an audience that hadn't come to see us.
During my time with Synergy and Cats Whiskers I had learned how to communicate with an audience and in that respect the support act was vastly more professional than the main act whose 'Yo!' 'Hi' and 'Heyeah' were good enough for their fans.
Phillips came with Clive to our first night and said that the rest of the audience came to see girlies. He had a mischievous twinkle in his eye. 'Just teasing darling, you were damned good and you gave a great performance. I know you can do it but I was still impressed.'
I waited for the curly one. 'Oh' he added 'the girlies actually

looked pretty good.'

A small crisis came sooner than expected; it took a week of steady improvement for Vickie's confidence to rise and with it came a slice of the rock chick to replace a portion of married mum.

Her 'We are here to play music/show respect' vocabulary faded and the thirty plus mum turned twenty-something and wore her hair in bunches. Her delusions of herself as rock chick and object of desire took a knock when the youngest member of the main act was heard to comment that it was 'like being on tour with your effin' mother'.

She remained sensible and focussed when performing but her increasing confidence brought dismissive responses to my gentle warnings.

'For goodness sake Al, it's only a few drinks after the show!' and her slightly offensive 'You've been there and done it darling. I really don't need a minder.'

I understood. During our early days in the business my respect for 'the wisdom of Soloman' as we jokingly called it allowed me to avoid making too many mistakes at a time when I thought I knew it all.

Liz, who had learned a lot during her six months as a professional understood Vickie's situation but kept out of it and by the end of the second week I felt that I had done all I could and let it go.

The band we were supporting was good if you like over produced heavy rock and were enjoying their success. It seemed that (in my judgement) 'thick chicks' were part of the scene.

I ignored them assuming that their attachment to the band added excitement to otherwise empty lives.

Almost immediately I realised that I was being an insensitive, self-righteous prig. I squirmed, felt terribly ashamed, suppressed a temptation to patronise and accepted everyone for what they were.

'Sextet' had chosen stage gear that was a little more racy than normal. Lacy tops in my case and cleavage revealing ones in Vickie's. Even so, compared to the hair, clothes and attitude of the main event we looked tame.

I no longer felt responsible for V but the worries resurfaced when she didn't return with us after a show one evening, arriving back at the guest house in the early hours.

Next morning, giggly and full of excuses she related the events of the evening.

'Just a couple of drinks, Tash is terrible, he made me laugh. One of those rough girls was there, she just went outside with that big roadie and' she lowered her voice, 'well, we guessed what happened, just like that, I thought it was disgusting.'

'Tash saw me looking when they came back and said "Your turn now Vick." I said 'I'm married.' and he said "Married is ok, available is all I need."

'Then Benny took my arm and we had a smoochy dance, and at the end I said 'thanks Ben' and came home. 'Well just a quick hug, he's ok compared to the others. Are they all like that?'

'Some. Ben's ok but be careful.'

A week later we all went to a proper party on the Saturday because we had two days off.

It was fun initially but I left with Liz when it started to get heavy. Liz was good at dealing with it and seemed to have fun and avoid getting involved at the same time. My technique was to be polite, friendly and un-engaged.

Vickie was late in again and Ollie told Liz next day that she had got tiddly and when one of the groupies went topless she giggled and said 'I wouldn't dare.'

This resulted in a comment about 'swinging mums' which led her to assure them she was a decent shape.

It is unwise to get involved in that kind of banter and according to Ollie she giggled, blushed, lifted her top and showed off.

He added a comment about her shape which rather confirmed that it was true.

Oh dear, I hope she hasn't been naughty, Clive will hate me and Chris will be cross.

I didn't know how to deal with it. I could confront her but if we fell out there would be nearly a month of bad feeling which would make matters worse.

I thought of asking Chris but he might do the 'offended man' thing so I asked mum if she could visit. Mum often has an answer.

She asked if I wanted her to stay and when I said yes and she made a non-mum joke asking if she would need to wipe my bottom for the next thirty years as well.

She would come on a Friday evening because Lisa went home to Chris or his parents at the weekend.

It brought home to me how much I missed her and how much the tour was messing up our lives.

Mum arrived and I felt some of the pressure release; V no longer regularly attended the after-show gatherings but she was spending a lot of time with Ben. I worry about Ben least because he is civilised and married, but mum's arrival was none too soon.

She gave Liz and Vickie a hug and we went to lunch together at a pleasant little café recommended by the theatre staff.

I never thought of Mum as someone who could be subtle but she worked the conversation around to her grandchildren, moved on to the visit she had made to the farm, told me that Chris and the children were missing me and mentioned that Clive had visited while she was there.

V asked how Clive was managing though she rings every other day and knew that his few problems were not serious. It gave Mum the opportunity to say that he was managing, then with a pause, 'obviously he misses you and Erin has been waking in the night crying. You are both so lucky to have caring husbands, it isn't easy to work and manage the children. Your mother has been filling in and Marilyn has been around to help him. Clive said she is an angel.'

I saw V frown. 'He would' she said in a meaningful voice.'

I understood her meaning, Chris said in a more candid moment that he likes Marilyn but she can sometimes give the impression that she is available. 'It's a waste really, she's attractive but she doesn't turn me on. Not many girls do, I'm probably too fussy.'
I asked him 'Who does?'
'Chloe possibly.'
'Chloe?? You mean Chloe from church whose husband is never there. Shortish with glasses?'
'Yes, slim, neat figure, lovely legs. I don't fancy her in a serious way but she's sort of sensible and likeable.'
'Huh.'
'Come off it darling. She's like you but you look lovely when you aren't wearing that sour face.'

Mum turned on the charm. We spent the next day together and she was a friend to V and Liz. That evening there was a semi-formal party. It combined a management check–up and the theatre outreach when they invited local business leaders. It wasn't the drunken after show gathering with a couple of groupies and some noisy or nervous fans but it still generated a deal of semi drunken behaviour.
I was tired; I could cope with the stress of performance but we had spent the afternoon rehearsing and the 'party' offered an opportunity to chase the management accountant. This extra activity and a single drink combined to make me feel so weary that I went home early.

The girls and Mum came in late, chatting and giggly as they passed my room and I caught the words '…I never thought that you would.' 'So what else did he say?' and 'As if! I'm a respectable married woman…' followed by the words 'Aren't we all?' and laughter.
Mum left the following evening; Rachel my sister is only six and she didn't want to leave her for long.
She said quietly to me before she left that she had spoken to V

and wasn't worried.

'She is' I was told 'less inhibited than she would at home and Clive wouldn't be very happy about her friendship with that nice boy Benjamin. Of course' she added 'you can never be sure but I think it is just a friendship and she sees the situation as a chance for some harmless fun.'

'Thanks mum, I shouldn't feel responsible but I can't help it.'

'Mum...'

'What.'

'Ollie tells me one of the girls went topless last night.'

'Yes. Don't look like that?'

'What happened?'

'Just one of those groupie girls showing off, apparently she does it quite often.'

'And?'

She smiled. 'I said to Victoria that you get more interest if you hint at things rather than be obvious and she said 'Like what?'

'I said that if you were a decent shape, not wearing a bra could be more interesting than an open display.'

'Was that all?'

'I'm being interrogated by my daughter again.' She pinkened slightly. 'Victoria said "I will if you will."'

'And?'

'I am still in fairly good shape and I was wearing a loose blouse so it wasn't obvious.'

'Unless you are smooching with someone and their hands start roaming.' The pinkening increased.

'You came here to put V on the straight and narrow and end up leading her astray.'

'Don't be silly darling, it gave me the chance to be on her side and have a little fun which is rare at my age. You should try it.'

She was right. I joined in with V and Liz a little more often, enjoyed some modest fun, ignored my friend's behaviour and on the last evening the three of us let go a little, some possibly more than others.

We decided to embarrass the band by behaving like older teenagers, short skirts, fancy tops that sort of thing. It was good to be treated like a rock chick rather than a married mum and it is flattering when hands must be discouraged.

I spent much of the evening with one of the management team because he was intelligent and straightforward.

I was viewing the evening through a modest haze of drink when I noticed that Ben was getting amorous and V seemed to be hooked.

Later in the evening Liz eased away from an admirer, approached me and asked if I had any plans, meaning had I any plans for the management guy who was smooching with me.

My plan was that when tiredness balanced enjoyment I would leave.

'No. Shall we go?' I thought for a moment 'Give me a couple of minutes?'

I thanked my friend for an enjoyable evening, was eased not unwillingly onto the terrace, was appreciated, disengaged and after a kiss I returned to the room. Liz was waiting and as we crossed the dance area we broke into a giggly boogie before heading for the door.

I noticed that V was missing; too bad, I was still feeling happy in the afterglow of management approval.

My mildly naughty evening had assured me that I was still attractive and required firm resolve to keep the appreciation at an acceptable level.

I woke the following morning with a clear head, feeling comfortable, slightly disappointed that the tour was over and desperate for a wee.

Sitting on the loo, chin in hands staring through the open door at the unmade bed I wondered if I should have shown more concern for Vickie.

"Not my problem" I told myself but I was aware that if there was a problem the blame would fall on me.

V was late for breakfast and was seen by Liz in the corridor outside her room talking to Ben.

Had he just arrived to collect her or was he leaving? When I joined her later she was uneasy and I couldn't decide if she was elated or unhappy.

Poor darling I thought, if she has misbehaved then let it be an enjoyable romp, please don't let her fall in love.

I drove the girls back to our homes late that afternoon in our van loaded with equipment. It was a tiring trip and I was looking forward to seeing Chris and the children because I had been home only twice during the tour. Chris had asked if he could come to a second show and I had made him stay overnight.

After I had dropped off Liz, the drive went from quiet to silent and we were nearly home when I spoke to V.

'Try to let it go.'

'It isn't that easy.' She looked miserable.

'Listen best friend, I don't know the situation between you and Ben but forget it. Be nice to Clive and enjoy putting the children to bed. Promise!' 'Tomorrow come over and we can have a chat and an inquest.'

'I'll see you tomorrow.'

I can only say that when we met for coffee next day she talked, was candid and surprised me with some of her admissions. There were more 'dates' with Ben than I knew and she admitted a close friendship.

I knew her very well; she was a decent person but in the right situation it is easy to be seduced unless you are very strong willed.

'It was difficult; it was super having a new friend.' she told me 'I had to keep reminding myself that home, the children and Clive were important.'

Maybe there never was a fling, perhaps that was her problem.

'Her parting shot with an unexpected attempt at black humour was 'Why is there always a dark side to enjoying a little bit of fun.'

Mum is very up together but her assessment had not taken into account that girls have a different attitude these days.

I understood V's liking for Ben, I had spoken with him on several occasions and had lunched with him once. Performers are not always rounded people and the nature of their business can make them wary and careful with what they say.

Ben was good looking and friendly. He admitted that he was taken with V describing her as a real darling, and good fun even though she was married.

After lunch we walked back to the theatre together chatting amiably.

During our conversation, he asked me where I learned guitar saying that there were some excellent girl guitarists but many were copies or they tried too hard. 'You do some pretty good riffing and you do simple very well.'

I explained that Chris had taught me the basic riffs and let me develop them in my own style.

He asked 'Chris who?'

'My husband' I told him, 'Chris Phillips, you may have heard of him, he was part of 'kR.'

Ben frowned then raised his eyebrows.

'Chris Phillips, I half recognised the name. I know you from acting and I know you are married but I didn't realise that Alison Smith is Mrs Phillips.'

'He was a damned good guitarist;' he bit his lips, 'I'm not being negative if I say he wasn't a virtuoso like Tony but he was solid and sometime brilliant and he could sing and perform. He was the kind of player we hacks aspire to be.'

Ben was very good and I assured him that he was certainly no hack.

'He did a great job with one 'kR number, fast, bass and guitar playing in harmony. What was it called?'

'It was called 'Loose Fit'. He was playing triplets and he had some input to the lyrics that were quite clever and funny. He got no credit because Bruce wrote the song.'

'Bruce, yes it was a shame, the band was on its way to the top. You were…' I inclined my head 'you were the girl who tried to save him.' I nodded. It was an uncomfortable memory that made me feel queasy.

'That was before you were Mrs Phillips, you were with Bruce, part of the band?'

'Yes, no, yes. Yes before I married Chris, no I was never Bruce's girlfriend or anything else, yes I was a backing singer and occasionally rhythm guitarist.'

'Wow, hard to believe, talented, lustworthy and lovely to be with.'

'Say it again.' I teased.

'What do you mean?'

'Tell me again how wonderful I am.'

We laughed together.

'You are. Three out of three is a f…damned good score.'

Ben says the right things, I am beginning to like him. Move over V.

'Tell me,' Ben continued. 'Chris had a reputation as being an ok bloke, is that right?'

'He's ordinary and he treats everyone the same; unless he is being hassled or he's under pressure he's a lamb.'

'I'm sure he is with you.'

He glances across admiringly. I have a second momentary tingle. 'No kidding. I never met him but I was talking with a sound guy who worked for 'kR and he said he was fussy about set up and snappy sometimes but mostly he was matey and easy going.'

'He is if kept in order.'

'I'm sure Mrs Phillips can keep order.' He gives me that look again. 'I need to say that Alison has qualities that promote serious interest.'

I smile at him. 'Thank-you.' I put a hand on his shoulder and we stop momentarily; I lean over and kiss his cheek.

Why should V hog the only dishy member of the band.

'Right.' He kisses me in return. They drop slightly, thank goodness we are entering the theatre to set up the equipment.

'Thanks for the lunch.'
'We must do it again.'
Sadly, we never did.

CHAPTER 11

A new lease of life

Phillip's Story

My date with A was not well received by Victoria but her invitation to a barbeque assured me that our friendship was back on track.

Alison would be in Swansea baby-sitting for her son Simon but my sister was coming to stay for the weekend and she would accompany me. We had been friends since childhood and following my divorce she had taken on the role of protector.

I was sure Vickie wouldn't mind if I took her to the party.

I had a very busy week at work and few opportunities to speak to Alison. She left a message saying that she wouldn't be in church but would catch up with me sometime. In my uncertain state I wasn't sure if she was avoiding or reassuring me.

The barbeque was...well a barbeque. Overcooked chops and suspicious chicken in tasteless rolls, the whole saved by home-made salads, rice or pasta dishes and on this occasion some perfect cold sliced beef.

While we were getting ready, my sister had speculated on the nature of the local society and my role in it.

'Phil darling you are a lamb to the slaughter, I'm sure some of the ladies are very nice but it would do no harm to check them out.'

I told her she would meet them at the barbeque and her response was 'Don't tell them I am your sister, don't lie, just introduce me as Sheena.'

Our evening had an uncomfortable beginning; I introduced Sheena to Vickie who smiled falsely, gave me a disapproving glance, said 'enjoy, must speak to other guests' and turned her back on us.

'Your friend Victoria?' Sheena offered a wry smile, took my hand and we began to circulate.

I spent much of the evening chatting with Clive; we had got along well from our first meeting and inevitably the conversation turned to my date with Alison.

'Not a lot to tell but I enjoyed the evening. We went to the theatre; the play wasn't great but the performance was good and afterwards in the pub we had a chat.'

'What did you think of her? Sorry to be inquisitive but I have a soft spot for her.'

'She is interesting and seems to be a decent person but....'

'Ah the 'but'. You couldn't quite get a clear picture.'

'No I couldn't, it was as if she was two people, I don't mean literally, I mean she seems really sensible and open then suddenly she clams up as If she has remembered something awful.'

'She lost her husband a couple of years ago; it was quite sudden and she took it badly. We worried about her for a while because she was verry unhappy and a bit irrational but she seems to be getting over the worst.'

'I knew she was widowed. You reckon that's why she gets sad moments?'

'Sometimes, but other times it's the old artistic temperament. She always was one for the ups and downs.'

'I see.'

'Don't get me wrong, ninety-nine point nine per cent of the time she is the real girl, kind, normal and well balanced but if something upsets her sometimes she will internalise it and be miserable, sometimes she reacts. Most often she withdraws until she can sort herself out.'

'Really. She seems to be a lovely person.'

'She's lovely, I've lusted after her since we first met, great body when she was younger, probably she still has. Her mother looked good into her fifties, not bad even into her sixties.'

I made allowance for his being happily tiddly.

'Great body? Interesting.'

'Beach holidays. We went abroad with them several times. Al was a surprise, brave girl. I could tell you a story, café in France, she saw this couple, young girl with an older guy and Al decided to put her straight, wow. I was cringing but... ' he frowned 'where was I?

Al, quite shy but on the beach, she and Vic, both of them everything off. Hard to' he thought, 'not get hard.'

We laughed but I felt slightly miffed that he had seen Alison naked. It wasn't jealousy it was 'I wish I had been there'.

'Always had a soft spot for Al but she was totally in love with her husband. Vick has a soft spot for you, do you fancy taking on Vick and leave me free to pursue Al.'

He was drunker than I thought.

'Nice idea but I don't think either of them would go along with it.'

'Good idea though.'

We got back on track and began to discuss other members of the village.

It was an interesting conversation and I learned which of the village ladies to avoid. Clive was a friend and a useful source of information.

Before she went home next day my sister gave me a detailed report on her evening.

Vickie was not at all impressed by my turning up with another woman (my sister is eight years younger than me and men find her attractive). Later in the evening she had been more friendly and Sheena's conclusion was that having another woman in my life implied a lack of commitment to Alison which was seen by Vickie as a good thing.

The general opinion of the gossips was that Vickie and I were having an affair and my date with A had caused bad feeling between them.

Alison on the other hand was a source of mixed reports.

"She has always behaved in a respectable manner as far as people know but I understand she had a wild youth. The general opinion was "She is very charming but of course you know what entertainers are; you see the face they want you to see."

It seems that with her husband barely cold she went back to singing with a rock band and had an affair with the singer. It showed that she was insensitive and foolish for someone of her age.

My sister's opinion was that reading between the lines she was mostly well liked and the gossip was based not on knowledge but on stereotypical ideas of rock stars.

Several other pieces of information had come to light. After her first singing career ended she had worked as an actor for several years "and you know what actors are like."

I didn't.

The one confirmed fact my sister told me, was that she had appeared naked in a film.

'It came up in conversation with Vickie; Clive was told to find the DVD and he loaned it to me. Here it is.'

This fact was un-welcome but as soon as my sister returned home I had to watch it.

The film wasn't too bad; quite well shot with several good performances and a story line that was just plausible. Its flaw was that it didn't know whether it was a comedy, an adventure or a smutty sub-carry-on farce.

Alison's first appearance gave me a shock, the slim attractive woman I knew was a slim attractive girl. She was wearing a t-shirt with a 'king Rock chick logo, had a leather jacket slung over her shoulder and was saying 'Cheers guys, see you' to some motorcyclists'. She then turned and walked towards the camera putting on her jacket. I was fixated by the nipples jiggling under the t-shirt.

The scene continued with her straddling a large motorcycle and fastening on her helmet`. She wasn't Marianne Faithfull exuding sexuality, she was the girl-next-door being cheeky.

The lead character then appeared and a smutty conversation began. I had never liked the actor playing the lead; presumably he was talented but the talent was well concealed and my principal feeling was a wish to kick his ass.

Alison's role was to transport the lead character to a commune in Scotland.

She was first taken to a hotel where in a bedroom she was seen tucking in her t-shirt and zipping up her jeans presumably after she had been bedded by the hero.

During this scene much filming was saved by their conversation which explained the reason for the trip. There were then shots of Scottish scenery and a tracking shot to a window in a small castle.

The scene then changed to an interior that said 'country house in Surry' rather than dingy castle and there followed a rambling dialogue between an unconvincing professor, his assistant and an irrelevant secretary who looked like a stripper on her day off. This informed us that the professor was searching for an ancient occult document of great value.

There was then an extended scene where an expert on ancient documents played by a very good actress was seen opening and reading a letter after which she picked up the phone and contacted the 'professor"

The ploy enabled her to establish her expertise and move the plot on a considerable distance. Quality tells and not only had she the skill to make her smutty exchanges amusing but the film started to come together.

The next shot followed a large motorcycle as it travelled down a country road and then cut to its arrival at the coast.

A panning shot of an empty beach ended to show Alison hauling a small motorcycle onto its stand. She took off her helmet and shook out her hair; her worldly motorcycle chick character was established by her cocky confidence but her looks were still girl-next-door.

The man took her hand and they descended on to a deserted beach; both looked remarkably fresh after a three hundred mile trip on a bike.

Some poorly dubbed dialogue informed us that they needed a refreshing swim.

Alison threw down her bag and took off the leather jacket. The man was already taking off his jeans.

'Race you.' he says and my heart gave a thump as she lifts her t-shirt to reveal lovely breasts in close up.

The scene changed to show her jacket and t-shirt lying on the sand.

A pair of jeans lands on it, her briefs follow and the camera pans away to show a naked girl trotting down the beach.

There is a fade and the next shot shows the couple returning from the sea hand in hand before lying down behind a dune.

I felt tense but …I re-ran the few seconds of A as the t-shirt came off followed by her rear as she headed for the sea then the scene of the two returning. The rear looks plumper than expected, the legs shorter and the pert teenage breasts of the first scene are larger and swaying. I re-ran the section again and it was clear that the naked girl was not the Alison. Later in the film there was a scene at an unconvincing orgy when Alison, this time wearing a long white shirt and revealing long legs is 'seduced' and subsequently is seen stripping out of focus in the background. The swaying bosoms confirmed that the stripper and the girl in longshot were stand-ins but I still felt a little upset. Young Alison was lovely.

I didn't see her until Wednesday. She was in the village cafe with a slim blonde woman that I knew. When I spoke to her she looked up, acknowledged me with a slightly cool 'Hello Phillip' paused and said 'This is Caren; perhaps you have met at the club.' 'Yes, we have played together. Hi Caren.' She smiled and responded but my mind was elsewhere.

Sheena's plan had yielded useful information but it had created a small problem which I hoped would be easily solved.

'Can I join you?'

Another pause 'Yes of course.'

'I'll get a coffee.'

By the time I returned my initial sense of being rebuffed had become a worry; Sheena's piece of fun had created a coolness in Victoria, might it have upset A? Surely not, she had been a wild child, a pop star. Was she acting?

I sat down and jumped straight in. 'Missed you at the barbie.'

'I was in Swansea, I told you.'

'Yes. It was a double shame because my sister came for the weekend and she would have loved to meet you.'

'Oh yes,' her response was neutral, 'Vickie told me that you came with a friend.'

'My sister.'

'This is Caren, from the tennis club.'

It was a rapid change of subject. 'Hello Caren. Are you the one I spoke to just now or a different one?'

Alison said 'That's my line' offered a smile and I fell in love again. I couldn't say exactly why but something about her was appealing and it wasn't sex. Perhaps it was.

That was probably where our real friendship began.

Our second date was an entirely different affair. Alison had been sent tickets for a concert by a band that was around when she was still at school. It had survived to the present day with a fluctuating core of the original band supplemented by bewildering number of transient members.

She had met several of the original members when, during one of its low periods the band had supported 'king Rock on part of their last tour. One of its members I was told had been *her* guitarist when she was running her own band.

I was growing increasingly fond of the older woman and references to her busy and varied life as a rock singer sat uncomfortably with my feeling for her.

I couldn't explain those feelings in any practical or real sense though who is to say what emotions are at work at an unconscious level. I think it was a wish that I had known the young girl she had been combined with a hope that she really was the person she now presented.

The tickets were free, had been sent by a management acquaintance with a note that we could go backstage after the show.

I collected her early in the evening since we were to have a pre-show meal and it was probable that we would be late home. I knocked, this time on the correct door and after a few moments it was opened. Alison looked stunning; I don't know how much time she had spent on her appearance but she looked wonderful. Her hair was in a layered bob and her makeup was just enough to enhance her looks. She was wearing a shortish skirt, a glittery top and black tights which should have been wrong but wasn't. I took in the vision and wondered how she had got it so right.

She was speaking. 'Hello, come in. Am I alright? Not too 'mutton'?'

I was aware of a hint of perfume and had difficulty in believing I was dating this exotic creature.

We entered the lounge and the youthful vision became an attractive woman in her forties,

'Vickie and Clive are coming, I had some spare tickets, I hope you don't mind, we will pick them up on the way.' Then suddenly, 'Oh Phil I am sorry I should have asked. It won't spoil the evening and we can arrange another date, just the two of us' she coloured, bit her lip 'if you still want to. I am hopeless.'

I finally managed to speak. 'You look wonderful.'

'Do I? Thanks Phil, I thought I should make an effort after last time.'

'Last time you only looked lovely, this time...I don't know what to say...young and lovely.'

'Don't exaggerate! Thank-you, I still love flattery,' She laughed

happily. 'Let's go.'
She grabbed a short suede jacket from a peg.

Clive and Vickie were waiting for us and came out of their gate as we got out of the car.
'Hi Al, looking great.' Clive opened the rear door.
'Goodness Al, I thought we were going to a concert; I didn't know you were hoping to perform?'
Vickie is usually kind but not always.
Alison didn't seem to mind and didn't comment; I remember her "Not too mutton" and hope she isn't hurt.
'You are right Vick, she looks fantastic.' Clive is impressed.
A looks up and I see a hint of smugness.
Vickie slides into the car and smiles at me. She is displaying more boosie than I have seen before and looks pretty dishy herself.
I raise my eyebrows appreciatively smile back and mouth a 'Wow'.

The concert was loud; it was not my kind of music though their live performance was much more exciting than their records. The band had formed in the early seventies and its remaining original members were half a trend older than me so the music was before my time.
Alison had come alive at the start of the concert, had slightly embarrassed me by swaying in her seat and waving her arms like a teenager. A glance had shown the girl she had been, lively and excited.
Vickie was sharing the excitement and I was reminded that these two still gigged and retained a feeling for performance.
I had already come to terms with age and a sense of exclusion when at the end of the concert we were taken back stage to 'meet the band'.
Alison had met three of the original band on a 'kR tour and Carl their current lead guitar had been part of her band on her Cats Whiskers' tour.

We were taken to the dressing rooms which were open, busy and noisy; Alison seemingly in her element slipped into the room, looked around and waved.

A f**k**'nell! was heard followed by more friendly bad language and she was gathered up and hugged by a sweaty aging freak with thinning dyed long hair.

'F' me,' the freak exclaimed 'its Smithy. F in hell' it repeated 'lookin great. Hey guys, s' Dorian Gray'. A second freak appeared. 'Hey guys remember Smithy?' said the first.

The second squinted through puffy eyes and after some profanities that expressed pleasure offered a sweaty hug and kiss. I noticed that that his sparse hair was carefully arranged.

My perfect woman was un-phased and obviously pleased to be remembered. After an exchange of compliments and more hugs she called us into the room to be greeted with indifference. Clive and I found ourselves sidelined with little to do except admire some battered but expensive guitars.

Vickie on the other hand was standing next to Alison and sharing the interest.

Clive nodded towards the girls where V was doing her wide eyed virtuous married woman routine which is mostly genuine.

'Vick likes to be chatted up.' Clive echoes my thoughts.

At that moment Vickie catches my eye, realises we are commenting, looks offended then turns her back on us and continues her animated discussion.

'These days I assume she's too old to pull.' Clive adds.

I get a twinge of guilt; am aware that she could pull me.

'Not sure about our Al though.' He becomes confidential. 'I thought that when I reached a certain age I would be less interested especially in older women. The trouble is that as soon as I feel comfortable with Al as a friend she turns up looking shaggable.' He looks at me quizzically.

'No mate. Hardly know her, chaste kiss is all of it. I know what you mean though, when I collected her tonight she looked about thirty-five.'

One of the aging rockers, Carl I think has his arm around her and is easing her across the room. He is being very familiar and she is heard to say quite loudly 'Carl, behave!'

I don't know if she is offended or pretending.

Carl picks up a guitar and they converse; he starts to play and A sings; there is a brief lull in the chatter and several people turn to look. After a few moments they turn back to their noise and activity and I get a mischievous pleasure seeing her disappointment.

She turns to Carl, finishes a verse and pretends that it was just for him, and after a brief conversation, looks up, smiles and eases across the room to join me.

'Carl was my guitarist when I had my own band' she tells me unnecessarily 'I soon remembered why I always kept him at arm's length; he wanted me to sing a couple of verses from one of our songs. It was fun.'

She changes the subject. 'I am sorry, this is boring for you and I must give the impression of an under dressed old woman trying to recapture her youth.'

I bounce from slight annoyance to feeling protective and risk an arm around her shoulders. 'The woman' I whisper 'looks very youthful.'

She turns her head away and squeezes my hand. 'Thanks Chris you always say the right...' She stops and goes rigid.

'I think I had better collect Vick.' Clive taps my arm and moves away.

Vickie has removed her jacket; her low top reveals an interesting amount of bosom.

A is red faced, she grips my sleeve. 'Sorry Phil I don't know why... shall we go?'

'Yes, good thinking. It was interesting to meet the band but I'm ready to go if Clive can drag Vickie away.'

Al nods. 'Vickie was quite shy when we first met but now she makes the most of every opportunity; I will need to prise her away.'

It took five minutes for the three or four aging rockers to be spoken to, kissed and captured on her phone .

We had only just left when I remembered I had left my coat. I returned to fetch it and caught '...yeah, she always was. The other one's worth a shag too, she'd be up for it if she was on her own.'

I left and joined the others.

Al had recovered from her moment of anxiety and was on a high. 'Lovely to be remembered.'

V & A sat in the back of the car on the way home giggling intermittently and I caught snatches of conversation.

'I could see that, straight for your bottom, pretending it's just joshing but....'

'I expect they always try it on if they fancy a woman, it's sad and disgusting as if they never grew up or moved on.' '....and they are all married or separated... must live in hope.' 'I wouldn't... you would...whisper.' Giggles.

Clearly the interest isn't limited to the sad old rockers.

After we had dropped off Vickie and Clive I insisted on driving Alison home. 'If not' I said 'I will need to walk home with you.'

I think she was pleased to be taken to the door but her willingness to 'save me the trouble' left me in doubt as to whether even a kiss would be allowed.

She didn't leap out of the car, which was an encouraging sign so after a pause I put an arm around her and kissed her. Her response was a peck on the cheek; I tried a second kiss.

'You must think I was silly behaving like a teenager tonight but it was the circumstance. In a situation where everybody is hugging some people take advantage so I usually avoid the hugs and shake hands instead. Some draw a wrong conclusion but I don't care.

I'm sorry if don't always respond naturally, I told you that I really only had one relationship in my life, the others were brief and seemed necessary at the time. Only two' she added quickly 'whatever V may imply. I'm very inexperienced when it comes to sex and things so if I panic don't be offended, it means 'I'm uncomfortable' not 'get lost'.'

'I'll take a chance.'

The hug became a cuddle, the cuddle modest exploration. She was warm and comfortable kissing, tightening then relaxed when I searched for what proved to be a shapely breast and enjoyed the moment, kissing her and gently massaging, at one point she giggled like a girl then held my hand and said 'Oh dear,' bit her lip and said 'getting silly.'

'It's important to be silly sometimes, it keeps you sane.'

I put my hand on her knee and slid it up the nice leg to the hem of her skirt; I was behaving as if I was thirty years younger. The hand was contemplating its next move when she gripped my wrist and said 'You don't need any more disappointments tonight.'

'Nothing about you disappoints me except that I wish I had met you thirty years ago.'

'I was happily married then.' She patted my cheek, adjusted her bra and eased out of the car. 'Will we make another date?'

'As soon as we can.'

'Yes. Next Friday? I have a rather busy week.'

'That's ok.'

'Phil..'

'What?'

'What I said earlier, I'm not going to rush into anything intimate, I made one mistake' she stopped and reddened 'if you decide I'm unsatisfactory I'll understand and I expect we can be friends.'

'I like you enough to live with any limitations; if you were more available I wouldn't be so keen.'

I meant it but her involuntary admission had sent a chill around my heart.

She blew a kiss and was gone leaving me frustrated but happy. Whatever the limitations I liked the whole person and for a woman in her fifties she had great body.

She invited me for tea on the following Thursday. 'I could show you some videos of the band if you are interested.'

'I would love to see them.'

She gave her cheeky smile. 'I'll believe that when you have seen them.'

Alison, I discovered, was no cook. The neat crust-less triangles of sandwich were a little dry as if they had been made that morning, the cake was slightly burned on the surface and the salmon and cream cheese blinis had become soggy.

It didn't matter, we took our tea into the lounge and she sat beside me on the settee.

'Are you sure you want to see my video history?'

'Of course I do.'

'Ok.'

She pressed play and I had my first glimpse of Synergy at work; after five minutes she stopped the performance and spoke.

'So long ago. Chris was the guitarist.'

I looked at her. She turned her head and smiled. As she leaned back I slid an arm around her shoulders and she snuggled in.

The song? Not great, decent with a hook and well performed but one of those you only vaguely remember; it was never going to be a big hit. The girl beside me? Bright eyed, singing with a sense of suppressed joy. Her wonderful husband? No sign of the easy-going charmer she had described; the impression given was youthful determination with a professional face.

There was a short break and a new performance began with a DJ shouting over it. Her husband, now looking cool played an intro and there she was, more confident but still looking very young and lovely. The camera pulled back and the heavily built guitarist was missing replaced by a girl playing keyboard. The camera cut to a close up and she smiled, perhaps she lacked the bubbling joy of Alison but she was lovely looking.

It was a better song with a better arrangement and was well performed. A voice beside me said 'It got into the top thirty.'

'Brilliant.' I was admiring the young girl.

'Sue, she was my best friend. She was killed in an accident, it was awful.'

'The girl playing piano?'

'She was twenty-one.' A's voice had changed. 'Everything went wrong. I don't want to talk about it.'

'No.' I squeezed her shoulder but she rolled away and stood up. 'Shall we see k'R in action.'

She knelt down and busied herself removing the disc and inserting a memory stick. I had witnessed a small incident from the past generate a moment of deep unhappiness.

'kR were good. I remembered the band and some of their material.

The songs were strong and well played, good harmonies and clever mixed rhythms. The video began with some back stage activity, instructions, banter and preparation a few seconds of which showed A's grim-faced husband carefully strapping on a guitar, checking it with a tuner the size of an effects pedal and shouting something to one of the team.

The backing singers didn't make an appearance until the third song. They wore short skirts and tight tee shirts with a 'kR logo. Alison looked lovely but I was distracted by her companion, a pretty blond girl with a pony tail who looked very sweet. Both girls were more than alive, they were wild.

At the conclusion of the show the band did a tribute to the Beach Boys; it wasn't their style but they did it well.

The girls came to the front of the stage and Alison picked up an acoustic guitar while her husband took his microphone centre stage. He had been visible mostly in the wide shots of the band, now I saw something of the real man; fired up, smiling professionally and talking confidently to an audience of five or six thousand; impressive.

His tension didn't transfer into the song, a medley of California Girls and Breakaway and his singing was pretty good.

Bruce, the girls and the keyboard player were harmonising and with a great band behind him the performance was pretty special.

I couldn't take my eyes off A, front stage, singing and strumming and when her husband joined her in the harmonies she looked as if she was in heaven.

When the final cheers faded and the performance ended I turned to her.

'Fantastic.'

There was a hint of tears. 'Yes. It was.'

I kissed her cheek and stood up; her emotions were too deep for me to deal with.

'Cup of tea?'

She nodded.

When I returned with the tea she was replacing the SD card in its case.

'I put everything special on hard drives and memory sticks as well, I couldn't bear to lose it.'

I poured the tea.

'The other singer, the pretty blond girl, she seemed familiar.'

'Really? Have you ever paid for sex?'

I was shocked.

Victoria is right, she is easy to love but very difficult to get close to.

It was two months of developing friendship before I asked if she would like to go away for the weekend. I had discovered a little more about an intelligent, kind and well-preserved person and had grown very fond of her.

That was the positive side, the negative was an unpredictable fragility that could destroy a moment of affection and prevent total commitment. Less tolerant friends would have described her as "a bit of a nutter".

We were to be away for only one night, she had booked the hotel and the room had twin beds.

We had a comfortable journey and had gone to a local restaurant for a relaxed and enjoyable meal.

Back in our room I had undressed and wearing just pyjama

trousers I walked around the bed and put my arms around her. She rested her hand on my arms and kissed me, held me then flapped her hand against my back. I was aware that I was hugging a middle-aged woman but she was slim, youthful and desirable.

My hand slid down to her bottom and suddenly she was easing away saying 'I don't want to commit!' like a teenager having a tantrum.

She threw herself on the bed and covered her face. I sat next to her, lustful, confused, annoyed but concerned.

Perhaps my friends were right, she was mentally unstable?

She recovered, swung her legs off the opposite side of the bed and turning, wiped her eyes and said 'I am sorry, so sorry, I thought I was fine but I'm not. I know it is ridiculous, sex is such a minor thing these days, you can do it with a stranger in a phone box and the media tells you that it is ok.'

She turned away....'unless you get pregnant or diseased then it is the fault of the authorities! I'm not like that, it isn't something trivial to me, it is lovely and it matters. I am really sorry Phil, I know it's stupid but I did warn you.'

'Alison...'

'You had better find someone else, Vickie would be far better if she wasn't married. I feel stupid even saying it but I still have too many hang ups.'

I agreed with her, my relationship with Vickie had permitted a small degree of intimacy but Alison was perfect except for her ability to throw my emotions all over the place.

'I don't know what to do.'

'Do you want to pack up and go home?'

'No! Can we stay and have a normal day just spending time together.'

'Of course.'

'I'm an old woman, lucky enough to be taken away for a weekend by a kind man and I'm behaving like a scared teenager who has been picked up by a stranger. It isn't you Phil, you are lovely, it's a flaw in me and it gets worse as I get older. I could just do it but

I want….' there was a long long pause while her middle aged/ youthful face sought an answer … 'I don't even know what I want.'

She turned her back and lay down.

The rest of the weekend was normal except that there was a dark shadow over our relationship.

Our friendship was still intact when we next met in the café, she was the same friendly person. We had an evening out at the cinema and parted with a hug and a kiss when we returned home, but the shadow remained and our friendship seemed to be in neutral, established but going nowhere.

I phoned a couple of times and she wasn't at home when normally she would have been.

I found I could control or suppress any jealousy and I had no temptation to check up or confront her so some good came from the situation. Our friendship was established and I was happy with it until by accident I discovered there was someone else.

I thought I was past the age where hurt stays with you.

CHAPTER 12

Girlfriends

It was Thursday, I had finished my mornings work at the packing station and since returning home I had seen and spoken to no-one.

My afternoon was spent painting the shower room, my mind distracted by reminiscences of incidents from the past.

By five the painting was finished; what next? Dinner is my next task but I'm not hungry.

I open the fridge, find half a quiche and switch on the oven, I open a small can of beans and empty them into my smallest casserole dish. The quiche goes into the oven, the beans into the microwave. By six fifteen I have eaten my dinner, nothing has changed; it was still Thursday and I was still alone.

It was a time in my life when the world was turning, I was moving on from all I knew and I no longer felt an integral part of what was. Time had overtaken the culture in which my life had been lived; I was an outsider learning to adapt. I never expected, never wanted to own the world (perhaps briefly when I was nineteen) but my life ran on normality, small grief's, a few thrills, love, small achievements and satisfaction. Loss, humiliation and loneliness were new. It was my new norm and I accepted the situation; I wasn't unhappy but my life was constantly unsettled by tiny anxieties and discontent.

Friday passed; shopping, the hens, a visit from Marilyn bringing the quarterly rental for our field and goat's cheese in exchange for eggs. In the evening there was choir practice.

Saturday was similar, a visit from Lisa and the children; small hugs and they race out into the drizzle to search for eggs. Lisa tells me that she is having a night out and that she has a babysitter.

'Bye mum, love you, see you Monday'. Kisses from my grandchildren and they are gone.

I make soup and eat it with dry bread, I can't be bothered.

It is late October the weather is gloomy and it is already dark; I'm not enjoying the book I'm reading, it is too much trouble to check the business accounts or learn the song we are adding to our set. Why should I, the band may not exist in a few weeks.

I wonder if I could play bass when Liz leaves; should I get Chris bass from the store room and try some songs? The thought makes me miserable. Television is a last resort but I am too fidgety and restless to settle. It is seven twenty-five and the phone rings.

'Hi Al.' It is Vickie.

'Hi V.'

'Al, I'm bored, Clive is watching football again, are you busy, could we go out for the evening? I know it's late to ask but I need to do something or I'll go mad. I don't mind if we only have a chat in a pub but we could go to a club if you like? I'm in a rut, I don't want to feel I'm past it as well.'

'Can't wait V darling, your call is the answer to a prayer. I'm fed up too.'

Clive was heard muttering in the background.

'No chance darling.'

'What was that?'

'Clive suggested that you come round and share a bottle and I go clubbing.' 'Shut up or I might.'

A drink with a friend at the 'Moon' is just what I need.

'Give me time to change; I will be with you in twenty minutes.

Oh, and thank Clive for the offer.'

I rushed upstairs to wash, change and add a touch of makeup.
When invited to parties as part of the band or during my brief acting career I would spend an hour getting ready and Chris would comment that I looked only a little more glam than usual.

A little interest that boosted my self-esteem was always welcome but a lot of interest always needed careful handling. I was never available, it was wise not to cause offence and I didn't want to put a strain on Chris' tolerance.
I didn't support his silly notion that decent girls don't but paradoxically, experience suggested that 'nice' girls tended to have more fun because they had the moral space to be a little naughty.
To be fair to Chris' I don't think his comment was meant literally, he meant that people you can trust don't hurt people they care about.
The promoted lifestyle seems to be that morals no longer apply, this based on the infantile premise that morality was simply about avoiding pregnancy. Try applying the principle in poor countries where there is no welfare, backup or social support.
A glance at Mosaic law and Christian and Islamic rules of guidance show that they are for individuals and the collective benefit of society. Sinning was a word that meant steering a ship off course, possibly onto the rocks; it was used to describe actions that could send your life on to the rocks.

My actor friend Danny told me that he had been in love once but after a bad and hurtful experience he had learned to mistrust motives, to take what was available and enjoy the moment. He also said that my niceness generated friendship but my good looks demanded seduction and he was afraid he might fall in love again.
I told him it was a no-win situation because if I capitulated, I wouldn't be the girl he wanted.
He conceded that he was happy to settle for sad old sex with the

best girl he knew and worry about spoiling a friendship later. Danny was fun and tempting but his 'best girl' retained her reputation.

Many of my friends had taken different paths to mine, some were successful and most gained the wisdom to deal with the consequences and make changes when things didn't work out. Only one, met at youth club reunion had supposed he could repeat his mistakes and achieve a different outcome. Drawn into conversation with him my first impression was of an unhappy fortynager but he seemed content enough as he described a failed marriage, infidelity and his current relationship before sounding me out as to my availability.

Why, I thought, does he imagine that I would exchange a lovely husband for a selfish uncommitted waste of space.

Long training allowed the thought to pass without a change of expression.

My evening out with V was low-key, but a mumsy conversation tucked into the corner of 'The Man-In-The-Moon' with my best friend, was a sanity saver.

There had been some mild interest from a couple of decent looking men in their forties when we ordered our drinks. It had been gently rebuffed because I needed a relaxed evening with a friend.

'Not interested?'

'Only in an abstract way. I used to get nervous with strangers but I learned to deal with this kind of situation.'

'Did it happen often?'

'Sometimes, mostly like tonight, someone showing mild interest in a friendly non-threatening way. A few times I had to deal with more determined seducers and I learned to say 'Not interested' in a positive way.'

'Not always.'

'Yes always. What do you mean?'

'Chris told me about your fling…'

'Do you mean Gary. That wasn't a fling, I was in a desperate situation where I needed someone to give support and reassurance. It was never a secret, Chris knew.'
'Not that, the other time.'

I felt a small shock. She couldn't know, no-one knew about the time when wrong circumstances all came together. Chris tired from working and looking after the children, my thirtieth on the horizon, worries that in my absence Chris might be straying.
I had gained a part in a single episode of a detective series. It was filmed on location and included a couple of actors that I knew and also a star who was spectacularly attractive. Over the short time we worked together I was flattered by his attention and during one conversation was reduced to giggles when interrogated as to whether 'Ms Perfect' was as perfect as he had been told.'

'I don't know what you mean.'
'Yes you do. Chris was normally relaxed when you were working but he actually admitted he was worried. It was when you were filming, just before your thirtieth.'
'Nine months before! He wouldn't have known.' What a stupid thing to say.
'Tell me about it.'
'No!' Vick was a close friend but sometimes she was too inquisitive.
I was quiet, remembering the incident and making a decision. It was a long time ago, a few exciting days when I enjoyed the attention and the interest of a very attractive man. Vickie seemed to think it was a serious affair.
'It was one weekend; I was unsettled at the time and things just came together and made things difficult.'
'Chris knew,' said Vickie quickly, 'he told me that you couldn't stop talking about one of your actor friends and he thought you might be misbehaving because you were trying to be normal but not being you. He was unhappy and I was upset for him. We…

tell me what happened.'
'I've just told you.'
'No, the details.'
'There's nothing to tell. We worked together for a week and became friendly. One evening we had a meal together I drank too much and fell under his spell.'
'Go on.' Vickie was quite excited.
'Honestly V I had no idea you were such a pervert.'
'Meee? Go on, tell me.'
I gave her my sad shake of the head.'
'Stop prevaricating, what happened?'
'At the end of an enjoyable evening we went back to our rooms. When we reached his room I said goodnight and stopped momentarily for a kiss.'
'Oooh! Was it good, he has reputation as a stud. How long…?' V went red. 'I mean how long did it last.'
'What, 'it' or the relationship?'
'Both.'
'The only thing I lost was my reputation; I was known as a 'good girl' if you want to use that expression and when someone saw me going into his room they assumed the worst.'
I changed the subject.

It was on the way home, thumping down the lanes that I decided I should explain a little more.
'I had better tell you about my night before you get the wrong idea. I was enjoying a kiss, the kiss was extended and he eased me into his room saying 'Not in the corridor'.
'The kiss became a cuddle and I became lost in the moment but aware that a yes or no moment was looming.'
'And?'
'I knew I should say no but things began to get more intimate… take that expression off your face, I'm sure you've been in the same situation many times. Haven't you? I waited.
'Maybe. What happened?'
'I had no strategy and I gabbled 'I really enjoyed the evening but I

don't do this, I really don't.'

'He kissed me as if he hadn't heard, released me, made a dismissive gesture said 'A delightful evening, goodnight good girl' and turned away. I stood for a moment then drifted back to my room.'

'Was that all?'

'Yes except that things get about; my friend Danny had a minor role and he was very cool with me when we met next day. We had a good relationship and I was really hurt when he said 'I hear someone was sucking up to our star last night.'

I blushed and said 'What do you mean?'

'It's not my business but I gather that someone was seen going into his room in the early hours.'

'Who was that?'

'Al treasure it's too late to play the innocent. The grapevine says "Dined, donged and dumped in one evening" I wish I knew the secret.'

I could feel the tears coming and said 'You shouldn't jump to conclusions; you know that isn't how I behave.'

He shrugged and didn't comment but he certainly didn't believe me.

I returned from a memory that still made me cringe, Vickie was still talking.

'I'm not surprised Danny was hurt, he was keen on you.'

'And his friend Maurice was keen on you.'

'Maurice asked me back to his flat and I was tempted but something stopped me.'

'I didn't stop you, I just said 'think about it'.

'Well, it spoiled my evening. You seem to have a mission to stop me enjoying life.'

'That's so mean, you make me feel like a wet blanket.'

'If we didn't get into positions where we are a bit naughty we wouldn't have any fun. Wouldn't you like to forget your inhibitions and just live.'

'I did when I joined Tony's band and it was a huge mistake. My emotions were still in a turmoil and I fell into the hands of a professional seducer.'

I was suddenly tired of the game.

'I was glad that I hadn't been seduced; Chris was less grumpy at the weekend so I told him about the situation, I admitted that I had been a bit starstruck but there was no way I would misbehave. He was less concerned as if he had accepted... Oh my god!'

Something that I had half known became clear.

'You were having an affair weren't you?' I said it quietly then wished I had kept my mouth shut.

Vickie stiffened

'No! We were friends, I mean affectionate friends but there was never an affair.'

She stopped. 'Confessions are supposed to be one sided.'

I was unsure how to react, had half-known but I couldn't afford the revelations of a long-ago incident to become an open wound.

'What happened?'

She ducked her head. 'Things did go a bit further once; he trusted you but he knew the pressures when you were working and he could never be sure could he?'

I waited.

'I called in one weekend and could see that he was really unhappy, not like Chris at all; I asked what was wrong and he opened up and said he thought you had fallen for an acting colleague. He had been worried for a week and then you made an excuse to stay away at the weekend.'

'It wasn't an excuse, the shooting was behind schedule.'

'Clive was being a pig at the time. He was mentoring a 'wonderful' girl trainee; you met her, he brought her home once, the pretty one that was so confident and treated him like a boyfriend.'

'And?'

'I was sympathetic and things got out a bit of hand.'

We sat in silence.

I had considered the possibility twenty-five years ago when my friendship led the crew to wrongly assume that I had been bedded by the star. I was treading carefully because if the story had got back to Chris it could have been damaging.

V's admission hurt.

'You know what Chris was like, he hated deceit, he felt guilty about you and was upset for me.'

I turned the corner into Vickie's Road.

'You were so lucky he could easily have misbehaved; several of the girls and women in the village had the hots for him.'

'Perhaps he had the hots for them.'

'I don't think so. It's silly but I felt that he was my special friend and I didn't want him to stray with anyone else.'

'Does Clive know?'

'No! Of course not.'

I stopped the car outside her house.

She began to open the door then turned to me.

'I'm really sorry Al, it really was just a silly moment please don't let it spoil our friendship.'

I knew I could get over it but at that moment I was feeling angry.

'Goodnight Vick!'

I drove away.

If you have only a few close friends they are very important.

CHAPTER 13

Coming to terms with age.

Vickie and I have been best friends for many years and at one time or another I have told her all there is to tell about my early life as a singer; there were high spots but most of our life was unexciting and tiring.

Telling it how it was hasn't discouraged her and several times she has mentioned her need to 'live before it is too late'.

I know what she has in mind; parties, (I must organise one) fun, meeting people and maybe romance. She also reminded me of my promise to go clubbing which I had forgotten.

I expect she needs to be reassured that she is still attractive. She is trim, good looking, has worn well and gets interest from several admirers but obviously that isn't enough.

It worries me because if she is determined to become a fiftyenager chasing romance her actions could wreck her marriage and our friendship.

'Do you think we are too old to go clubbing?' The subject was raised again in the village pub after choir practice one evening.

'I don't expect there is an age limit, but why would you want to? Most of the people will be youngsters looking for fun or office groups having an evening out. I suppose there will be some people like us who have done the fun but are still looking for enjoyment.'

'Oh shut up Al, you sound like Chris at his worst.'

'Chris was very thoughtful.'

'He was a darling and I loved him to bits but sometimes he could out-preach an archbishop.'

'Don't be unkind, I'd give anything for him to be here talking in his logical, sensible way; I often stopped listening but he didn't mind. Sometimes I remember an incident' I was suddenly seeing the past 'and I can hear him in my mind and I want him to be here and he isn't…and he never will be!'

'I know Al; I miss him too.'

'You don't know!!' People were looking and V recoiled. 'You can't know.'

We sat in silence for a while.

'Sorry Al.' She pats my arm. 'Can we get back to the present. Shall we go out next Saturday? I need a shot of being silly, getting dressed up or down and dancing the night away. I want to feel free like you.'

'Freedom is being content with what you have, I would kill to have Chris alive' I dragged myself back under control 'I feel my age and I'm lonely.'

'Not very lonely. You've had two dates with my best manfriend.'

'Dates? A snack in Thornbury and a calamitous evening at the theatre'

'It put a few noses out of joint, I can tell you. I overheard "What do you expect with her background?" and there was…'

She repeated a few of the comments. 'There was some comment when the two of you had lunch, now you are dating seriously your popularity with the local ladies is zero.'

My god, a lunchtime snack and a visit to the theatre and my reputation is in tatters; I feel ill-used and hurt.

'Now perhaps you understand why I was cautious when I was working in a business where the grapevine was terrible.'

'Maurice once asked me if Chris and I were separating. I told him it was nonsense and he said that my affair with Danny had caused a rift.'

'I said "There is no affair and there is no rift." and was given an 'I understand' look and a comforting pat on the arm.'

'Danny was keen and we sometimes did lunch and we had been out in the evening a couple of times. I made it clear that we were no more than friends but speculation decided we were an item, the speculation became rumour and completed the circuit as fact. Chris had come to visit and we had a lovely weekend but gossip concluded that he arrived unexpectedly to 'check up on me' which confirmed that our relationship was rocky.'

'I told you before that my past is a lot less wicked than many of our respectable friends.

The subject returned to clubbing; I needed a night out and Vickie's mild pressure was enough to persuade me. I don't feel old and I don't look old; Tony said ......lots of things.

Chris seldom objected if I needed my space but I wished that he was here to ask. I'm not looking for a relationship certainly not in a club but it would be good for my self-esteem if someone showed a little interest.

I shouldn't think like that, I have a new friendship and I don't want to spoil it.

We went out the following Saturday.

V arrived in a short skirt and a crop top that revealed too much cleavage. The top and the cleavage were covered by a lacy blouse but I knew from beach holidays that there was minimal distance between crop top and exposure; energetic boogying could be embarrassing.

I settled for a v-necked green dress which went well with my recent cut and tint.

The tint was a concession to my hairdresser, my few grey hairs are hardly noticeable but she persuaded me.

I agonised over undies, decided that no one was going to see them and settled for some comfy maroon briefs and a matching slightly padded half cup.

V won't have it all her own way.

I was looking forward to the evening, mildly concerned that I would feel out of place but confident that I could cope.

It was easy, a nervous bus ride, a short walk and we joined the queue. The youngsters would arrive later, probably as we oldies were leaving.

Once we were in the flashing, suffocating gloom of the dance floor we could have passed for a couple in their thirties. Most of the dancers were young, many I guessed from work or collage but there were a few women and men who were older or looked older.

There was also a sprinkling of the over-made up and underdressed who would be more attractive if they dressed to suit themselves rather than copying fashion.

We joined the dancers and I slowly let go. After fifteen minutes I needed a break and headed to the bar where a young man spoke to me. He was about thirty and acted like a student trying to be sophisticated; I was confident that I could deal with him and responded.

Why not, interaction is part of being alive.

When I had bought a drink (how much?) we moved to a less crowded area and managed a semi-conversation. I asked what he did, if he enjoyed it and wished I was young like him. (Off putting but gaining a small compliment).

We returned to the floor where V was engaged in a middle-aged version of flashdance with a rather dishy looking partner.

Proof of my theory? Two attractive, tidily dressed women gained some interest in a room full of young girls some of whom might have been more attractive if they had less on display.

(What am I saying? Chris leave my mind alone!!)

After some wonderfully uninhibited dancing with my new friend, I claimed breathlessness and we eased back to a point as far as possible from the harsh thudding oppression of the loudspeakers.

Here we were able to converse in only moderately raised voices and when by chance the conversation turned to pop music, I mentioned that I had sung with a rock band in the eighties. He showed interest then, realising that I must be at least fifty he blanked. He wasn't totally put off, my looks hadn't changed and we returned to the dancing where I let go again.

Vickie was missing but returned shortly afterwards and joined us; her lacy blouse looser and the crop top at danger level. She waved, tucked her blouse across and smiled excitedly; she was enjoying her evening.

After some more energetic dancing I needed another rest and headed with my friend to the bar where we picked up our previous semi shouted conversation.

He asked what kind of band I had played in and if it was local. I told him that we formed in Bristol but we had subsequently toured the country.

'You toured? Professional?'

'Yes. We were called Synergy we had several hits.'

'Really? Cool.' It was obvious he had never heard of us.

'I was also with a band called 'king Rock.' I made it a question. He frowned and then some kind of connection was made.

'Yeah. I seem to remember when I was a kid. Yeah, my older brother would know, I think he was a fan. 'He's here, I expect he would like to meet you.' 'Don't go away, I'll fetch him.'

He returned a couple of minutes later with Jason.

'This is Alison, we've been dancing.' It seems I was a now a trophy. 'Do you remember her? She was the singer with a band you liked 'king rock. Do you remember, when we were kids?'

He didn't.

'You must, you were a fan when you were a teenager; this is Alison, you had her picture on your wall.'

So, Jason must be nearing fifty, I feel a little younger.

Light dawned slowly. As it dawned the vacant stare became more focussed. 'Alison?'

'Yes, Alison Smith.'

'Hey, you were great.'

'Were' is a rubber bullet but I thanked him. 'Alison Phillips, I was married to the guitarist Chris Phillips.'

'The blonde guy?'

'That's him.'

He is impressed. We chat, he's ok, more interested in the girl in the poster than me, but ok.

'Coming?' he extracts me from his brother we join the flashing noise.

We boogie for an extended drum and bass session, it's just noise but it doesn't matter; I feel free. I also begin to feel tired and we return to where his brother is waiting. It is eleven, I have enjoyed the dancing, the interest and two bottles of lager. I am sober and the last bus goes in half an hour.

I make an apologetic farewell to my new friends and get a momentary hug. Their night is just beginning.

Vickie is still dancing enthusiastically; her crop top has been pulled up but is working well. She is still with Darren who must reckon he's in with a chance.

I gain V's attention, point to my watch and mouth 'bus'

She shakes her head and mouths 'Not yet.'

'Yes!' I nod and point to my watch again.

She shouts in Darren's ear and he shouts back. I recognise the signs.

With a frown she leaves the dancing. 'I'll follow you soon Al, Darren says he'll give me a lift if I miss the bus.'

'I think you should come now, Clive will be worried if you are late home.'

'I'll be fine' she shouts 'I'll probably ... bus ... tell Clive ....staying with you, ...late.'

There was nothing to say. I take her arm and shout 'Be careful.' in her ear.

She turns away. 'Of course ... liberated.'

'Don't get too liberated.' I shout tartly

She laughs, '...chance.'

The crop top says she has a chance.

I made it to the bus and was home at twelve fifteen after a rapid walk from the main road and a nervous scurry down our dark lane I entered the kitchen. There was a message from Vickie on the ansa-phone. "I rang Clive and said we were just leaving, see you soon."

We? I didn't hear her come in.

I was up early showered, dressed and having my breakfast when she appeared wearing my bath robe looking tired. Other signs suggested that she was rather embarrassed.

'Good morning Vick.'

'Hi Al.'

'Were you late in.'

'Not very.'

A long silence.

'He said I was dishy and I said "I'm too old to be dishy" but he told me that I didn't look old.'

There was a long pause when she found a cup, added milk, picked up the teapot and poured herself my second cup of tea.

'Thanks for coming out last night, I really enjoyed the evening; when we were dancing I felt more alive than I have for years. It was as if a cloud had lifted.'

'Shall I guess that when you left the club he asked if you would like to stop for coffee before he brought you home.'

V blushed. 'He lives just off the A38 so it was practically on the way.

I didn't stay long. I know what you are thinking. Sometimes you treat me like a teenager; Darren was quite keen but if he thought he was on to a good thing he was disappointed.'

'I'm pleased to hear it.'

V laughed. 'We did have a bit of a cuddle and he was interested in the usual way.'

She looked into her teacup and pursed her lips. 'We thought we were liberated when we were young and when I said no, Darren was ok but

I think he was expecting a yes'.

'There was quite a lot visible to encourage interest and....'

'What?'

She was wearing undies under the dressing gown and half a love bite was visible just above her bra.

'Some of his interest is still visible.' I tapped my left chest.

She looked down and covered herself.

'You had better check if there are any other give aways.'

'There aren't. 'She looked down and smiled 'At my age that's a compliment. The problem is that when he brought me home he...'

'What?'

'He asked if he could see me again. That was what made me feel good; It showed that he was genuinely interested.'

'So will you?'

'I shouldn't should I?'

'It's not a good idea. You might not want to say no a second time.'

'Of course I would. Goodness Al, I've had a fun evening, it isn't the start of an affair. He's probably ten years younger than me' I raised my eyebrows 'maybe more.'

'I know I'm being a wet blanket but if he wants to see you again he is probably thinking sex.'

'Thank-you Mother, I wouldn't have thought of that. Listen darling, a young man showing an interest has done me a lot of good. He's not as bad as you think or I couldn't have risked a cuddle. I did promise to see him again and I decided before 'mothers warning' that it will be just the once and very discreet.'

'Is that all?'

'Of course, just some of ego massaging.'

'And a bit of' I patted my chest 'massaging?'

'Shut up Al!'

'And the rest?'

'There isn't a 'rest' but thanks for telling me about this.' She lifted out the top of her bra and looked. 'Oh dear, that is awkward.'

The subject was not raised again. She confided that she had enjoyed her second date and I was told "Only a bit of fun, don't say anything and don't play mother hen!".

I hoped she hadn't been too naughty; Clive would be furious if he knew of her 'bit of fun' and I know from experience that there is a point when emotion kicks in, fun becomes passion and 'being sensible' is just words.

After Chris' death when my emotions were shut down and my defences were low, I had sleepwalked into a relationship, had accepted mantras like 'free woman', 'enjoy life' and 'live again' and was totally unprepared for Tony's casual attitude.

What was for me a commitment was for him a transient sexual exchange, mildly interesting because I was a change from his usual cheap tarts.

It was painful to admit that I was a temporary crotch for an aging rock-star. (Yes, the spelling is correct!!) Thankfully common sense kicked in, I reconciled myself to the fact that the commitment was one sided and walked away from the situation.

Vickie, apart from her admission of a second date remained her normal self, showing none of those signs that are so obvious to close friends, the smugness of a secret knowledge or despondency from being used and rejected.

I concluded that the situation had given a boost to Vickie's sense of self-worth. I knew her pretty well, her manner and all the indications suggested that there hadn't been an affair and an emotionless quickie would be out of character.

During our conversations about her friendship the subject of another 'fun' evening resurfaced.

'I enjoyed our evening we must do it again, perhaps a club in Bristol.'

'Yes, maybe. The music was too loud but it was good. (And that from a girl who performed with a major rock band.)

'You're not keen I can tell. Still, you did it all when you were young.'

'Don't start that again.'

'I'm not but I expect there were a lot of parties, clubbing, glamour and being featured in magazines and newspapers.'

'Local newspapers when I got married. The closest I got to

glamour was the publicity photo shoots and I found them embarrassing.'

'Embarrassing? V's eyes opened 'Rude?'

'No, but the circumstances were iffy; changing when there were people about and photos that reduced us to sex objects. The clothes weren't particularly revealing, you would see more on a beach but it felt like wearing a bikini in church. I could probably find the proofs if you are interested.'

'Of course I am.'

I went to the study and searched the bottom drawer of the filing cabinet. There was a dusty folder that said Syn/kR/KR pub. I extracted it and carried it back to our lounge.

I sat down at the table with V leaning over me and opened it. On top was a photo of Sue, the last of the (fairly modest) nudes that were taken of her. I turned it over.

'Is that you?' V reached to take it from me.

'No, it's one of Sue's indiscrete ones that ended up in a magazine.'

'Let me see.'

I showed her.

'Goodness. I don't think Clive would be pleased if I appeared in a magazine like that. She does look very pretty, fancy that.'

'That is the worst one thank goodness.'

'She returned the photo and I passed her the next one.

A great heave of happy sadness overcame me. There I was, twenty-one, long legs and sparkly eyes looking wonderful. At the time I was very unhappy but youth and good looks shone through; I passed the next and there I was holding hands with Sue, both of us looking lovely.

Vickie picked up the photo. 'Al, you look fabulous, I mean, so glam...no not glam, like you but so alive. Don't show them to Clive, he has a thing for you and if he sees them he will be in love again. Did you ever do any like Sue?'

'I was asked when we were in our first season; Chris told me to ask Sol.

'Sol said 'Photos of our Al sitting on the wall looking dishy and feeling special enough to agree to some bikini shots on the beach followed by a studio session...'

'Not neccess...'

'...where you are persuaded to take your clothes off.'

I told him not to be rude and he laughed and said 'I'm saying that it's easy to get sucked in and it's probably wise to say no.'

'I did once let Chris photograph me because I wanted to stop time like Sue. We took a lot of care with the lighting so the results were good.'

'Naughty?'

'No. Nude but not rude. Although...'

'Another confession?'

'No. When Chris was taking the photos I said that I couldn't understand the mentality of girls who took their clothes off for a living. He said 'Really?' then when we were finished he came over and kissed me and said I looked utterly gorgeous.'

'That's so sweet.'

'It wasn't. The sod turned on the charm then he picked up the camera kissed me and said "a couple more looking fabulous and a bit naughty?" I was feeling loved and loving so I showed off. Afterwards he said "I reckon that I can sell these for a couple of grand. You could start a new career as one of the girls you couldn't understand."

'I was furious because the sod was showing me that given the appropriate charm I enjoyed showing off as much as the girls I was judging.'

'Did you keep the photos?'

'There were none, he only pretended to take the last ones. Your hero could be an absolute righteous bas... when he wanted. Have you ever been photographed with nothing on?'

'Clive once took some Polaroids and I was asked by a friend but I was too shy and Clive would have said no. Anyway, all they want to see is your bits.'

'Yes, it isn't the nudity, it's the voyeurism that makes it grubby however the pervs try to justify it. When we went naked on the beach it was fun, completely different.'

'Yes, I felt safe.'

'Me too, we are all a mixture of things; mind, knowledge, personality, culture and beliefs. Your body is just part of the whole and since most men think with their willys if your body is public, they assume your bits are public too.'

'That is very profound Al.'

'No, it's not its Phillips striking from the grave....again.'

'Honestly V, I once asked your hero what attracted him to other woman and after a moment he said "Legs, face, figure then you check out personality". That from a man who was relatively sensitive and considerate.'

'I think you lived with Chris for too long.'

'Not really.' I went quiet and V understood.

'Sorry Al, I didn't mean it like that, he was always caring even when he was having fun and if he came in that door now...'

I looked with an awful momentary hope

'...I would race you to him.'

She hesitated for a moment. 'Sorry, that was thoughtless

CHAPTER 14

Near Disaster

Alisons story

'I'm afraid I gave in to Vickie's demands to go clubbing again.

I had enjoyed our previous evening, even the whistling in the ears brought back memories of concerts with 'kR.

We arranged to go out on a Friday night, myself wanting to try somewhere different V keen to repeat our previous visit.

Was she hoping to see Darren? If the right person showed interest. would I enjoy a fling?

It was unlikely, the chance of meeting someone who was intelligent, attractive and interested in a middle-aged widow required expectations far higher than my own. If the unlikely happened I certainly wouldn't be sucked into relationship.

I dressed a little more attractively than before, settling for a strappy dress with black sparkly tights.

The black lacy or the half cup? I could probably get away without one. I quickly dismiss the thought and stick with the maroon that I am wearing.

'Lord, please don't let me look too 'yesterday' or mutton.'

I checked in the mirror, decided that the dress offered just sufficient exposure; a hint of cleavage covered by my gold locket with a diamond heart. Except for a diamond ring it was my most expensive piece of jewellery. I hoped it would be mistaken for something pretty but cheap.

Was the dress too short? It was about three inches above the knee, probably exactly the wrong length to be fashionable.

It doesn't matter, who will notice an older woman in a room full of twenty or thirty-somethings; I am going to enjoy myself.

Vickie's v-neck offered more exposure (and access) and her skirt was a fraction shorter. Thankfully she still looked like my best friend.

My hope that we would share a fun evening was short lived. We had barely arrived when I had to deal with Victoria's badly acted chance meeting with Darren.

I wasn't cross, was happy to dance alone and more than pleased when a nearby dancer smiled at me.

I wasn't initially impressed by my companion. To fully appreciate him I needed to mentally shed ten years or more. He was confident with restrained fashionable looks that would have turned my head when I was seventeen'.

I wasn't seventeen but was flattered and my new friend, after establishing a link nodded towards the bar where a semi conversation allowed an exchange of names. Here he gained a brownie point when he told me he found women in their thirties or forties more interesting.

The good evening that I hoped for became a reality, fun dancing, a few drinks and some fragmented conversations that bridged the generation gap.

We were becoming friends when at 11 o clock I told him my husband was collecting me. He must have seen my wedding ring and guessed I was married (if only).

He concealed any signs of disappointment and took the statement with a nod of the head gaining a second brownie point a kiss and a genuine 'Thanks Stuart, you have been very kind to an older woman.'

'An attractive woman, and I don't mean good looking.'

'Thankyou.' I offered a second kiss on his cheek. 'Seriously, when I was a professional singer I met all sorts and I learned to make judgements.'

'You were a professional entertainer?'

'Yes, a long time ago. Can I be candid?'

He nodded.

'I have enjoyed the evening but I am surprised that you spent time with me, you are an OK guy who could easily find a nice girl.'

I couldn't believe what I had said, so pompous I sounded like Chris.

'I think I have found a very nice...' he paused 'older woman.'

He smiled and raised an eyebrow with a 'What d'you reckon' gesture. I understood why V was tempted.

'Thank you again but I must rush. Bye.'

I wasn't going to chase V or cover for her, either she was on the bus or she wasn't. Our paths had crossed several times; she looked happy and was enjoying herself. The little jacket over the v-neck was neat but failed to conceal the movement permitted by her push up.

It was a week later that Clive called in on a Saturday; it was unusual but he was always welcome and I offered him tea. We had spoken only a few words before I knew that something was wrong. I fetched some biscuits but when I returned had thought of nothing to say.

'You know you are always welcome Clive but I thought you visited your parents on Saturday and then went to football?'

Silence. Clive looks at me then at the table. Small warnings.

'Is everything ok? You aren't yourself.'

'No, I'm worried and annoyed. You've been leading Vick astray and I don't like it.'

'What do you mean? I don't go astray myself.'

'You seem to forget she is married, dragging her to clubs, I thought I could trust you to look after her.'

A good friend is angry with me; I am shaken and I begin to panic. 'Of course you can trust me you two are my best friends. Whatever is the matter?'

'I think she's having an affair. Is she?'

'No, no I don't think so.'

'You should be able to tell me, you are the one who has been taking her out to discos or clubs or wherever.'

'I haven't, she... we agreed we could do with an evening out.'

'So why has she started telling me you need a night out and you are taking her with you?'

Oh goodness, what can I say? Do I let her down and defend myself?

'She thinks I had lots of fun when I was young; I suppose we are at an age when we need to feel we are still alive and we thought it would be fun to go to a club. We've only been twice and we did get a bit of chat; it's gratifying to get attention but it was nothing serious.'

'Well that confirms it.' Clive looks angry.

'No, it was just fun, we just had an enjoyable evening dancing. I told her we needed to be careful and she said 'Don't be silly, it's ust fun, not getting involved.'

'When was this?'

'The last time was a week ago.'

'Has she seen the same bloke since?'

'There was one chap she danced with on our first visit, and they met again when we went last week.'

'She was home late.'

'She might have missed the bus and taken a taxi, I only just caught it.'

'She's seen him in between.'

'Why do you think that?'

'Blank ansaphone messages, not home when she normally is and she took a day off from work; said she was feeling ill when she went in but she didn't come home.'

'I would have said something if I thought it was serious, I haven't because I'm sure there is nothing to say.'

Clive looked upset 'I thought you were a friend but you stick together. She was out last Wednesday and the one before.'

'She went to the cinema with me last Wednesday.' I am getting upset.

'Clive darling, please don't be cross with me, you are my best friends and I need both of you.' I hugged him. 'Honestly I haven't led her astray. I did warn her to make sure that a fun evening doesn't get serious. I'll talk to her tonight and find out what I can.'

'Suppose it is serious?'

I hugged him again. 'When I was young I had opportunities but I loved Chris and I could never be casual about physical things. Vickie is more sensible than I was at the time.'

'Sorry I was cross with you Al darling. If she is being deceitful, I'll need your friendship.'

I met V that evening and after a few preliminaries I leapt straight in.

'What's going on, have you been seeing Darren again?' She looked up, startled and I saw the beginnings of concern.

'Clive knows about it.'

She tightened.

'I did see him, he asked me to come out one evening and I had a free evening so I thought it would be alright; it was just an ordinary enjoyable evening.'

I interpreted the unsaid.

Vickie was continuing. 'I know it's wrong and I was reluctant but when he phoned and asked if we could meet I thought it would be ok.'

I filled in the details. 'Have you seen him often?'

'No, only once except when we went to the club.'

'Am I your best friend?'

'Yes, of course, I couldn't tell anyone else.'

'Then you must end it or you will mess up your marriage. I don't want to know any details because I need to be able to tell Clive that it isn't serious. Does Darren know where you live?'

'No, when he dropped me off at your house it was dark.'

She was silent.

'If you see him again you could might generate a fantasy about starting a new life.'

'Don't be so melodramatic of course I won't.'

'You might and I can tell you what will happen if you did.'

'A, you are such a know-all. What?'

'Three weeks of sex before fun with an older woman becomes boring, then you have a row and split up.'

'You are so cynical, he said he loves me.'

'Of course he did, he's enjoying some fun with an up-market lady.'

'Don't be bitchy.'

'I'm not,' I was getting desperate 'I can understand how you feel but you can't maintain the pretence much longer.'

'I am being very discrete.'

'You are not! Clive knows something is going on, he came and asked me about it and I told him that I will find out what is happening.'

'What? You mean you would tell him?'

'I don't need to tell him, he knows something is going on but not how far it has gone. I want to tell him that it is just friendship.' I looked her directly in the eye.

'So you would tell him.'

'For goodness sake V, the situation is simple, Darren is having fun, you are enjoying the attention, your husband knows something is going on and I am trying to mend the situation before its irreparable.'

'I don't want to lose Clive, I just want a little excitement in my life.' 'What shall I do?'

'If you don't want to lose Clive and your current life you must forget Darren now. The situation is already past the point where you can pretend it hasn't happened.'

V was getting upset which meant I was finally getting through.

We sat down together and as the sniffles turned to tears we hugged.

'It's not fair'

'I know, if you were single I wouldn't even comment.'

'You would!'

'Perhaps but it wouldn't matter. Downplay it, admit you were silly to let a casual meeting become a friendship. Clive wants to believe that it was a mild friendship.'

'How do you know?'

'Men do, the ones worth keeping.' 'Vickie darling did you?'

'Oh Al.' she looked at me, 'I ...'

'No! No! I didn't ask, don't say anything.'

'I was going to say it feels wonderful having someone interested in me.'

'Is there any evidence, I mean were you seen together, did you write or text? There are no photos or anything?'

'No, I phoned him from work to make arrangements, I didn't write but...'

'But?'

'He did take a photo of me.'

I thought about it. 'On your own,'

'Yes, just me. He said I looked lovely.'

'You must let him down gently; better still he must be pleased to get rid of you. You could say you think you might be pregnant. Sorry I know nothing happened.'

V smiled. 'No, and it's hardly likely.'

'You could say your husband is a very jealous man; you think he is having you watched and could get violent. That will probably make him suggest you cool it for a while.'

'I don't want to cool it, I know you're right but I feel as if my life is in colour.'

We were silent for a while.

'Do you want me to talk to Clive first? I'll say that it was just a friendship and you didn't realise it looked serious until I spoke to you.'

'I suppose. I just want to carry on and hope no-one finds out.'

'No-one except me and Clive which probably means half the village. I can minimise it or tell him everything I know. Your decision!'

'Don't be silly Al...oh you mean it.'

'Yes, it seems so ordinary, just a new friendship but for Clive it is destructive.'

It took a long talk to get our friendship back to normal. Uncertainty was followed in close order by annoyance, an attempt to get back at me, and reluctant acceptance.
Eventually she took a deep breath and said 'I was afraid this would happen. I suppose I want my normal life with family and I want the fun as well.'
'We all feel like that.'
'Thank you horrible know all Alice.

The next day I had my talk with Clive.
I started by saying that he mustn't worry because as far as I could tell it was just a friendship and Vickie was going to explain that evening.
He asked what I knew and I told him that V realised it was an unsatisfactory situation; she had seen him only a couple of times and simply enjoyed having a new friendship.'
I assured him that I wouldn't lead her stray and that I was relieved that her friendship hadn't developed too far.
He wasn't very happy and I gave him a hug.

I heard the V's story the following day. The situation wasn't resolved, there was coolness and some suppressed anger but the incident was seen as embarrassing silliness, not as a destructive relationship.
'I couldn't tell the whole truth,' she bit her lip 'I couldn't say that Darren thought I was available and that he was interested in my body.'
'I said that I was surprised that a young man would be interested in me but I felt in control which is why I saw him a second time. I knew I shouldn't but I felt flattered by the interest.'
'Clive was getting annoyed and said 'How much interest?'
'I was getting in too deep; he knew it wasn't just chatting and tea and cakes so I admitted it was a little more than just friendship.'
'He said 'You had better tell me.' so I told him that it was mostly dancing and chat but I allowed some cuddles which was

a mistake because he started to get interested and I had to be a firm with him.'

'Other things?'

'No! He did show interest but I'm too old for things like that.'

'Not old, attractive, understand why another bloke would fancy you.'

The conversation continued for a while and I began to feel relief that her relationship wasn't broken. It would take a while before the incident was forgotten but I thought I understood Clive; if V had become obsessed to the point where she didn't bother to conceal things it would have finished her marriage. Clive was cross but was prepared to forgive her lapse.

That evening, on my own again I mulled the situation over in my mind and found that I was shaking. Close friends mean so much to me.

Vickie in confidence to Al.

I wasn't entirely honest with you because you said that you didn't want to know everything. It was just a hug and some kisses on our first meeting but on my second visit we spent the day together and I went back to his flat unsure how things might develop.

I didn't intend to be seduced but we were a bit more intimate; I thought my tum and the few stretch marks would be off putting but he was complimentary and it was a struggle not to respond. I was relaxed and foolishly I let him take a photo of me.

When you tackled me I think the friendship was over. I was upset and was trying to feel positive and minimise things at the same time.

CHAPTER 15

Happy and Sad

Sarah invited me to holiday in France with the family.

I couldn't turn down the opportunity of spending time with the grandchildren but I was aware that I would be the 'old person' in the group and was unsure of my new role in family orientated situations.

Would I be granny, out of touch, excluded from conversation, too old to join them on the beach, an embarrassment when wearing a bikini?

Mum had joined us for a week during our Summer Season; she had borrowed one of my bikinis and Dave had been (far too) appreciative and treated her as a girlfriend. Mum was ten years younger than I am now but I don't think I will be an embarrassment,.

The family hired a Gite near the coast at the end of May; Simon and Beth couldn't come but Sarah and Lisa were there with their husbands and my five grandchildren.

On our first night, I asked if they minded having mum with them. Sarah's husband smiled and said 'It is like having another sister with us and it will be even better if you share the child minding.'

I was happy to share the child minding equally happy to be included as one of the adults when we went to the beach, visited places of interest or had an evening out.

The girls were kind and inclusive but several times I was hit by a moment of intense loneliness.

It happened, I dealt with it; a deep breath, a moment of unhappiness, I re-adjust and join the living.

We went frequently to the beach where I lay comfortably under a sunshade while the grandchildren had noisy fun. I took them swimming, delighted them by screaming when they splashed me, splashed them back and swung them around in the water until I was dizzy and exhausted.

I found the social interaction in the mix of generations slightly difficult because culture changes meant I no longer knew what was acceptable. Whether to wear a bikini or not was the first problem. My daughters went topless and were happy to run around playing ball with the boys and the children.

Sarah who is sensitive to my feelings asked and answered my question.

'Let me guess mum, you don't know whether to join us.'

'Yes, I don't know if I am too old to wear a bikini?'

'Of course you can mum, you are practically the same shape you were twenty years ago. I thought you were wondering whether to go topless.'

'Oh no, I wouldn't want to embarrass the boys.'

'The boys won't mind if you decide to go naked; they would probably appreciate it.'

'I don't think I will go that far.'

'Your decision, we might and you are welcome to join us.

The younger generation are more casual than I was; they don't need to justify their attitude, but they do seem to accept a 'choice without knowledge' regime promoted by the media as if it were balancing a system that enforced meaningless restrictions. Morals are just rules of guidance that help people to live reasonably satisfactory lives but all we hear is a one-sided bellow telling us to get back in the gutter.

I settled into my role and enjoyed a lovely holiday. I started wearing my bikini without a suntop, then the suntop without the bikini top.

I was treated as one of the girls and when we went for a swim I took my top off.

Jogging back up the beach I was aware that I was jiggling rather than flopping and felt much more comfortable. Sarah's intelligent if rather stolid husband told her later that her mum was 'damned tidy for her age'.

Towards the end of the holiday on a deserted beach and very hot day and girls went naked.

'Coming mum?'

Sarah's husband had taken the children to a play park. Could I?

Oh what the hell, I may never get another chance.

'Are you sure?'

'Of course.'

I slipped off my bottoms and joined them walking down the beach. Most of me is pretty firm and tidy if not quite to modern standards.

'I hope I look so good when I'm your age.' Sarah is so kind.

Lisa's husband looks up when we return from the sea; his eyes sweep over me; I blush but he smiles. 'Three lovely ladies, lucky me.' he says.

I returned home to pile of correspondence, most of it business related, some bills and charity letters, but one from mum, one from Sol and one from a solicitor.

I read the one from Mum first. It was mostly small talk, hoping I had a good holiday; the sort of thing that was generally sent as a text or if it was trivial enough, on face book.

There was one serious item and it was a sad one; Uncle Gerry had died. He was the oldest of mum's brothers, in his late eighties and, when I last saw him, hale and hearty.

He was always so kind and interested in what I was doing; I enjoyed his company and his unselfish advice. I would miss him. We had gone through a very lean patch in the early days of Synergy and though I didn't know it at the time, Uncle Gee had helped with support for clothes and essentials.

Mum said he was lonely after Auntie Clare died so I always tried to visit when I was in Bristol.

He had three children; one lived nearby and was supportive; her brother Alex lived in Yorkshire and visited when he could but Ferdy, the youngest only appeared when he needed money. Chris called him Ferdy the Infrequent.

The legal document was opened with some trepidation. A fine? A summons? Neither, a delightful surprise; in his will Uncle Gee had left me his car, an MX5, his beautifully kept pride and joy. He had shown it to me when he bought it and taken me for a drive. His last car, 'an old man's pet' as he described it. 'Stupid, but I get pleasure out of it.'

I told him it was lovely. And so it was, silver with a fold away hardtop, fun and comfortable.

I read the instructions saying where and when I should collect it and cried again.

When I collected it and signed the forms the memory of that drive with Uncle Gee came back; his elderly face, lively and delighted, sentient and enjoying his 'small pleasure'. Now he had died, would never smile indulgently at me or call me 'Duckling' or 'Treasure'. A whole lifetime of good and bad experience of learning to accept and care about others was gone; I was hit by a rush of sadness tinged with fear.

I drove the car home carefully and on arrival cleared a space in our garage and put it away. Something would have to go

It was easier than expected with Clive advising me to sell the other two and buy a small estate car. The Polo provided a decent sum to the kitty and the old Suzuki was part exchanged. For several thousand pounds I could ill afford, I found myself possessed of a smart second-hand Jazz Hybrid.

The legacy had cost me money but I was feeling pleased with myself when I drove the Honda home. Clive had come with me to the dealer and had been very helpful so I asked him in for coffee.

I was generous with my thanks hugging him and offering a kiss which was accepted with 'You are worth it Al.'

'Thank-you for your help, you are a good friend.'

I offered a second hug and Clive whispered in my ear 'Sorry Al ...' then gently patted my bottom.

I knew him well enough not be offended but I didn't want to encourage him.

'The hug was to say thank-you Clive, it wasn't encouragement to take advantage.'

'No darling, I hope you don't mind being appreciated.'

The hand continued to explore and appreciate despite a more assertive 'Clive, don't be naughty!' 'That's enough! What would Vickie say.'

He kissed my cheek. 'She enjoys it too. I'm fond of you Al and I am a normal man.'

'Not normal' I said 'a very special friend or I would be offended.'

'Thanks darling.' He kissed my cheek and with a 'Bot still lovely' he left.

I felt warm and pleased rather than offended; it was good to have a friend who could show affection without expecting a response.

CHAPTER 16

Incidents

Alisons Story

Vickie and I had been close friends for thirty years. Our tastes and attitudes were different enough to maintain interest but our codes and philosophies of life had sufficient commonality to smooth over any problems. We met often and as would be expected, much of our conversation was mundane; family, work, people and village incidents were analysed, discussed and put to bed with a suitable judgement.

Our friendship flowed comfortably along punctuated from time to time by conversations that revisited supposedly exciting incidents from my past life but seldom from hers.
She is of the opinion that everyone in or on the fringes of show business is at it like knives. It is true that the nature of the business enables the misuse of position or power and actors are under pressure to accept demands that would be actionable in other professions. Considering that parts of the profession are attractive to drop outs and wasters, it is to their credit that most of the people I met were surprisingly well balanced.

We had been shopping in Bristol and after visiting mum had gone to a cafe in Bedminster where by chance we met Andy. It was an awkward meeting because our relationship was that of estranged friends.
On the drive home I was quizzed on the depth of our

relationship and disappointed her with an assurance that it was no more than friendship. The conversation then drifted to other imagined seductions.

The traffic was heavy and I was concentrating on driving so I minimised the distraction by exaggerating one of the few serious attempts at seducton that had an amusing outcome.

'I was seriously propositioned once' I told to her 'It happened when I was setting up my egg business.

It was a difficult time for me; the acting and singing gigs had dried up because I didn't have the time to chase work, I was missing the excitement and Chris was complaining that he was overloaded with work and was expected to spend more time looking after the children. We were both stressed and short tempered and there was a small cloud over our relationship. We had our ups and downs and we always dealt with them by giving each other space.'

'Several months earlier Chris had done some backing work on an album that Tony was producing and we were invited to a party connected with the launch.'

'There was a possibility of picking up some work so I made an effort to look good. Maybe I overdid it, the top was lowish and Chris made an unkind comment about putting the goods on display which was hurtful because he was always supportive.

At parties we tended to split up but keep in contact and get back together regularly but that evening we had drifted apart and I was being given the come-on chat in a very effective way by someone in management.'

'The guy was straightforward telling me that I came across as a lovely person which added to my talent and good looks was very appealing. I had heard similar before but reassurance is never wasted.

A few drinks, a dance and some further chat and I was being told that "the world has changed, these days a girl has a right to enjoy herself."

There was truth in his assertions, the new generation had been brought up to do as they wanted. 'Choice from ignorance' was the mantra, there was no explanation that morals help us to avoid many of life's problems.'

'Some people saw relationships as career moves or image acquisition, love, even friendship had no part in it.

It was also true that most of us like to 'enjoy ourselves' though many (love you Chrissie) would be very hurt if their beloved 'enjoyed themselves' with someone else.'

'When my companion told me to forget my old-fashioned attitudes and enjoy life I admitted, helped by too much champagne, that there was truth in what he said.

Time was passing; was I wasting it?

The problem is that infidelity has its price, small if you have nothing to lose but devastating if you are happy and content.

I asked him 'Would you be happy if your girlfriend strayed?' and he prevaricated saying 'Everyone should enjoy sexual freedom without anxiety, regard it as a pleasurable activity that does no harm.'

(No harm? Hurting and losing my soulmate, breaking up my home and sharing my children?)

'Perhaps I should.' I said, then 'You are right, I should. Ok, tonight is the beginning of a new me.'

'He smiled and said 'Good decision lovely Alison.'

We were sort of smooching, I mean dancing and conversing; I let things relax then held his arm and said 'Who is that guy over there, the one in the white jacket?'

He told me and I looked up and said 'Thank you for loosening my silly inhibitions, I really fancy him, I wonder if I can pull.' Then I smiled turned and moved away. Just for a moment he was really annoyed.'

'For people like him sex is a transient pleasure that gives a little substance to what is probably a self-centred life.

I think I understood the motivation; he was trying to relive his youth and I would briefly offer interest as a new partner.

Sadly, nothing can ever replace the joy of youth or the magic of your first love.'

'I was lucky, I found my soulmate and floated in a world that was mostly happiness and contentment though it was sometimes unsettled by anxiety or jealousy. Without Chris I might have continued to search for my perfect partner becoming a little more damaged and discontent with each encounter. The partner, if he existed and found would probably have little time for the imperfect person I had become.'

'I told you about the model we met, the very pretty one that Chris fancied. She showed me some of her portfolio and she looked lovely. It was only a few years later I was shown a horrid magazine with pictures of her actually doing it.'
Chris said "You wonder what she is doing now? One day a lovely eighteen- year-old and a thousand days later, each minutely grubbier than the last she's an over made-up slapper.'
'It made me angry. Militant feminism bangs on about freedom and choice as if everyone was wealthy, well-educated and strong minded. Most young girls are ignorant and easily deceived and feminists can't deal with important issues like exploitation so they agonise about gender signs on lavatories rather than teaching morals.'

'You are getting boring Chris.'
'What do you mean...what?' 'Oh you beast! Sorry!'
'You do go on sometimes.'
'You started it!' I backed off. 'I know I was lucky otherwise I might I have ended up like the girl in the magazine?'
'I don't think so, we have our silly moments but we wouldn't allow ourselves to be exploited.'
'No, I could never take my clothes off for money.'
'You did darling or have you forgotten.'
'That was different! Vee! You've really got it in for me today. It's not the nudity it's about exploitation; girls being deceived and bullied is wicked.'

I don't think we had these soul-searching conversations very often but we talked a lot and V did seem to get a vicarious thrill from my few failings.

It was in the café after pilates that I told Vickie that when Terry and I were together in 'Cats Whiskers he was my best friend and saved my sanity.
'What was he like?' she asked me.
'Not like anything, he was just an ordinary bloke who was a very good drummer. We were good friends and he got on really well with mum but he was a bit reserved with Chris.
To be honest Chris wasn't totally relaxed with gays or anyone who was slightly left field. He wasn't negative or anti, he treated them like everyone else but he tended to be over-considerate. Sensitive people can see this as patronising.
He was pretty well balanced and he realised that in any minority there are small groups of extremists who want the world to revolve around them. Chris reckoned that as a minority of one he should respect people who showed respect to others.
He had a theory that when the media owners promoted minority interests it was done to disempower the majority and destroy the socialist revolution. I can remember him saying to Sol 'Everybody should be in the 'everybody' gang.
He said he was a left-wing conservative because he supported the idea of collective people power as a balance against the power of the rich and powerful.'

I had started to ramble like Chris and Vickie wanted to get back to Terry and our friendship.
I told her that we lost touch after Synergy folded; a letter once or twice a year then an awful one saying he was HIV. He was dismissive about it but I was really upset because the person I knew was kind and caring and I always assumed he was careful.
'I wrote and said I would come and see him. It was just after Princess Di had done that visit and I thought she was just wonderful. I mean I'm sure she had advice and knew there was

negligible risk but there was a lot of uncertainty and it gave other people confidence.

I went to see him and discovered he was far worse than I expected; he had some support but not enough and I knew I had to help him.

Chris was very iffy about it because things about Aids weren't well known. He was upset about Terry but mostly concerned about me.

I went and found a bedsit near to Terry's flat; I couldn't do much but I was there and shopped and talked and made tea. He was grateful for my help and it broke my heart because all I could do was be there.

Chris came to visit once and was quite nervous. When they met he was shocked and did that man-thing where they become strong and positive. It was loveable but nonsense.

Before he went home he showed his real feelings and sat on the bed, hugged him and said 'So sorry mate.'

I saw him out, holding his hand and he became angry and said 'It's all wrong, what can we do?' then the silly boy started to cry.

He went home the same day and at the station he kissed me and said 'Darling you are wonderful. Tell Terry I'll pray for some comfort.'

I said 'I think it has been sent' and he frowned then he understood.

'Yes it has darling. I'll still pray.'

I was there for about two weeks then I came home to catch up.

While I was home he went into hospital. I went up and stayed for a few days calling every day then I had to come back for a gig and he died while I was here.'

'I couldn't grieve or feel satisfied that I had helped; I didn't even have the sense of release by being there when he died. I don't know how I felt but it was mostly dissatisfaction, not knowing and helplessness.'

'He saved me once when we were on tour. I had a casual date with a man who seemed decent enough. We enjoyed a chat and a meal but when we went back to the club to collect my kit he attacked me. Terry had been having a late drink with some friends; he heard me crying and rescued me. He cared about me like a brother and protected me.'

CHAPTER 17

A Critical Time

Alison's story

The weekend away with Phil was a mistake.

I liked him but I was unsure about the strength of my feelings and I suppose I was testing myself.

Despite reservations I was looking forward to it; I enjoyed the drive and the day's activities but when the critical point arrived I didn't want to go to bed with him.

It wasn't Phil's fault, he ticked most of the boxes but my relationship with Tony eighteen months earlier had left a scar, my self-confidence was low and when I asked myself "Am I ready for this?" I was reduced to blank minded helplessness.

That night, lying in a separate bed feeling sorry for myself I realised that I didn't need sex and I didn't want the restriction of commitment. I hoped Phil and I would remain friends but that was all.

I began to consider Vickie's attitude; would a brief fling suit my needs? If so, could I retain my wider group of friends.

It was a cynical and selfish thought, the antithesis of my moral code. I tried to rationalise; it might be fun but the answer was no, it wasn't me.

I had a wonderful thirty-five years with Chris; the sex ranging from heavenly thrills of our early days through giggly naughtiness to happy fun and contentment when we were older. I had several opportunities to misbehave but they were seldom difficult to resist, only once had looks, charm and personality combined and infidelity was avoided because sophisticated me turned into a gabbling, nervous schoolgirl.

Several days later, mulling over the problem for the tenth time, the rational side of me began to understand what had happened. It took a very painful admission to begin the process.
I had always taken male interest for granted but had never made use of it because I found my perfect partner and enjoyed fun, love and passion.
I wasn't the glamorous sexual animal with a strong moral character that I sometimes thought. I enjoyed sex but I needed love.

In my mid-fifties I face the real me and admit that my moral superiority and my good behaviour were the result of an average sex drive and a happy marriage.
Perhaps I was being too hard on myself, things are never black or white but the basic truth was there. Mum knew how important Chris was for me; she had even told me how lucky I was to find someone exciting who adored me.
My 'other men' such as they were had used me and moved on.

Where to go? I still liked Phill, probably in the right circumstances I could have a full relationship with him but (another of Daves horrible expressions came to mind) it would be sympathy sex, token, passive and unsatisfactory.
I would stay true to my nature and if Phil was content we would remain friends.

I was over the worst of my grief; it never went away but these days it only intruded intermittently. My happy time was over and I needed to move on.
I hadn't mapped out my future but sensed it would be my present with a few changes but I needed to break free and create a gap between the past and the future.
I wasn't even sure what break free meant and wrote down a few

suggestions that included crossing continents in a camper with a guitar, a singles holiday that took me to remote places and an office job that surrounding me with people.

I avoided the subject of sex, I was free, cautious maybe but free and if a situation arose where someone was right for me then perhaps…. maybe.

My mind drifted back to the young man I had met at the club a month earlier. Surely, he wouldn't be seriously interested in a fifty something mum even if she did look younger. He had said that he liked 'attractive older woman'. On our short acquaintance I had assumed and dismissed his interest but now realised that I had felt a stronger attraction to him than to Phil.

.

What did I want, a comfortable relationship or excitement? My 'wise' advice to Vickie was "don't" but she was married with a caring husband.

My mind revolved again, it wasn't that different, V had wanted and found excitement, had stepped back because she had a lot to lose; I was free to do as I pleased within the limits imposed by self-respect and common sense.

It wasn't an issue that could be sorted overnight; I would need to be sure of what I wanted, sure of who I wanted and in what capacity. At fifty-five I was nervous about stepping out of my comfort zone but it was an age at which I couldn't prevaricate for long.

Nervousness is a familiar state when you are performing and something you learn to overcome. I had discussed the subject at a dinner party with Sally and Andrew. They weren't close friends like V and C but we knew them well because Andrew had worked with Chris at Rolls and his father had worked for Chris' consultancy.

Caren from tennis was there with her partner together with Sian, Sally's sister, recently divorced and towing a new man.

It was an enjoyable evening talking with fresh faces and quietly watching Sian's new man trying and failing to establish himself. (Just as well because the relationship lasted barely a month.)

Whilst the men talked about engineering (not all the time from the laughter that followed one of Chris' foul stories), the girls had discussed nerves, depression and vallium.

Later that night I raised the subject with Chris and he told me that for the first year as a professional he had been nervy and stressed but knew that he needed to show confidence because it is a major part of performance.

I was glad we hadn't discussed nerves at the time.

I was naïvely confident that he knew what he was doing; things often went wrong and with Dave and Sol he would pull things together and set them back on course.

He did lose his temper a couple of times. The first time I was terribly upset, almost frightened but Dave shrugged and said 'Silly sod, he should get cross more often not wait until the pressure is too much. Go and give him a hug girl and tell him we all love him.' 'Go on now.'

I was in tears because I didn't know the angry person who had walked away from us. I followed him, put a hand on his shoulders and said something meaningless like 'Alright?'

He was in tears and I felt a huge rush of compassion, threw my arms around him and hugged him until he relaxed. He kissed my cheek and whispered 'Sorry. Thanks darling, I need to know someone is on my side.'

I said 'Always' and with that all his confidence came back.

'Let's give it our best shot' was our motto. The words stuck in my mind, I would make my decisions and go for it; I would wear my sensible head and if made mistakes they would be corrected and put behind me.

I decided to start my 'new life' with an evening out at a club. I would go on my own and become one of the aging women trying to recapture their youth.

Wrong thinking! Most of we older women would simply be

enjoying the evening having a little bit of fun.

I decided to go to the club I had visited with V on the same evening as before. It was unlikely that Stuart would be there and even less likely he would remember me but familiarity with the surroundings made the venture less stressful.

I clung to Chis' advice to 'go for it' and took an age to dress trying very hard to get a right the balance between looking good for my age, a touch of glamour and simplicity.

Boosted by a feeling that I had got it right I drove to Gloucester for my evening out.

Age doesn't eliminate nerves but experience enables you to suppress them.

Passing through the shabby tunnel that led to the dance area required a conscious effort of will.

Danny, a friend from my acting days had once appeared in a reduced version of Henry V and when we first met one of his encouragements to me was 'Stiffen up those sinews Al'.

When he got to know me better it reduced to a more oblique 'You need some stiff sinew Al darling'.

Once inside it took a few minutes to acclimatise aurally and physically; a brief prayer and I joined the dancing. Thirty years of performance in a world of light and noise was good preparation and I relaxed and let go; I could dance well and I reckoned that I looked pretty stylish but even shedding ten years I remained an older woman in a sea of youngsters.

I wasn't alone, there were a number of older ladies enjoying themselves but mostly they were in groups.

I retired briefly to the horrid loo where a dubious looking girl acting suspiciously gave me a threatening look.

Returning to the dancing I settled down to enjoy the release when a hand touched my shoulder and a voice in my ear shouted 'Mrs Alison'.

I recognised the voice immediately and as I turned my smile admitted that I had hoped to see him.

'Hi'... Stu.'

He joins me, we continue to dance and there is a link; there is nothing between us and he is probably fifteen years younger but he did remember me.

I forget my age, switch on a younger me and Alison the performer lets go.

Stu looks a little surprised but I sense that he is impressed.

I notice a 'What does that silly cow think she's doing?' expression on the face of an overweight youngster but I don't care.

After a while we retire to the least noisy corner and semi-converse; it is a pattern we repeat for the rest of the evening; I like him and he seems interested in me.

When tiredness starts to take the pleasure out of the evening I indicate that I must go and Stuart offers to see me to my car. We leave together and he walks with me through the car park. I don't feel nervous being escorted by a stranger but I feel light headed after hours of pounding rhythms.

When we arrive at my car we talk for a moment and he asks me back to his apartment in a way that lets me say no without giving offence.

I say yes.

'Great' he smiles 'it will save me a twenty-minute walk; I need to be up early.'

He guides me back to his apartment and I begin to feel a nervous thrill. What am I doing?

'I live a little way down the next turning on the left' he says 'but if you carry on to the main road you will know where you are.'

I do so; the road is the A38 and it will be easy to find my way home. He is being very considerate.

I back into a garage entrance, drive back up the road and turn right

'Just here.'

I stop outside a small block of modern apartments and after a moment we get out.

'This,' I think as we take the stairs to the first floor 'is not a student flat.'

It turns out to be a large and expensive apartment.

Nerves creep in again, what am I doing? I can deal with it. Deal with what? The big let-down when he realises I am over fifty or...a thought creeps into my head unbidden, capitulation and scary sex because I am afraid to say no.

Neither. I think I can spot the signs that tell me to back off or get out and there are none, Stu seems an ok guy.

'Coffee, Tea?' Take a seat.

I choose a smallish white leather armchair. 'Do you have peppermint tea?'

'I think so; there is probably rose hip if not.'

'Fine.'

'Would you like to see the flat?'

He briefly opens the doors on two large bedrooms, a study, a superb bathroom and a kitchen which is beautifully equipped and makes mine look very 1990s. He fills and switches on the kettle which matches the other table top items and we talk while it boils.

He is pleasant looking and personable; I judge that he is in his late thirties possibly his early forties. He hasn't indicated that he is horrified to discover he has brought a granny home.

I catch a glimpse of myself in a mirror. Not bad, thirty-nine maybe forty...whatever in this light.

I ask what he does and he tells me that he is a doctor specialising in mental health. I don't know what to think.

'It is important to stay grounded,' he tells me 'I find visiting a club from time to time is a huge release.' He tells me a little about himself; I discover he plays in string quartet and for fun, in a folk duo.

I tell him about myself; not too much, that I am a widow and that I run an egg packing business.

It may be professional skill but he is easy to talk to. He hasn't made any kind of move and I don't know if it is reassuring or worrying. I finish my tea, decide it is time to leave and I thank him for inviting me to see his flat.

'A lovely flat.' I tell him as I stand up collect my bag and jacket and move towards the door.

I am puzzled, he doesn't seem to be put off by my age, there are hints that lady friends are not unknown and there is a suggestion that one is or was permanent.

We walk to my car.

'I like your car he says. Alison...' here it comes... 'you don't meet many smart women in the clubs; a few but they often have issues. I like you.'

'He puts his arms around me and kisses me. I am startled but I respond and enjoy a few seconds of being kissed.'

'Will you come out with me on Saturday? For a meal, I would like to take you to my favourite restaurant.'

'Yes ok. You don't mind taking your mum?'

'Only when she makes foolish and unnecessary remarks.'

'Oh.' I feel suitably put down.

'In my professional life I cannot make rapid assumptions but I am off duty and with you I will take the risk. You seem to be sensible and well balanced and you know that you are attractive. Leave reassurance to those who need it.'

'I...' Damn. I don't know what to say. 'When I was young I received quite a lot of interest in the girl but less in the person. My marriage gave me the confidence I needed. I'll explain another time.'

'Ok Alison, I don't usually analyse beautiful ladies unless I am charging them for the privilege.' He kisses me and smiles. Honestly I am human outside work. I had better give you my phone number.' He finds and passes me a card.

I slide into the car, reach into my bag and search out one of mine. He glances at it, leans forward and kisses my cheek, says 'Good night Alison' and steps back.

As I pull away he gives a small wave.

My head is in a whirl as I join the A38 and head for home. A voice that I try to suppress keeps saying "You've pulled".

CHAPTER 18

Watershed

Alisons Story

By Friday I had rationalised the situation; he must have realised that I was older than I looked and had politely got rid of me. His card said that he is an M.D. but it might be a persona he adopts when pulling; his apartment was very up market but maybe it is rented.

If he was genuine he could have picked up a young women, why me?

He rang and we arranged to meet.

My head told me that our friendship could only be temporary but I was having an adventure. I felt ridiculously pleased that an intelligent younger man wanted to see me again.

I was in the same happy mood on Saturday; a mix of nerves and elation because I was taking risks and feeling wicked.

Phil called in mid-morning, enjoyed a coffee and a chat and left me feeling guilty. We were good friends and but early feelings of affection hadn't grown and a new beginning seemed unlikely.

I didn't feel passion for Stuart either but I am excited by his interest.

On Saturday evening I decided to impress and dressed to stun. If it was over the top too bad.

It was. Had I been dressing for a showbiz party twenty years earlier it would have been fine, but for a date at a local hostelry with a stranger it was embarrassing.

The face with its minimal makeup was fine and the boosies still quality but the half-cup combined with the low top would have put them on display when I leaned forward so both were changed.

The dragon patterned skirt (at fifty-five?) showed my legs to perfection and my nicks when I sat down. I changed it for a plain blue denim and with my standard black tights I looked like me.

I always knew how to look my best but didn't always get the details correct; I would ask Chris and sometimes he would offer a suggestion that helped me to get it just right.

I was ready with twenty minutes to spare and sat in a state of nerves listening for his car. He arrived a little early and I made myself walk to Chris' study to await the bell.

When it rang I walked back down the passage through the lounge and dining room to the hall and opened the door.

Wow. He is very smart and looks young.

'Good evening Alison. You have a lovely house; difficult to find but worth finding.'

'Thankyou Stuart, come into the lounge.'

We pass through the dining room. 'Take a seat.'

He looks around the room in the normal way of a first time visitor, seeing the contents but getting a sense of the owner.

'It used to be a farmhouse' I explain 'it's long but narrow and not as big as it seems.' 'These rooms and the kitchen are the full width of the house. There's a passage from that door' I pointed 'to the study at the far end. There is a shower and toilet and a little store room on the right of the passage.' 'The main bedroom is upstairs and there are three others; two really, we added an en-suite to our room so the fourth room is just a box room.'

'Do you have a brochure?'

'What?'

'I like the house but I'm not in the market for one this size.'

I feel foolish but recover 'Don't be rude.'

'You can show me around if you like.'

'I've told you everything. I love it but something always needs redecorating; this room and the bathroom are recent and our bedroom and the en-suite are... I meant my bedroom.' I correct myself. He notices, reaches out and pats my wrist.

'I was admiring the guitar.'

'My husband's guitar. We played...I still play in a band.'

'It's fun isn't it, and therapeutic. The guitar looks expensive; a Gibson is it?'

'Yes. It hasn't been moved except for dusting since he...you know.'

'Yes, you told me. Do you never play it?'

'No. It doesn't suit my style.'

'So what do you play?'

'A fat Strat; does that mean anything?'

'I think so.'

'I had a wonderful Telecaster but it was so precious that I had to lock it away. Oh goodness! I forgot I'm talking to an analyst.'

'No, you are talking to an admirer.'

'Thank-you.' I run away from the potential familiarity. 'Would you like to see the Strat?'

I go to the office and fetch 'Ms 2'.

'I'm not really a guitarist; I play a little but I don't know much about them.' He strums a chord. 'Hmm!' he frowns 'it has life in it.'

'Yes, Chris chose it carefully and he modified...it does everything I need.'

'Would you like to demo?'

'Not now, you are supposed to be wining and dining me.'

'Let's go then.'

It was a lovely evening; I had been to the restaurant with Chris once or twice and the food was good if expensive. Stuart had booked a table in an alcove and in the seclusion with candlelight, chatter and warmth I began to feel happy. There was no pressure, just possibility and I felt in control.

The arrival of the bill brought a problem, it was far more than

I would normally pay and I headed off an argument by saying 'I would like to share this time.'

He hesitated then in an archaic way said. 'As you wish.' It was the only hiccup in a thoroughly enjoyable evening.

We drove back to my house with the talk still flowing easily and inconsequentially; when we parked in the drive I invited him in. It wasn't planned, it just happened naturally.

The rest of the night happened naturally too; a small brandy, a kiss and we went to bed.

I don't know why I did it; probably because Stu made me feel relaxed and in control.

When we entered the bedroom, he held my arms and asked 'Are you sure?'

I said 'No, I don't do this, I never have but I feel... I don't know what I feel, something to do with moving on. Sorry I'm useless.'

He kissed my cheek and I relaxed a little.'

Some-how I managed to undress without feeling silly and wearing just my briefs and a pyjama top I slipped into bed. Stu seemed to approve, offering as we became better acquainted, positive verbal and dare I say physical indications.

I was nervous; the situation was familiar and unfamiliar and when things became more intimate the nerves were released as a giggle. I shook my head and said 'Sorry, it is ok' hugged him, relaxed and gave myself up to the excitement; I was so relaxed that afterwards I fell asleep and shared my bed with a stranger.

I woke slowly next morning; a momentary shock at not being alone then drifting, wondering if it was all a dream and discovering that it wasn't. I was relieved to find that my briefs were back in place.

Stuart was awake and eased onto an elbow looking down at me.

'I suppose I must say that you are lovely or you will feign anxiety and make a silly remark about age in the hope of gathering compliments.'

'I will not horrid psychiatric person.'

'Good.' He smiled and pushed the duvet onto the floor then eased down my briefs.

'No! Don't!' I whispered and covered myself with my hands but he held my arm, kissed me then ran his eyes over me.

'Hmm, what shall I say?'

'Nothing! Shut up.'

I was naked, it was daylight and I was in bed with a stranger. I tightened mentally and physically and reached for the duvet with a free hand.

'You are lovely as you know very well' he looked me in the eye 'even allowing for your advanced years.'

'Ooh you...pig.'

'Good looking, a good body and the jiggly bits are pretty special. Is that sufficient or shall I continue until my comment is obviously insincere?'

'Pretty good yourself' I respond 'except when you exploit my weaknesses.'

He began to stroke then kiss me and almost before I was aware I was capitulating for a second time muttering protests like a mantra to retain my self-respect.

I had always been a shy about nakedness, even on the beach with Chris I behaved modestly. Now in middle age, with some effort, I could tolerate and appreciate the admiration of a stranger.

I was in a strange euphoric state when we breakfasted in the kitchen, part of me amazed and happy, another part uncertain and a little ashamed.

The latter part asked him 'Is everything ok?' and blundered on to repeat 'I don't do this sort of thing, I never did, I loved my husband and I haven't done anything like this since he died.'

(I had wiped from my memory the brief relationship with Tony)

'You regularly brought men home when you were married? I told you that you shouldn't need reassurance; it is a pleasure to be with you. Is that enough?'

'I meant as you know that I have never been promiscuous and I mean never. I need to justify myself.'

'Shall I risk shattering your confidence and say that I know you are older than you look and that you are less than perfect but the whole person is a very attractive package. You seem to have got life right.'

'I have tried. Thank-you for being kind and for a lovely evening.'

'We must do it again.'

'Yes.' I felt slightly hot.

Afterwards I showed him round the house.

My guitars and amps were in the study and after I explained about Sextet he asked me to sing something.

'Are you teasing or patronising?'

'Curious.'

'Ok.' I picked up the Ovation and offered a verse of 'Human'; it fitted my feelings. I was delighted to see that for the first time he was on the back foot.

'Hey!'

I scored a small victory, enjoyed it but didn't extend it.

'Very professional.'

'I was a professional for seven years, I still am part time. I haven't always been a desperate middle-aged housewife.'

He laughed, a big full happy laugh and I basked in the shared good feeling.

'Would you like to tell me about it? Perhaps another time.' He moved forward and put his arms around me. 'Would the desperate housewife like…' he whispered.

'No she wouldn't! She's still coming to terms with a self she doesn't recognise.'

'Is that so? I suspect that you have always been able to deal with your other self.'

'Perhaps.' I tried to think what to say. 'Chris and I were soulmates and it was easy to deal with admiration and interest.'

'And potential seduction?'

'It's easier to deal with serious interest if you love someone.' I hesitated 'Not always easy but I succeeded.' The force of my comment came to me. 'Now you think I am repressed, uptight and old fashioned.'

'No, I think you are sensible, cautious and unspoiled which is why you are nice to know. Have you ever considered that perhaps things were the other way around?'

'What does that mean?'

He gave me an amused look then held my arms and kissed me.

'Did the happy marriage shield the lovely Alison from the promiscuous Alison.'

'I don't need to be analysed thank-you.'

'Ok.'

Should I tell him? Why not. 'For your information Chris and I split up for over a year, I could have enjoyed myself but I never found a replacement.'

'He didn't deserve you.'

The subject was never raised again.'

He left mid-morning, kissing me and saying 'We must meet soon.'

It was as easy as that and I was left with few hang ups and little anxiety. It wasn't a new me, I hadn't become an unconcerned amoral widow; the real me was temporarily suspended while I explored a new situation.

Oh my goodness, I want to tell V and the rest of the world that I have a boyfriend who likes me; I laugh to myself, a wonderful bubbly releasing laugh.

Chrissie was the only person I could really let go with but I had enjoyed my night with Stuart. He is kind, intelligent and thoughtful; for a short while I am going to just let things happen.

I wonder what the choir would think if they knew their choir-mistress was having a relationship. I laugh again, at the imagery, wonderful emptying laughter that makes me feel good.

When Stu had left after our first night of love I sat in the lounge with the remaining croissant and the large cafetiere contemplating what I wanted from my new friendship, how long might it last, where I was going and what else I might do?

I had been slightly unsettled by his comment that I may have been a tart who hid behind marriage to maintain her virtue. He was wrong but I understood his thinking because I had capitulated on our first date. There was no psychology involved it was simply that meeting the right person had coincided with my need to move on.

I had never wanted loveless 'fun' encounters when I was with my own band partly because I still loved Chris but partly, as I now realised, because I was nervous with men.

I had always had love, friendship, excitement and stability and I would never have risked losing it for the few thrilling weeks of an affair.

My fear of the slippery slope, the easy slide from moral to amoral to immoral returned momentarily. It was ok, I was in control and the new situation wasn't sliding anywhere. Stu and I were friends because he was affectionate without being possessive.

For a few months I would adopt the philosophy of my actor friend Danny who was able to enjoy a short-term relationship and let it go without rancour.

I was going through the older persons equivalent of taking a year out.

I relaxed and my mind began to explore other activities.

The activities ranged from the sensible; Greenpeace, Sailing and Young Wives, through the foolish; bungee jumping, a renewal of flying and driving to Australia, to the naughty; posing for art classes, becoming an escort (at my age?) and naturism (I knew one lady who was a naturist)

The trouble with blue sky thinking is that you can be swamped by the nonsense. I had my phone next to me and recorded my ideas.

That evening I reviewed my 'possibles' hurriedly deleting the silly, the rude and those for which I was too old.

As I progressed the options thinned out I put my 'engage in

social support' option to one side.

The two most promising additions to my 'bucket list' were a tour of Europe and a second string to my musical activities. The first was possible if I stayed in cheap hotels and booked a mobile home for a longer stay, the second required a word with Marion to ask if her offer to join a Caley band was still open.

My relationship with Stu did not work quite as I hoped; the initial excitement lasted only for a few weeks but the friendship continued for a couple of months.

It wasn't all sex, far from it, we met irregularly, once sometimes twice in a week and most of our time together was spent in ordinary social activity, talking, eating, even shopping.

I might as well be frank, I could probably have counted our intimate times on my fingers. Pathetic for a 'desperate' widow who was moving on.

One Friday we went to the theatre; I had been asked if I would like to stay over and afterwards, when we returned to his flat I was invited to share his immaculate bed.

The next morning he was up before me and whilst I lay warm and comfy in his bed he came in with two mugs and said 'Tea?'

My sleepy mind said 'Is that all you can offer?' I was lying naked against the pillow and I pushed the duvet aside. It was something I sometimes did with Chris and he had always shown his appreciation.

'Tea first or it will get cold' said Stu.

The sleepy mind woke and cringed.

I had the presence of mind to pull back the duvet and say 'Thankyou.'

Stu was so good saying 'Thank-you for the treat darling.'

The relationship was good, but it included an upset and a silly incident that could have been catastrophic.

The upset was inevitable.

Stu stayed overnight on a second occasion; we were going to a show in Cardiff and since we would be late back staying with me was a sensible solution. On his arrival he offered a quick kiss and took his bag upstairs.

I was in the kitchen when the bell rang and looking up I saw Phil at the door; he waved and I went to open it.

'Hi Al he said, I was passing on my way home. I haven't seen you for a week and thought I would call, are you free?'

I was never any good at lying, hopeless when caught out and seldom had a strategy.

'Hello Phil, it isn't very convenient, I have a visitor. Can I ring you tomorrow.'

'Oh, I see.' He frowned. 'Yes of course.'

At that moment Stu came down the stairs saying 'I put my bag in the bedroom' and entered the kitchen saying 'is it OK if I have a shower…oh hi.'

I went rigid and saw instantly that Phil understood the situation and was very upset. 'Hi.' He said automatically.

'Sorry Phil, I will ring you tomorrow, don't worry.' What a stupid thing to say.

'Right! Bye Al.' He turned and walked away. I shut the door feeling awful.

'Just a friend.'

'I could see. More than a friend I think, I'm afraid he was upset to see me. I am sorry, I hope I haven't spoiled something.'

'No. I hope not, I will sort it out.'

Prevarication; I knew immediately that my friendship with Phil was ruined. It might survive but it wouldn't be the same because his 'perfect woman' (the description was a shared joke) had been caught whoring and the unspoken notion of fidelity was shattered.

The miserable feeling lasted until the middle of the concert, faded during the second half and I enjoyed the rest of my evening and night with Stu.

The silly incident was potentially disastrous.

Stu knew that I had been a professional singer and I had offered to show him our videos when he next visited.

When meeting him I took a little more trouble with my appearance and had decided that morning to wear a dress instead of the usual chinos and added my prettiest nicks. Well, why not?

I saw his car arrive, waved and opened the door to invite him in. His first words were, 'I have missed lovely Alison' and I barely had time to say thank-you before he kissed me.

'That was nice but you shouldn't take advantage of a lonely....' Before I knew where I was, he had eased me giggling into a corner and ignoring my less than assertive protests, lifted my skirt and took advantage.

My protest was serious because as well as postie and the milkman, friends often come to the door and if anyone saw me with my skirt around my waist cuddled into a corner being... intimate I would have had to leave the village.

Leave the village? the choice was emigration or suicide.

The phone call from Phil came ten minutes later and I was thankful that he couldn't see his red faced 'girlfriend' answering; her voice calm and collected, slapping at a hand that continued to show interest in her bottom.

The rest of the day was more satisfactory; it included a film show in the afternoon when Stu saw young me fronting Synergy and looking fabulous in concert with 'king Rock.

He was quiet during the playing but at its end he turned, looked at me and said 'Alison Rachel, you were a stunner. It would be hard to relate my lovely friend with the young rocker except that she has hardly changed.'

We went out that night to his favourite restaurant where this time I allowed him to pay; he had his reward when we returned to my house but he wasn't asked to stay the night.

After I had my shower next morning I returned to the bedroom and throwing off my bath robe smiled at my reflection in the mirror. A trim, middle aged woman smiled back but the slightly lop-sided smile was almost a leer. I was shocked.

During our summer season Dave had shown a serious interest in the prettiest of the dancers. We were leaving the theatre one lunchtime when she came out of a dressing room said 'Hi Dave' and gave him the same sort of self-satisfied smile.

Dave said 'Hi Penny.' then, as we moved away 'The little slut has just been shafted.'

I had just seen a reflection of the same smile.

My fling ended shortly afterwards. We had enjoyed an evening concert but when we returned to his apartment, I realised that something was amiss.

Stu made some coffee, sat me down and gently explained that his circumstances had changed and that reluctantly he would not be able to continue our relationship.

I knew from the start that our friendship would be short term but had settled comfortably into a situation that added an extra dimension to my life.

He talked on giving apologies and assurances that his feelings for me were genuine and it was hard to conceal my hurt.

Thankfully he didn't suggest that I would soon find someone else which would have made me angry.

As it was I was able to stand up, fetch my coat, thank him for his honesty and brushing aside further kindnesses say 'Please don't spoil things by prolonging the situation.'

I walked to my car, settled in and cried; when I had recovered, upset but only slightly miserable I drove home.

By lunchtime next day I had rationalised the situation; My fling had lasted longer than expected; it could have been sexual but mostly it was fun and friendship; Stu had told me that he liked me but I sensed from the first that there was someone else. He never said he loved me and though I liked him, I had never felt that strange feeling of love that had been an ever-present companion in my marriage.

I was reluctant to read the text that came next day fearing that my emotions would be stirred up. It was kind, apologetic and honest explaining that six months earlier his long-term partner had accepted a post in the North and there had been a trial separation. She had written and admitted that her action was a mistake, (mistakes let alone an admission of the same were unknown) such a concession could not be dismissed and she was returning to his life.

He had been surprised to find how much his affection for me had grown, how much he liked me and enjoyed my company. Making the break had been hard and he hoped I wouldn't think too badly of him.

Emotion welled up again; if he hadn't been suitable there never would have been a relationship but his note was no more than a slap in the face, painful but instantly over. I was able to text 'Having no previous experience of 'relationships' I am pleased to discover that I can deal with their ending.'

My affair was part of my period of change and though short it had been mostly good. The hint of a leer that I had seen in the mirror had shown me someone I had no wish to become. When the break came the upset was brief and less hurtful than I had feared but there was a brief and unpleasant consequence.

A few days after the break I received an unwelcome visit. A woman came to the door asking if I was Alison Phillips.
I said 'Yes I am' and was subjected to a torrent of angry abuse about 'desperate old whores who drop their pants for anyone'.
'Keep away from him or you'll be sorry.'
My visitor then lost her temper and slapped my face.
Shocked and with no opportunity to explain I reacted, stepped forward and punched her. She staggered backwards and grabbing her jacket I propelled her towards her car.
'Get out!! I know who you are and you will be facing an action for assault.' Her nose dripped blood over her smart jacket.
'I have no interest in Stuart except that now I feel sorry for him.'
She walked slowly to her car; shouted more abuse which assured

me that I was a sad baggy old slut. I tried to think of an equally abusive response but only managed 'Get off my property' before she drove away.

I returned indoors and collapsed on the sofa my insides in a turmoil.

When I was recovered from the shock I reached for the phone and with shaking hands phoned a solicitor friend in the village and asked for advice. He advised that I make an appointment to visit his office and give him the whole story. He could then advise on the action I should take.

There were no consequences except an apologetic text from Stuart hoping I wouldn't take action.

I ignored it.

When I was young incidents of that kind were quickly forgotten but I was alone and vulnerable and it dented my confidence.

I suppose things are never that easy. The ending of my friendship was harder than I pretended and one evening misery overwhelmed me. I threw on a coat and stamped down the lane to Geoff and Marilyn's farm thinking up an excuse to visit just to have company.

I mustn't make too much of the negatives; the affair was a new experience, the upset short-lived and it left no scars. Most importantly I had turned a corner and could live life on my own. I was separating myself from the past; my marriage was a wonderful time that was over. I needed to preserve the memory and start again. Six months wasn't much to ask.

The failings? Vickie soon knew that something was going on and I lied shamelessly. I think she must have hinted to Phil who questioned me whether our (passive) relationship was still on. I felt guilty because he was a good friend.

Sorry Phil, for a while I need a life where I am free and not beholden to anyone.

My needs are limited and if I follow mum's example I will still look good at 65 and maybe decent even at 75.

Chris once said, and I think it was original, 'Middle class isn't a class it is a way of life that produces fairly well balanced healthy and often successful people.'

I decided that I didn't want to remarry; unexpected because I liked having strong friendships but I had discovered that I liked being me.

CHAPTER 19

The Ceilidh Band

A new musical interest was one of the more exciting options that resulted from my review of future activities. I knew that Marion from pilates played in a folk band and decided to speak to her at my next session.

I was a professional singer/guitarist who had achieved some success in a hard business. Perhaps I saw myself modestly dismissing the appreciation of my skills by the other players and the more I thought about it the more excited I became.

It was a return to my musical roots... sort of.

Ali's Band (I still shed a tear thinking about it) and my musical career began in folk clubs and the kindness and tolerance of the audiences was very encouraging. On open mic. nights half the audience were nervously waiting their turn to perform and mutual support was part of scene.

On Tuesday after our workout I told V that I wanted a private word with Marion and would join her in the café. I waited until V and Caren had left, crossed the empty hall and spoke to Marion saying that I had always enjoyed folk music and asking whether I could come to one of her folk sessions.

She looked surprised and then said 'Of course, anyone is welcome. Are you sure it is your thing? We just play tunes for fun and some of us get together to play for Barn Dances. It's mostly

about the enjoyment of the music, we don't make any money.'
'I'm not looking to make money' I said 'I enjoy playing music especially in groups, I hope I have something to contribute.'
'I'm sure you will, I know you were a professional.'
'That was a long time ago.'
I was about to add "I still am" but didn't want to sound patronising.

I looked forward to my first session. Marion had given me the details, but unwilling to go on my own I offered to collect her.
I couldn't decide whether to take a guitar or a mandolin to the first session; I was competent on guitar and could read guitar music provided the tempo was reasonably slow and un-complicated. On mandolin I was slow, inaccurate and my reading was limited by my unfamiliarity with the fingerboard.
I considered taking my flute, but I hadn't played it for several years.

There was no problem with what to wear; something simple, probably whatever I had on except that I would change the flatties for my soft red leather boots and add a sparkly scarf.
I decided to take the Ovation; it wasn't ideal but my old Eko was precious because of its memories.

I was late collecting Marion deciding at the last minute that the jumper with coloured hoops was more suitable than the olive green one. It was at the bottom of the laundry basket so instead I changed my jeans for green chinos. The chinos were the wrong shade so I settled for a white t-shirt with a tartan shirt over the top.
Driving to the venue, a village hall about fifteen minutes away I felt a touch of nervous excitement. Marion had chatted through most of the journey telling me about the band; she sounded concerned that I might find the evening amateurish.
We parked in the small car park and collected our instruments from the boot. As we walked to the entrance Marion handed me a folder.

'These are some of the more popular songs we play, they include music and chords so you can play whichever you choose.'

I had been worried that I wouldn't know the tunes but Marion had offered a lifeline.

'Bless you Marion that's so thoughtful, I didn't know how I would manage if I had to play by ear.'

'Some people like to use music but most of us know the tunes.'

We entered the hall to find a dozen people standing or sitting around surrounded by their instruments; a couple had music stands and several were using tablets; it was a surprise, Chris had been transferring the data on our laptop to a tablet when…I shook myself, I didn't want to start the evening with tears.

Several of the people looked up when I arrived and Marion introduced me to a man who had been tuning a violin.

'Alison? Marion said that we might be gaining a new member; it's lovely to see you, I hope you enjoy the evening let me introduce you to…'

I was introduced to several people who were welcoming and gave a sense that they were comfortable with themselves.'

'Sit between Marion and Lyndon, he is our other guitarist.'

Lyndon looks up and smiles; he is one of the two youngsters, most people are fifty plus.

I set up my music stand, take the Ovation from its case and clip on the tuner. It is seldom needed.

I turn and thank Marion for the music folder and flip through the content; mostly single line tunes with the chords written over the top; most of the tunes are in G or D.

I put the folder on my music stand, select at random a tune that seems fairly simple and run through it.

We sit in a large circle and Arthur who welcomed me moves to the middle with his violin.

'Shall we begin with 'Taur Mor'. 'Taur Mor' he repeats 'we will take it slowly'. He looks at me and smiles encouragingly. I riff through the pages and find the tune, it is simple, dum-de dum-de dum-de diddly.

'Ok.' Arthur nods and we start to play; not all of us, I can read and play but I am unfamiliar with the style; after a stumble of wrong or delayed notes I pick up the rhythm. I am becoming confident when after three repeats the band stops.

'Faster than I expected.' I say to Marion.

'You'll get used to it; it takes a lot of practice to keep up with the better players.'

'I can play rhythm but I will need to learn the tunes.'

Arthur is speaking again. 'Shall we do the 'Astleys Ride' set? It was loose at the barn dance so let's take it slowly.'

'Are you managing Alison?' He looks at me.

I nod. 'Yes, if it too fast for me to read I will play the chords'

'Chords are fine, we need a solid accompaniment. Right, let's take this one at a steady pace.'

It is too fast for me but I get a feel for the rhythm and start to enjoy myself.

Mid-evening we stop for coffee and cake; I am introduced to and converse with several people. They are all enthusiasts and there is a good atmosphere. I know that there are always hidden problems and concealed rivalries but the general feeling is good. I return to my seat and speak to Lyndon. He responds kindly but is talking to an old lady and old ladies and guitars don't mix.

On the way home Marion asks me if I enjoyed the evening and will I come again.

'Yes, of course I will.'

I have had a lovely evening, have a new interest and a new circle of friends.

There is an unexpected benefit from my evening, I now have an incentive to practice the guitar and the mandolin. I was happy to strum an accompaniment for the assorted violins mandolins and flutes that provided the tune but I want to learn the tunes and stretch my skills.

For several weeks the house reverberated with a selection of tunes and I became familiar with the structures. I could read the music and it was really a matter of combining the two. It wasn't that easy, some of the tunes had difficult fingering but for most it was a matter of practice.

Within a month I knew many people by their first names, felt that I was reasonably established and started to play the melody on some of the tunes.

I think that Lyndon was relieved to regain his role as rhythm guitarist and was sufficiently impressed to talk to me as if I was a human being rather than an old person.

(Listen Lyndon my lad, this "old person" went naked on a French beach last year and the comments were favourable)

Progress with the mandolin was slower but ten minutes practice before tea every day was paying off and the fingering was beginning to improve. Another few months and I would be good enough to take it to a session.

The following week Arthur asked if I would like to do a gig and I said I would love to if I was free. I checked the phone and found to my annoyance that 'Sextet' was playing on the same day.

We only had eleven gigs booked for the whole year and it seemed perverse that one of them should coincide with my first invitation to play at a barn dance.

'Sorry' I said and without thinking 'I've another gig on that day.'

'You play in another band?'

There was no point in avoiding the issue. 'I run a band called Sextet.'

'Now I recognise you,' a voice over Arthur's shoulder 'I thought you looked familiar but I couldn't place you.'

Peter and his wife were talking to another couple and had overheard our conversation.

'Sorry Alison I didn't mean to interrupt. Your band played at our works dinner a few years ago.'

'I hope we were good.' Please don't let it spoil things!

'You were excellent' he turns to Arthur 'Alison is the singer and guitarist in a band, she is very good. Seriously,' he turns back to me 'you really were very good.'

'Thankyou. We only gig about once a month but this month we have two and one coincides with the barn dance.'

Please don't let him make connections with Synergy or 'kR.

'So you won't be able to join us that day.' Arthur is an organiser and my other activities are irrelevant.

'No, not on that date but I would love to when I am available.'

'Good, we have several performances and two barn dances in the next few months.'

I return to my seat and check my guitar tuning. Pete is talking to his friends and they look in my direction and smile. It's an inclusive smile that says they are happy to have me playing with them. I smile back and raise my eyebrows.

At the end of the evening, I went home on a high. Musically the sessions were not what I expected, almost all the songs were folk songs from Britain the US or Europe that had been the political, pop or love songs of their day and many were for dancing. There was a happy atmosphere; I really enjoyed myself.

I played my first pub session the same week; part of a new social group visiting and playing in pubs where a dozen of us would get together, enjoy the music and ourselves. As we were leaving, I had a second invitation to play in the band for a Barn Dance. The band had a core of six who co-opted people to make up numbers when needed. I was invited only because their guitarist was unavailable but I was still delighted.

I told Vickie about my invitation to play at the dance and she pretended to be jealous. Clive would be out with a friend from work on the evening of the gig and V was happy to accept my invitation and come on her own.

It was a nothing gig even by Sextet's standards but I loved it. I enjoyed playing, everyone seemed happy and some of the dancers were helpless with laughter when the dances went wrong.

My only disappointment was that as a performer I wasn't able to join the dancing and the dancers including V were having so much fun.

The following week there was an open session in our village pub, the nicer one. It was wonderfully relaxing, playing music and chatting with my new friends. The music was fun and I felt very alive in a warm cocoon of belonging. It was a situation that I had always loved and I regressed to being myself at eighteen with Chris and Dave in a friendly folk club. My teenage tipple had been orange juice and lemonade but by the end of the evening the older me was happy and rather noisy after two (or was it three?) G and Ts.

I may have been more relaxed than I thought because when time was called and we packed up, two of the band offered to see me home safely.

"Thanks, I'm fine,' I told them 'I only live ten minutes away." Clutching my mandolin I waved goodbye, tottered out of the car park and strode off along the main road through the village. Their car passed with a shouted 'Bye Alison, take care' as I turned down Church Road which led to our lane.

The tiddliness had made me very laid back because when I passed 'The Duke' some lads who were leaving shouted 'It's rockin' Granny. Give us a tune.' and 'Need a hand?' followed by sniggers and comments.

I waved, smiled and strode or tottered on.

The walk took a little longer than normal and I was chilled through by the time I got home.

The central heating went off at eight and the house was chilly but I had banked down the Parkray that was sometimes lit in the winter. Still in my coat I opened the door of the fire, threw on some logs and opened the vent. The glowing ashes flickered and small flames rose. I knelt shivering in front of the open door then rose, checked that I had locked the back door, took a biscuit from the tin, put the kettle on and circled the kitchen until it boiled. I poured myself a cup of hot water and returned to the lounge.

The logs had caught and warmth was beginning to flow from the fire; I squatted on the rug to make the most of it.

I was beginning to feel tired and a little nauseous so as soon as I was warm I returned to the kitchen, filled a hot water bottle and went up to bed where I half undressed, pulled on pyjamas and a dressing gown and curled up in bed.

I was just dropping off when the phone rang. Cursing I reached across and picked it up.

Marilyn's voice, urgent. 'Alison!'

'What…what is it, are you ok?'

'I am but you have a problem, your chimney is on fire. Geoff was shutting the barn and he saw the glow, there are sparks. He is coming round.'

'Oh.' Panic. 'I'll dress. Thanks.'

I put the phone down, my mind still fuzzy, threw off the dressing gown and pyjama trousers, dragged on jeans, shoes, a jumper and the coat that was lying on the chair.

Half way down the stairs I could feel the heat and hear the crackling roar of the fire. I realised that I had left the door of the Parkray open and knew that I had to shut it.

It took courage to enter the room, the logs were blazing and huge flames were licking up the chimney, the room was like a furnace. Panic was gripping me. I must shut the door, I must. I picked up a dining chair and with the heat burning my face I eased up to the fire from the side. I hooked a chair leg behind the door and flicked it shut. It swung shut then bounced back. I could feel the heat through my clothes as I gently pushed it shut and hooked the latch in place. The burning heat of the fire was reduced and I was able to pick up a poker and shut the vent.

I staggered back heart pounding and was relieved to see that fire had diminished slightly.

The bell rang and I ran to the kitchen and opened the back door. Geoff hurried in. 'Thank goodness you are ok.'

'I left the fire door open and the fire was roaring.'

'Is it shut now?'

'Yes, I realised what I had done.'

'Well done. It is easy to forget, we have done the same several times.'

We entered the lounge; the fire was still hot but the flames were less.

'Good. I'll check the chimney.' He hurried out and a minute later came back with the kitchen fire extinguisher.

'It's still on fire; the soot in the chimney has caught and the up-draught keeps the fire going.' I'll try this. Can you open the door when I say?

'I'll try.'

'Lift the catch and open when I say now.'

'Now.'

Using the poker I opened the door and the heat hit me, Geoff banged the button on the extinguisher against the hearth and pointed the hose up the chimney.

The fire began to roar again.

'Shut the door.' I pushed it shut with the poker and Geoff flicked the catch. 'Do you have another extinguisher?

'There is an old one in the barn and one in the car.'

'Can you fetch them, have you any old cloths?'

I thought for a moment 'There are some curtains we use to cover furniture when decorating.'

'Get them.'

I ran to the washroom grabbed them from a shelf of paint tins and ran back.

'Thanks. Get the extinguishers.'

I ran to the kitchen and collected my car keys; out of the door ignoring the cold I ran across the yard and opened the boot of the Jazz. I threw out the box of odds and ends and found the extinguisher slammed the boot and ran to the barn to fetch the second one. It was in an open cupboard and picking it up I staggered back across the yard.

Geoff had tucked the cloth around the vents and the fire had died back a little.

'Ok, we will try again, the same way as before.' I picked up the poker. 'My god, how long have you had this one? He was looking at the barn extinguisher.

'I don't know.'

'We'll try it.'

We repeated the process with the extinguisher then shut the door and the fire died back again.

'I think that may be ok, we'll see.' 'You were lucky. I've seen old extinguishers blow up in people's faces. I'll check the chimney.' He disappeared and I slumped back into a chair.

The stress of the last fifteen minutes released itself and I began to shake.

Geoff returned. 'The chimney should be fine, a few sparks but it will die out if it isn't fed.'

'Thanks Geoff. Sorry I'm so wet.'

'Wet? Nonsense, you did well; nasty thing to happen. I'll keep an eye on it for a while to make sure it doesn't catch again. The fire is damped down and if we starve it of air, it will go out and the soot will stop burning. The chimney should be ok but you need to get it swept.'

The shaking stopped; I was beginning to recover. 'I don't know what to say, I was tiddly and forgot about the fire.'

'Are you ok?'

'I think so. Thanks Geoff and thank Mar for me.' I stood up. 'I had a lovely evening and was feeling happy then this happened.'

'It was an accident when you were tired.' He looked at me and raised his eyebrows. He didn't say 'and drunk.'

'You acted a damned well in the circumstances. Don't get knocked back by it love. When you are a farmer life is a lot of work and full of problems and you can't pretend they don't exist, you have to deal with them.'

I nodded. 'I feel so stupid.'

'Are you ok now?'

'I think so. I'm not as resilient as I was.'

'None of us are. You remember how relieved Mar and I were when Rex came to join us.'

I did, Rex was their younger son and I could recall Marylin's delight when she told me that his partner had had a change of heart and was now committed to being a farmer's wife.

'Do you want me to stay for a while?'

'No, you need to get back…well, for five minutes…would you like a cuppa?'

'Good idea.'

He left about twenty minutes later giving me an encouraging hug and reminding me that I had successfully dealt with a nasty situation.

I stayed in the kitchen pottering and moving things. Restless, I went into the yard and checked the chimney, it seemed ok. The car was unlocked and at my box of goodies was lying in the drive. I returned it to the boot, locked the car looked at the chimney again and felt lonely.

I wished Chris was with me and in the darkness of the yard I became aware that he was gone, no longer a presence, just a memory.

Chilled and tearful I returned to the kitchen.

Chimney fires are rare now that most people have central heating and they are seldom dangerous unless you have a thatched roof. I often had a wood fire in winter; the central heating was expensive and I only heated the rooms I used. The fire used up the broken branches and prunings from our little orchard.

Chris would sometimes help Geoff when he needed an extra man and we would get a trailer full of logs in payment.

The setback didn't dampen my enthusiasm for the Caley band and I was excited to be asked to join them for a stint at the Sidmouth festival.

I had been to the festival once when the children were in their early teens and Lisa still a small child. They were at an age when 'fun' means lounging about with friends but after a workshop and a concert they changed from being semi-human teenagers and entered into the spirit of the event. They didn't want to be associated with us but Sarah who had always had a touch of the performer completed a flute workshop and decided that a hippy life drifting from festival to festival was the life she would choose.

At home with her peer group the festival was forgotten except as a source of stories which I hope were exaggerated.

The following week during the coffee break my musical past was revealed; Peter approached me with a smile and said 'Good Evening Alison.'

'Hi Peter, it's busy tonight.'

We conversed about family for a minute or two then with a twinkle he smiled and said 'I'm afraid your secret is out.'

I thought of Stuart and blushed. 'The internet' he continued 'I had a feeling that you were more familiar than Sextet.'

'Oh.'

'I had a poster of a band called Synergy on the wall. I was a big fan of the girls.'

'Oh. Thankyou. It's a long time ago.'

'You were also a singer with 'king Rock.'

'Yes. An awful name for a band but I didn't realise it at the time.'

'Great band though. Were you the girl in the video?'

'Yes, one of them.'

'The dark one, playing guitar in the final song when the guitarist was singing.'

'That was me.'

'I thought so, you haven't changed that much. Wow, that was stadium rock, I mean big time. What was your…?' He runs out of questions.

'I was a backing singer and by our standards it was 'big time'; the band was tipped to go mega but Bruce the singer died and the band died with him.'

'And now you grace our little band.'

Is he being sarcastic? My happiness takes a knock and I frown.

'That sounded quite wrong, I meant we are very lucky to have a,' he hesitates 'an attractive and talented star playing with us.'

Peter has always been straightforward. Happiness is restored.

'I love playing music with other people and this group is so friendly.' I smile at him. 'People sometimes get a wrong impression of singers with pop-bands. No one will ask me to sing will they?'

'No, well…. would you like to?'

'Sorry Peter just teasing. People do sometimes ask and it is always the wrong time.'

'If there was a right time and I asked discretely?'

'Perhaps. It's a long time since Chris and I were part of 'king Rock. and…' It all comes back and I am instantly desolate. It shows.

'Are you ok?' Peter looks concerned.

'Yes, yes I'm fine,' I force myself to recover 'the guitarist Chris was my husband, he died.'

'Oh?' Peter is making connections. 'Chris is Chris Phillips, he was your husband? I am sorry.'

'It's ok, I'm nearly over it but sometimes I have sad moments.'

I went with them to the Sidmouth festival staying with Lisa and the grandchildren in a small holiday cottage near the donkey sanctuary.

Life was good; there were moments of loneliness when I desperately wanted what had been but I could rise above them.

The recent family holiday had been enjoyable but challenging and now here I was in my fifties wearing short skirts playing music with my friends in the day, wearing a bikini on the beach (is that water cold) and dancing the night away in the big marquee with paper flower garlands in my hair like an aging hippy.

I just loved it.

CHAPTER 20

Holiday

Alison's story

My fling with Stu was fun and had some lovely moments but I was never comfortable with the situation. It was like a good gig at a dodgy venue; an enjoyable event but not really me.

I settled for sex and friendship and it provided a watershed between what had been and my future.

After I had turned the corner I was able to give a lot of thought to my future activities and made an outline plan.

I wasn't going to become an airline pilot or an MP, I wasn't going to found charities or hospitals. My future was going to be my mundane present, my business, the choir, music and volunteer activities. I would holiday with friends and enjoy simple pleasures.

I would add a list of 'to do's where my skills such as they were would be a benefit to the community.

My first action had been to join the Caley band, my second to invite mum to live with me. She is still active and fully compos mentis; she still drives and knows several people in the village.

It will be her choice; I made an open offer that allowed her to decide if and when she wants to join me. She said she likes the idea but needs to think about it and will let me know her decision.

My next project was a holiday.

I loved France; we had spent our honeymoon there and enjoyed half a dozen holidays with the children or with friends.

The thought of spending an open-ended holiday in the two-seater was exciting, the blue skies, the beaches, the cafes and the history were enticing but visiting them on my own brought anxieties and with the happy memories came a longing for the past.

I wondered if Vickie would be allowed to join me or perhaps Maggie who was finally free again having realised that her new partner was a freeloader. (I could have told her that before he moved in.)

She told me that when asked to leave he had refused, saying that he had given up his home, his job and his freedom to move in with her.

His home she knew was a rented flat, he was 'between' jobs and had contributed nothing to the partnership.

Her brother and a solicitor friend had explained to him that there was an easy or a hard way to leave and the man had settled for a handout to enable him to find new accommodation.

.

The holiday would need to be organised; how long could I afford to stay away, was the Mazda big enough to hold all the luggage and which parts of the continent would I visit?

I knew I could do it, but I didn't want to do it alone? I would ask V if she could join me.

I spoke to her in the pub after choir practice, telling her of my intention to tour the continent.

She left me in no doubt of her opinion. 'Lucky you, it shows the difference between our situation; if I had your car I would be gone.'

'On your own?'

'No, I would take you with me.' She smiled. 'I would take Phil if I was allowed. Are you hoping to take him?'

'No, we don't have that kind of relationship.' I changed the subject.

Later in the evening I returned to the subject of the holiday and said simply 'You could come with me if you were allowed.'

'On holiday? I don't know.' A smile. 'That would be super. When?'

'Early June?'

'I will start to work on Clive tonight.'

It was the end of May before our European trip was fully organised. Vickie had some difficulty persuading Clive that it would be two middle aged women enjoying the sights, food and scenery.

He seemed to think that it would be three weeks of sun, sand and sex. I conceded the sun and sand and assured him that unless we met thirty year old versions of Clive and Chris and they liked old ladies, there was no chance of the sex.'

Perhaps a small chance as my fling with Stuart had shown but I had no wish to repeat it.

V had unkindly suggested that my relationship with Stuartwas like hers with Darren except that I had been seduced and behaved like a silly teenager.

I told her that the two situations were quite different.

'Were they? An attractive, sensible older woman, picked up in a club by a charmer who says the right things? The difference is that that I didn't have three months of sex before being dumped in favour of an old girlfriend.'

I ignored her because she didn't understand the real situation, but later, alone in my bed the conversation came back to me and I admitted there were similarities.

I had met an intelligent stranger, we had each enjoyed the others company. There was friendship, affection and we got on well until his partner returned and he was obliged to let me go.

It was in the past and I had put the situation behind me but V's comment, however wrong, was annoying.

The next morning, showered and dressed with sun flooding

through the bedroom window the conversation was still on my mind. I hadn't been used, Stu and I were equal partners and we had enjoyed a lovely relationship. For me it was a unique situation and afterwards I was happy to return to being the real me.

I booked three days in Paris followed by a week in a cheap apartment near Antibes then six days at a hotel near Lake Garda; the rest of the journey would be pot luck staying in low-cost hotels like Ibis or in pensions.

It was a challenging journey but with Vickie added to my insurance we could share the driving.

She was a good, safe driver with a clean licence (unlike me) and I now had to decide which car to use. I wanted to use the Mazda with its style and open top but the Hybrid offered space, comfort and a huge reduction in fuel cost.

What the hell, it will be warm, a smart dress, jeans, shorts and t-shirts. Nicks can be washed and we will be in flip flops half the time.

We did a trial which showed that two modest suitcases a continental touring kit and tyre repair liquid just fitted in the boot with our shoes and wash bags. The folding hardtop took up a lot of space but there was just room behind the seats for maps (I wasn't totally confident with my sat nav), wallets, paperwork, money and tissues. The sunglasses, cameras (please don't think of anything else), hats, sunscreen, first aid and insect repellent were squeezed in to free areas.

We compared lists and I realised that I had made no allowance for water and snacks, that we hadn't included towels, swimwear, beach mats etc.

A tactical 'helpless woman' call was made to an accessory firm who suggested a boot rack and a top box at a price that would have used up my holiday spending money. Clive, having accepted that the holiday was going to happen did an internet search and found a large waterproof bag that sat on the boot lid and allowed the hardtop to open and shut.

It wasn't ideal but it was affordable and the extra space spared me having to trade a t-shirt for an extra pair of knicks in my bulging suitcase; more importantly we still had enough money to eat.

The car was emptied of all but the essentials and the paperwork, spare money and passports were distributed to safe locations.

I had the car serviced at our local garage explaining to Nick that we were going to tour Europe and would probably be covering several thousand miles. His look said 'I know what you are after' but he said 'Don't worry luv, I'll give it a thorough check; you won't have any problems, these cars are bullet proof.'

I was reassured.

The last few days before the holiday were frantic. Lisa had agreed to 'live in' to look after the house and my grandchildren would look after the hens. They knew them by name, regularly fed and watered them and collected the eggs. They were excited to be responsible for them but three weeks was a long time and they would need constant reminders and support from mum.

Lisa assured me that she could manage the business, the house and the children. 'Stop fussing mum.'

The car was packed, the bag securely attached, the boot crammed and we were ready to leave. Clive was being affectionate to both of us, offering me an excessive hug and a request that I should look after Vickie.

'We will look after each other.'

'Will you?' The remark was questioning but Clive seemed unconcerned and I sensed that he was looking forward to three weeks of freedom without V.

I had known them for thirty years, it was a close friendship but the intimacies of a relationship are often hidden.

I wanted to make a stylish exit with the roof down but rain was threatening so I settled for the safe option. After some more loving hugs from Clive (both of us) we pulled away waving and headed for Portsmouth. The expected shower didn't arrive but we were glad of the roof when, ten miles from our destination a downpour struck unexpectedly.

It was an uneventful journey, the car comfortable, the right amount of chatter, an easy crossing and an effortless run to Paris.

As we approached the city my mind leapt back to our honeymoon and a lump rose in my throat.

No, no, I am being silly; I control threatening tears and force myself back to the present.

'Al, are you ok.' V's voice from my left.

'Yes, just for a moment I was remembering.'

She squeezes my arm.

We had a great time in Paris, the car parked, feeling alive and free do whatever we chose.

I insisted that we visited 'La Musette' and walked from the metro with my head filled with music, Chris and the band.

What were they called? Manny Quin, the name came back.

I recognised the building but the venue was gone, La Musette was now a Vietnamese restaurant.

The visit was madness, more memories flooded back bringing tears and I stood on a busy pavement sobbing, with Vickie's arm around my shoulder.

Perhaps I crossed another emotional bridge, the remainder of our time in Paris was spent visiting museums and enjoying cafes and restaurants was happy. It made a good beginning to the holiday.

Our leisurely trip to the south where we had rented an economic apartment was fun.

The stopover at a 'Formula one' travel lodge was one long giggle, friendship, laughter and a shower in a cubicle the size of a telephone box that was bliss after four hours driving in hot conditions. At one of our stops we bought a new sunhat for V who had lost hers an hour into the journey; the buffeting as we passed a truck at seventy-five had whisked it from her head never to be seen again.

The following day we arrived in the south and looked for our small apartment. Locating it in a shabby back street was difficult and the nearest parking was a hundred metres away.

We entered with some trepidation; a narrow alleyway and concrete steps to the second floor from a small yard. Up the steps and we open the door.

It was small and plain but clean; we entered the kitchen which unlike mine was spotless, the lounge bedroom and shower room are the same.

That evening we decided to explore the town. Vick and I have remained slim and largely unlined and I thought we looked rather good as we left the apartment.

After a short walk to find our bearings we checked out a number of restaurants before selecting a small inexpensive one.

I remembered the heady days of our honeymoon when we had stayed in a mobile home but driven a Jaguar and eaten in expensive hotels.

After a pleasant but uninspiring meal we took our first stroll around the town. Whether it is the warm evenings, the character of the town, the smell of the food or just being on holiday I relaxed, felt younger and slowly immersed myself in the atmosphere.

We even received a few smiles that suggested we were worth a glance

I say this because next day, to our surprise we actually pulled.

It was a chance encounter when one of a group of men smiled and said 'Ca va.' I smiled back and said 'Ca va bien'. Later when we were swimming our paths crossed again and a conversation in a mixture of languages resulted in our being asked out.

We prevaricated and were told, 'You think, we ask again later'.

I guessed they were all in their mid to late forties.

V asked what I thought and I said 'We could give it a try but we must be cautious and make it clear that it is just an evening out. Are you sure you want to?'

She looked at me then did something I had never seen, she pulled out the front of her bikini bottoms looked down and said 'what do you reckon?' then she giggled and said 'Clive does that.'

'They wouldn't be interested …would they?'

'Clive is. Not' she added 'that they are going to get it.'

'So, what is the answer?'

'Let's speak to them and if they seem ok we can give it a try.'

We checked it out and asked our friends 'where to meet and where to go.' A meeting and a night out with strangers would happen only in a public place.

We judged that they were civilised and agreed to meet the older pair at a club in the town.

Since my encounter with Stu I was more confident and prepared for social intercourse which meant chatting and dancing, the intercourse did not include sexual activity.

I was having my 'year out', it was a transition period, a rite of passage from my old life to the new and it had already brought a different kind of confidence.

We went in a mood of nervous excitement; the guys were tidy and seemed decent; hopeful but not threatening. A lot of dancing, several lagers but no funny substances saw us going back to their apartment where despite good intentions I enjoyed another drink a cosy chat and some smoochy dancing that cost no more than a fondled bottom.

I hinted that I might be more available on a second date and my partner having decided that I was worth a second attempt escorted me home.

By the time V returned I was feeling guilty about leaving her alone.

She isn't promiscuous but I was concerned that I had left her in a difficult situation. I was relieved when she returned not long after me looking relaxed.

My 'Hmm, are you ok V?' was met with 'Yes, fine. I must have a shower.'

She had been in the shower for a couple of minutes when her voice shouted 'Al, can you get my shampoo.' I found it and passed it to her.

After a while she appeared towelling her hair. I gave her some time and said 'Was everything ok?'

'Yes fine. Why did you leave, you seemed to be enjoying yourself?'

'I was but he was starting to get interested and I didn't want him to become a nuisance.'

'Did anything happen when you came back?'

'We had a kiss at the door.'

'Naturally, Mrs Perfect is always sensible. I was going to come back with you but you suddenly disappeared and my friend was also getting interested. I think he assumed that he was doing an older woman a favour.'

'Really Vick when it comes to resisting temptation you are hopeless.'

'I'm not. I enjoyed the interest but the hands began to roam. Despite your doubts about my ability to resist I've only been naughty once in thirty-five years of marriage.'

'Twice.'

She frowned. 'Don't be mean Al, you know that was an accident.' There was a silence.

'Sorry V, we were stupid to go out with strangers, they were ok but you never know.'

'I suppose it was a bit silly; my only problem was that the roving hands had sharp nails. Al could you see if I am ok, I'm a bit sore in places.'

'What do you mean?'

'Sharp nails, I just told you.'

'Do I have to …alright if you want. Now?'

'Yes.'

We went to the bedroom and she slipped off her pants and knelt on the bed.

We knew each other well, had seen each other naked in showers, changing rooms and on the beach but this was more intimate.

I put on my glasses and inspected; there were a couple of small scratches on her bot but that was all.

The ridiculousness of the situation hit me and I giggled.

'What!'

'Nothing, I really don't want to inspect your bot. It looks ok, Germoline should be fine.'

'Could you?'

'Me? Tttt...I suppose.'

I found the germoline, applied some to a tissue and unwillingly dabbed at the scratches and the reddish bits.

She squeaked and clenched 'Al! Oooh! That stings.'

'Are there any other parts that need medication?'

'There are not!'

V was happy to spend the following day on a different beach lying under a sunshade wearing a brief bikini. Any 'discomfort' must have been minor and was forgotten when we walked topless down to the sea. We couldn't compete with the youngsters but were trim enough to feel un-embarrassed.

Perhaps there was also a confidence that we could 'pull'.

The rest of the holiday was largely uneventful. We got to know a pair of married couples at Lake Garda and one of the husbands showed interest in a very discrete way. He was lovely, I wished his wife could have been spirited away but sadly she was lovely too. Damn, damn.

By the end of the week the husband and I were good friends and I was wondering if I found someone like him whether my decision not to remarry might be reconsidered.

CHAPTER 21

A Word with Dave

About Chris

At different times people have asked me was Chris a good musician or did he find a good singer and have a lot of luck.

Alison was attractive, she had a lively personality and a good voice, she developed her skills and became a good singer and a good performer.

There are hundreds of 'good performers' with good voices and even if you get the break you still need luck, dedication and a certain amount of compromise.

Her musical career was successful partly because the band was better than its individuals but she was a quick learner and Chris gave her the confidence to be a good frontman.

Her acting career was brief but quite successful and if you also consider the number of highly competent unemployed actors, suggestions that she had made use of her assets are unsurprising.

Who knows; she was a nice girl but she wasn't perfect.

Chris was fussy in his choice of girlfriends; he fell in love with Al on their first meeting and she was his soulmate. After they were married he remained faithful as far as I know, but he was no saint.

I was surprised that he resisted Sue for so long because she was innocent, very pretty and it was clear that she adored him.

It was a bigger surprise when he gave a job to Sarah; she was good-looking but she could be deceitful and manipulative and she always had her eye on the main chance; not really Chris' type. He admired her because she had a hard life and he described their relationship as a supportive partnership.

It was true but it's also true he was shafting her and 'supportive partnership' was his hypocritical way of minimising their relationship.

Thirty years later she admitted to me that she had been fond of him.

He was a competent guitarist with a decent voice and a great ear for harmony. He worked at his guitar skills and got steadily better and more confident.

The proof came when Bruce Kay asked him to join 'king Rock; Bruce learned his art in the sixties and seventies then created a team that produced a great band. Chris wasn't asked to join because he was all they could get; Tony was Bruce's first choice and when he was injured Chris was their choice to replace him. That is a big accolade.

I'll give another example.

About ten years after 'kR broke up I called on Chris on my way home from Gloucester. His band was playing as a trio that evening in a pub near Chipping Sodbury; it was a big pub but no big deal.

Al was visiting her mum and would meet us there.

'The lazy cow will arrive after the kit is set up looking lovely, being charming and full of excuses. Would you like to come along and watch?'

He meant 'Come and help me to set up'.

I went.

Half an hour before the start Al still hadn't arrived and Chris was worried in case something had happened. He phoned her mother who said she had gone to see Maggie in the afternoon.

He put the phone down and made a comment that must have set her ears burning.

When the band played as a trio Chris played bass so he gave me his keys and asked me to dash home and get his guitar; he would delay the start, do twenty minutes, take a short break then do a long set.

I got back ten minutes into the gig and I thought Al must have arrived. Big surprise, Chris was playing bass and singing with the drummer singing harmonies. Together they were much of the sound you would have expected from a good trio. He did sone more song and some chat with those who were listening and came off.

He was furious but obviously very worried about Al because his first words were 'Where is she?'

He pulled himself together and said 'Listen mate, can you remember any of the Synergy stuff?'

I said 'I think so.'

'Right payback time, let's make a set list.' He laughed because he had put me on the spot but it was a false laugh, he was worried.

It took a couple of minutes to set up the amp and get the feel of his strat and five more to try a few intros.

He picked up the bass, made a few adjustments, and we were on. I was introduced, played the intro and we went into the first song.

I hadn't played for a long time but after a few minutes it all came back; I guess hours of practice fifteen years earlier had fixed it somewhere in my brain.

The sound with the fold-back (no such luxuries with Synergy) was far better than I remembered; I was playing with a pro who had come a long way.

I played a solid rhythm and the bass just filled out the sound, it sounded so good I was wondering whether I might re-join the band.

We were halfway through the set when Al rushed in clutching her guitar case; she was red faced and obviously upset, more so when she saw Chris face.

We finished the song, played one more then took a break.

Chris didn't say a lot but a dozen years having to lead bands and fight his corner had hardened him.

He wasn't unkind, a gentle but assertive bollocking that reminded her that she had let the team down; she took it well because she knew the score.

(She would never admit it but she was exactly the same with Sextet.)

She stuttered an explanation; she had gone out for a meal with Maggie and forgotten. 'When I remembered I nearly had a heart attack, I felt so ill.'

It was like a private soldier telling the C.O. that he had forgotten he was on guard duty.

'Really glad you are here Al,' I said, 'we were getting worried.'

She gave me a look of gratitude.

'Right, last two of the first set and the whole of the second, if it's convenient.'

'Yes, sorry.'

'Thanks Dave, you were really good.'

They moved away and there was a whispered argument. Al walked away with her face set.

She came back after a few minutes with her guitar joined Chris and they went on stage, she said a few words to the few who were listening and went into her first song.

Chris was never cross for long, especially with Al. As soon as they had finished the set and an encore he changed completely, put an arm around her and said he hoped she hadn't rushed.

'Of course I did, I raced out and left Maggie to pay and walk home.'

'I owe her.'

'Never take risks darling, never' he stroked her arm then held it, 'I might get grumpy if you are late but I'd be distraught if you had an accident.'

I made sure that he gave my favourite girl a hug before I left. It was a good excuse to hug her myself and whisper 'Take care, I

would be as upset as the old man if you had an accident.'
'Silly darling, as if.'

I did once wonder if I had misunderstood him. I was chatting
with Diane, a lady for whom I had always a
Had a great admiration; we were talking about why some people
were attractive.
She mentioned visiting Chris after Sue's death, partly to help and
also to keep in touch because she felt that he and her daughter
were right for each other. She drifted off the subject saying how
unhappy he was and that she had done her best to be comforting
and friendly and reassure him that life would get better.
'The silly boy said it was very kind of me to visit and I was his
only girlfriend... I mean it was a kind thing to say.' she blushed.
I knew they were good friends but what she had said implied
more than friendship.
I gave her a meaningful look and she stumbled and stuttered
saying
'I mean it's unusual for a mum to support her daughter's ex-
boyfriend and obviously it depends on the person but we
became good friends'
'And you felt that you could trust Chris? He's my best mate but he
is perfectly normal and vulnerable to kind, attractive women.'
I looked her in the eye.
'Chris is also trustworthy. He would never say anything that
might be misinterpreted, he wouldn't.' Her cheeks had gone red.
'Nor would I.' She kissed my cheek and whispered 'No.'

About Chris and Al

Their relationship wasn't perfect but from the start it was good
enough to take a few knocks.
Al was innocent and unspoiled when they met and Chris was
very lucky to find her when he did because she enjoyed attention
and had already had one unsettling experience.
It broke his heart when he had to choose between her and Sue.

It would have been no contest as far as I was concerned despite Sue's pregnancy but at the time Al was becoming self–centred, asserting her independence and being difficult.

My feeling was that Chris made a morally decent totally wrong decision; right or wrong, having committed himself to Sue he was very loving and when Synergy folded the marriage seemed to be working. Then she died in an awful accident.

He found Al again, but she was damaged, I don't mean physically or sexually, but she had lost her some of that lovely open-hearted trust. She regained it slowly and was almost her old self by the time of their marriage.

When she regained her confidence she became friends with Sue's sister Liz.

My feeling was that she was overcompensating and that the friendship was a mistake because Liz was as pretty and rather naughtier than her sister.

Several years later they formed Sextet together so I guess there were no problems.

There are often incidents that point up a relationship, it was a real love match, but that didn't mean they never fell out. Chris' marriage to Sue was really a series of misunderstandings that got out of hand and the subsequent bust up was a huge error of judgement.

It was the small things that were funny.

I've said that Al had miserable moments when she would grumble and complain and you need to remember that Chris was an unsophisticated twenty-two-year old.

He was very good with her, kind, supportive and tolerant, too tolerant sometimes and when he was under pressure he would snap long after he should have said 'for f**** sake shut it.'

I remember one evening when we went to a jazz club.

Al had been having a difficult day struggling with a new song; it may have been period problems, a subject never mentioned but when you are living close together you get a sense of timings.

She tried to be civil but she came to the club because she was unsure about Chris' interest in Sarah and she didn't want him to go on his own.

From the moment we left it was 'We won't be late will we?'

'I am feeling tired today.' 'When does it finish?'

When we arrived 'It's too loud.' 'Can we sit at the back?' 'It's horribly smoky.'

The tables were like card tables with paper cloths and candles in jars; first she kicked the leg of the one next to us and spilt drinks, then 'There isn't enough room I feel trapped.' then 'Its too stuffy.'

She wasn't normally like that but she was miserable and it came out in a series of grumbles. Chris was tolerant but I could see he was getting irritated and eventually he snapped.

She had complained 'I'm cold there's a draught.' And when it was repeated the third time he stood up picked up the candle on the table and set the tablecloth on fire.

'That should 'f***** warm you up then.' He said and walked out.

Al's scream drowned out the band. I splashed beer on the cloth and put the flames out then legged it after Chris. He was outside hooting with laughter.

'Dave mate did you see her face.'

Al followed me out in a fury and slapped him shouting 'You stupid dangerous sod!!'

'You said you were cold, I warmed you up! Stop bloody complaining.'

Al slapped him again and called him a 'stupid pig', then 'Silly sod.'

Someone came out of the club and shouted 'That's them, hey you buggers!'

We legged it, ran into a park and hid in the bushes, Al too, breathless with laughter just loving the excitement and being part of the gang. A total transformation.

Chris was rather shy with women and he disappointed several who fancied him but don't be misled, he was as randy as the rest of us but only if he really liked a girl. Girls liked him if they met him because he was kind and always tried to be interested.

About Al

It is difficult to say what brings success to an entertainer because there are so many factors. Talent, luck, inside knowledge, stamina, commitment and perhaps compromise. We had all those to some extent and our compromises were minor, mostly songs, clothes or image. Sometimes when to kiss arse and when to keep opinions to ourselves.

Al normally wore jeans with a cardigan over a tee-shirt and her stage gear was a fancy top, a skirt and black woolly tights.

The management told her that she must try harder which meant show more flesh, either low necks or short skirts.

It generated a memorable comment, 'No point in the low neck, nothing to show so I will have to show my nicks.'

All bluster; she avoided anything provocative and the 'glam' dresses she eventually wore (with the black woolly tights) were elegant or pretty and only modestly revealing.

There are a lot of people out there who help others even if the kindness is partly self-interest. We had some luck getting started; the right place at the right time, a lawyer friend who got a decent deal and a manager who was parsimonious but reasonably honest. That is unfair to Maurice who was pillar of rectitude when compared with some of the villains in his profession.

'Synergy' started as an amateur band and its professional face was the result of hard work and the help of the two Terrys, particularly Sol. Thanks to the collective talent and a lot of subtle changes in musical direction the band achieved modest success. A couple of our releases actually charted, pretty lowdown but sufficient to gain a little exposure on the box which led to better tours in better venues.

Al had a tough time when we started, she had a strong moral character, was grounded and was able to deal satisfactorily with most problems but it took a long time before she learned to be assertive with aggressive people.

She was trim and good looking and when she made the effort was very attractive; unfortunately the interest and flattery she received gave her an inflated opinion of her charm. Most young girls are attractive and most men are not particularly demanding. Al's added attraction was her niceness and perhaps her virtue.

The only time I ever saw her lose her common sense and behave stupidly was when we went to the states with 'kR.

Tired from our flight and probably jet lagged we had gone to an after-show party.

Chris was missing (catching up on sleep) and Al was very wound up because she had discovered that Sarah was part of the band.

The party was a rather tacky gathering; apart from one of the groupies who was topless and showing off, the only item of interest was Sarah.

I was smooching with her and catching up on her news and Al was being chatted up by Bruce who was teasing her about the topless girl. She was reacting in a rather aggressive way and I think someone may have spiked her drink because earlier she had punched a guy who annoyed her (totally non-Al) and she was lucky not to get a slapping.

Shortly afterwards I heard her say 'For goodness sake Bruce I do not behave like that, why would I?'

A minute or so afterwards I heard her say loudly 'No, that's nothing to do with it, I could if I wanted!' then, a little later 'Alright I will! Just to shut you up.'

There was some slow smoochy music playing and Al who was a good dancer started to move in time. It wasn't how she behaved and I was more interested in young Sarah but I glanced across occasionally to watch and I realised that she was pretending to strip.

She was in a funny mood and actually started to take her clothes off; top then skirt and inelegantly, her tights. She looked lovely in her pretty undies and I assumed that would be it but she continued to dance with a 'See, I can if I want' look on her face.

There was a small circle of watchers and a few moments later there was a coarse cheer.

I turned back and there she was arms raised, bra in hand showing off. I enjoyed the sight of my favourite girl with her titties on display but when she turned her back and wiggled her bot I realised she had lost it and that she might take off her nicks. There were half a dozen semi-drunks encouraging her and if she stripped completely the situation might turn ugly.

I needed to act quickly so abandoning Sarah I grabbed her discarded clothes and while she still had her back to me, covered her top bellowed 'Fantastic!! Cheers for the lovely Alison!' and rushed her out through the door.

It was a bit of a scramble, cheers and boos and some resistance. She was confused and not helping but I treated it like a loose maul grabbed the back of her nicks and gave her the bums rush.

Once we were outside and I had dragged her well down the corridor she became more rational and realised she was half naked.

'Dave! What are you doing? Oh my god!!' She acted as if it was my fault, went scarlet clutched the clothes around her and ran to her room.

The next morning when I went to collect her she had a headache and pretended to remember nothing. She was more concerned that Chris was sharing a room with Sarah. (But not a bed) I told her.

I don't remember anything of the sort. I expect Dave was drunk and fantasising!

Her introduction to acting was in a rather poor film. Chris told me that she was so excited when she received the offer that he had to be supportive. He always suspected that she was there to show off her assets and when she refused, she was pressured into a compromise. She was shy about nudity but she was normal and whispers said the cutting room floor showed a significant compromise.

It did not

She was good in her role and it led to a part as a barmaid in a long running TV series. She was convincing playing a tarty version herself and it gained her a couple of small parts and a support role in a film.
I was told that she was strongly tipped for a significant support role in a major film but she turned it down. Well, that was her story.

My take on her 'career' was that she could play variations of herself very well but when she needed to act her limitations were obvious.
It was demonstrated by the shortness of her 'career'.

It don't visit often these days because my wife is mildly suspicious of our friendship and believes that I still have a thing for her which is true.
I did visit recently and we had a lunch together in her kitchen.
In the middle of lunch she gave one of her appealing looks and said 'Dave, there is something I always wanted to ask you.'
Oh yes, I thought, what now? 'Go on then, ask.' And out of the blue came 'Who was Samantha.'
'Samantha who?'
'Don't prevaricate Dave.'
'It is long forgotten, why ask now?'
She put her head on one side, did a fair impression of herself at twenty and demanded an answer without having to say anything. Well, damn her, if she wants to hurt herself let her.
'Chris' chorus line.'
'What?'
'You remember his chorus line?'
'Yes. Some silly girls, they used to congregate at the front and chant for one of the boys. They put me off several times.'

'A dozen or more and they were Chris' adoring fans.'
She frowned in a way that dismissed the possibility. 'What about them?'
'They were Samantha.'
Light dawned slowly and with it came upset.
'They? I thought that Samantha was someone that he might...'
'That what?'
She said nothing so I said nothing, she can imagine what suits her.

People have asked what she looked like and it isn't easy for me to describe her. She had a nice face, attractive from all angles with a hint of freckles, very slightly large front teeth, beautiful eyes and dark chestnut hair. Her mother I once described as being a little like Hannah Gordon or was it...never mind, it isn't accurate but there was a loose similarity.
The best guide I can give came from Chris. Al was working away and I had visited and stayed for dinner. We were watching TV and Chris said 'she would be my dream girl if I needed one.'
I wasn't paying a lot of attention and said 'You surprise me.' He said 'No, not that one, hang on...' the scene changed '...that one.'
'Really? Maybe... I could see a slight similarity to Al; not the same but a look that was appealing. I think the actress' name was Jane Snowden. It's amazing how things come back to you.

If we are going to be ruthlessly candid then I might as well give my opinion on one of the main aspects of her character. She was in a profession where there was a lot of very attractive and talented competition and some rough tough competition if you like pornography with musical accompaniment.
She started her 'girly' band to show Chris that she could hack it on her own. The band was pretty good and Liz certainly enjoyed playing the crowd, even her friend Vickie, who I had thought of as a rather innocent girl gave a different impression when onstage but the 'Rock Chick' element was mostly show.

Al was brought up to understand morals rather than learning

them and forgetting the moment a hand went up her skirt and she was nervous with men.

She liked to think she was liberated but Chris told me once that she was no great shakes in bed, willing but rather passive and unadventurous.

'I'm not complaining but' and he became very confidential 'Sue was more lively and Sarah, well not for the long term but when she was willing...'

'So you are saying Al is no good in bed? I will happily relieve you of the boredom.'

'I didn't say that. Let me think of an example that a lecher like you will understand.'

'Let me hear it.'

'You have a date with Diane.'

'Good start, I'll settle for that.'

'Ok. You take her out for the evening, and when you take her home she allows a cuddle on the doorstep. Ok so far?'

'It certainly is. Could you arrange it for me.'

'She asks you in and you decide to go for it. You discover that she has a decent body. Still ok or are you getting bored?'

'I'm trying to imagine it.'

'Di surrenders and invites you to her bed; the sex is enjoyable but nothing special. Was it a waste of time?'

'Bedding Di a waste of time? Are you kidding me?'

'I'm telling you that Al is adorable, the sex is a bonus.'

About Sue

It was a common mistake to assume that Sue was a waste of space who traded her virginity for a place in the band.

Total nonsense; Sue joined the band with Al's approval long before Chris lost the struggle to resist her.

He was as randy as the rest of us, but he showed respect to relatively innocent girls like Sue and he would never have asked her to join the band if she hadn't been a good musician.

It is a fact that even moderately successful bands rely on talent coming together to create a good sound. Sue wouldn't have contributed enough to kick start a band, but she was good enough to keep it rolling. She was a grade six or seven pianist and musically was far more competent than the rest of us.

Once she became confident and began to perform and enjoy herself her looks added to Al's gave the band a gimmick.

It certainly wasn't ABBA at the Hollywood Bowl or even Brotherhood of Man on TOTP, it was 'Girl Next Door' at the local Country Club which can be even more attractive.

Trev, the guitarist on their last tour was asked by a journalist 'Is Susie any good?' He said 'Musically she's fine, she's beginning to get a feel for rock, she adds to the sound, and the audiences love her.'

'But is she any good really?' the guy persisted.

'She's a good musician, she's also kind, pretty, has a lovely ass and decent legs. Most of the audience come to see the band but some come to lust after the girl.'

Di.

I remember when Al's mum came to visit on our first summer season; it was a Tuesday and the weather was glorious; the wind had died and the town was simmering in the warmth of the July sun.

Al and Diane hadn't been seen since breakfast and there seemed little prospect of them reappearing before tea, so I suggested a visit to the beach.

'We might find a couple of lovelies to keep us company.'

'You might' Chris told me 'but Al's got a sixth sense where other women are concerned.'

'Let's have a pasty on the seafront then we'll do a quick recce of the beach to find you some talent.'

The recce was a waste of time, the beach offering nothing to stimulate my interest. There were a couple of girls sunbathing but they were the kind I tended to avoid. There were two girls having fun in the sea but even from a distance I reckoned they were too young.

Farther down the beach there was a bikinied pair who might have been of interest but they were accompanied by several young men.

'So? Do we admire the sixteen-year-olds from a distance?'

'I have no interest in girls who may be under age.'

'Liz is only fifteen.'

'That's different Liz is Susie's sister. Let's go and admire the bikinis.'

We were about half way to the group when Chris spoke.

'Would you effin believe it?'

'I would indeed, our Di looks damned good in a bikini.'

'If that was you and me with a group of girls Al would get ratty and make sarcastic remarks.'

'As no doubt you will.'

'I... well I can't now can I? Hi Al! Do you *mind* if we join you?'

'Just the right hint of sarcasm I would say.'

Al turned, was immediately defensive. 'Oh! Hi Chris. Mum and I thought we'd go to the beach. Come and join us.'

The lad chatting to Di looked surprised

'Diane,' I ignored the rest of the gathering, 'looking good my love.'

'Thank-you David, even misplaced flattery is appreciated.'

'No flattery, the simple truth.' I sat down and noticed that the lad next to her was glad to be spared the embarrassment of chatting up a mum.

To be fair to the lad, Di looked a nicely preserved thirty something; I think the bikini was one of Al's but Di was a little more rounded and the top was pleasantly revealing.

I spent the next twenty enjoyable minutes admiring and chatting to her eventually asking if she would like to come out to a club after our evening show.

As we were leaving the beach Diane told Al about my invitation.

'You don't mind do you?'

She did; definitely displeased, dumfounded is probably the right

word; she clutched Chris' arm, gave me a murderous look and said 'I suppose so. We'll all be very tired after the show. That doesn't matter, we'll come with you won't we Chris.'
'Must we…yeah, well ok.'

I collected her after the show; she was wearing a sleeveless dress that displayed cleavage with some buttons undone to show her legs.
Al wasn't at all happy so I stirred it a little.
'Looking great Diane, stick close to me or you will gather a flock of admirers wanting to take you home.'
Al found her voice. 'David! Stop being silly! Mum, don't encourage him!'

It was an unpromising start to an enjoyable evening.
Al was chatted up and danced with her admirer quite unaware of her double standards and my prediction about Di proved correct. When Al eventually returned to our table and saw Di dancing with and enjoying the attentions of a good-looking predator, the situation triggered the other side of her standards.
I was asked why I wasn't looking after her mum and gained a few brownie points when, at a break in the dancing I recovered her, giggly, slightly tiddly and delighted by her encounter.
My subsequent questioning as to whether I was a satisfactory substitute provoked a reply that she had been asked (she whispered) if she was up for it.
'I asked 'What?' and he said 'Sex darling.' I said 'Thankyou but I am married.' He whispered something very rude and then said 'A shame, you are lovely and perhaps you should find out what you are missing.'
'If you are keen' I told her 'he isn't the only one who is interested.'
'Really David! You are just as bad, why you imagine…?'
'Well young Di, it is because I would like to find out more about the real you.'
'Would you?' She slapped my wrist but she was smiling.

The evening took a turn for the better when we left the club.

Diane collected her jacket and I helped her on with it suggesting that since the weather was warm maybe she would like to walk home by way of the sea front.

'David is going to walk me home along the seafront.' she said to Al.

Her daughters look would have killed a lesser man. I loved the girl but she could be a pain so as we walked away I put an arm around Di's shoulder and we headed for the seafront.

Diane's parting 'Don't worry, we won't be long' may have helped but I could feel the knives hitting my back. I discovered later it had taken a lot of reassurance to prevent Al from following us.

It must have been half an hour before we returned to the hotel.

Chris tackled me later. Alison had spent fifteen minutes pacing between the lounge and the front door before panic set in; my ears should have been on fire.

'I hope you didn't otherwise Al will give me hell.' Chris told me.

'I wouldn't tell you if I had mate. Sadly I can reassure you that I didn't. More accurately, like many promising young ladies she wouldn't.' 'That said...'

'What?'

'She's got lovely firm tits but her refusal to let me get any further was even firmer.'

'They are nice aren't they you dirty sod.'

'Me? Have you? You pervert, not with Di surely?'

'No I haven't, don't be disgusting! She and Al were coming to a party and Al went sick so Di came on her own. We both had a few drinks and a bit of a cuddle when we were dancing.'

'And what else you swine?'

'We stopped on the way home and had a brief snog. Di said in her straight-laced way 'I'm only a little bit tiddly and I think I can trust you to take advantage of me.'

It sounds like a nightmare, snogging your Mil but you know Di.'

'So what has happened since? Any more naughties you pervert?'

'Certainly not, it was a one-off situation plus alcohol and we stayed friends.'

CHAPTER 22

Thoughts from the Grave

Twenty years ago Chris had a guitar stolen at a gig; it was the back-up 335 supplied during the US tour. It wasn't the precious one used in the video but it had been regularly used with 'kR and had some provenance.

The guitar was insured and the payout coincided with a small unexpected windfall of monies from 'kR.

I had given up acting and the egg business was becoming stable so we had some spare time and decided to build a secure room in the loft.

The roof space was accessed via a large hatch with a fold away step ladder and our first task was to cough our way over the joists and decide where the room would go. Our second task was laying additional insulation and boarding it with chipboard panels.

The new floor covered half the roof space and once it was safe the children were allowed to come up and join us.

Chris, always looking for something to worry about decided that the roof needed to be re-felted. With much of our windfall spent paying a roofer we had no option but to build the room ourselves.

The house is long but narrow and even a quite small room had insufficient headroom at the sides.

We built some wooden frames with plywood on the outside

and glued insulation into the spaces. The frames were screwed together to form a large shed which filled the space between roof and floor.

There seemed to be a lot of unnecessary pieces of board lying about but if I had asked why, Mr Grumpy would have reminded me that he was a structural engineer.

An electrician was called in to add lights and power and the inside was finished with hardboard panels.

Mr G then realised he hadn't allowed access to the rest of the loft. I offered a suggestion, was given a pitying look and left him to it. Next day I was shown a hole fitted with a plywood door that gave us access to the rest of the roof

I bravely mentioned that the gap round the door might be a source of draughts and was sarcastically asked how I would draughtproof it.

I asked if he could put a panel that was bigger than the hole on the inside of the door.

'I could!' he said and muttered about the extra work.

I was subsequently invited back to see the new door, it was the old door fitted with a panel that overlapped the hole; on the back was a slab of insulation. 'Lovely, well done. It is big enough.'

'Yes. How often do we need to get to the roof?'

A month later we had the offer of a grant that enabled us to properly insulate the rest of the roof with glass wool.

I appreciated the insulating properties but hated the feel of the material. I asked Chris if glass dust was as dangerous as asbestos. 'No' I was told 'asbestos is carcinogenic.' Then he thought and said

'I don't know really, asbestos fibres scar in the lung, I don't see why glass fibres wouldn't do the same.'

Now he tells me.

The painting and decorating never got done but the room did acquire an old carpet, a small filing cabinet, a narrow wardrobe for storage and a couple of chests. I added a tiny armchair and a heater.

It was used as a store room for expensive or loved equipment that was seldom used including Chris original Strat, his 'kR 335, the lovely Tele I inherited from Sue and my precious Eko. Sometimes I would go into the loft and play one of them; sometimes I cried.

The filing cabinet contained legal and financial documents (Chris kept duplicates in a tin chest hidden in the barn) and copies of our original videos transferred to CDs then to SD cards. We also stored our scrap books and photos. Cardboard boxes from our washing machine held Chris violin, guitar bags, posters; a couple of shoe boxes held pedals, harmonicas tools and spares.

It's funny how you get moments of panic; after the chimney fire I brought down two of the guitars and put them with some photos and memorabilia under my bed. I could bear to lose some of my life but not all of it.

I had gone to the loft for the SD cards intending to transfer the videos to a memory stick which I would keep by the TV.

Whilst there pottering and wallowing in nostalgia I noticed Chris old briefcase lying in the washing machine box. I picked it up, hugged it then opened it.

It was full of small items; spare strings, a tool bag, capos, a bottle neck, a box of screws and a small box labelled EL84 which had four little bulbs inside.

In one of the compartments was an exercise book which I had seen but never read and tucked into the cover, a large envelope containing some photos. I felt a nervous shock run through me and stood frozen for a minute or more before finally removing them.

The two on top were those of Sarah that Chris had rescued after Bruce's death. The next two were originals of Sue's magazine photos; she looked very pretty and far too young. The next three were of mum thirty years earlier when she was younger than I am.

The first two were studio photos and she was wearing a v-necked dress that I remembered.

In one she was standing elegantly smiling at the camera looking like my lovely mum. The other was similar but rather cheeky; she had her foot on a stool and the dress had ridden up to the top of her leg; she looked almost glam. I felt happy that she looked young, sad that it was so long ago.

The last one gave me a shock. It was a normal photoprint and she was posing modestly and elegantly but she was wearing only a happy smile. Oh mum, you look beautiful but it's disturbing.

The first pages of the exercise book contained a set of brief notes on performance starting with 'Be yourself' and 'Always look confident and engage with the audience'. There was much more; the next five pages of the book contained a list of our songs with their keys, the instruments used and the various effects, some scrubbed out and changed. On the sixth page was scribbled 'Just a thought' and I started to read.

Chris' writings

It was at a party; I vaguely remember the guy, a semi-hippie who probably had a degree in philosophy, had lost his way and drifted onto the fringes of the rock scene. I had been explaining my take on Christianity and he had listened, dismissed it as humanism and turned a deaf ear to my suggestion that there wasn't a lot of humanism in society before Christianity became embedded.

The talk drifted to aliens and his attitude changed. 'Listen,' he said grabbing my sleeve 'suppose there are aliens amongst us.'

My experience was that conspiracy theorists could turn the speculative interpretation of a small area of uncertainty into proof positive whilst ignoring overwhelming inconvenience of proven fact.

I began to lose interest.

He recognised that the shutters were coming down. 'No seriously,' he jumped straight in, 'supposing Adam was the alien.' My glazed look must have become obvious.

'I mean,' he continued, 'suppose Adam was Lucifer. The bible never said he died but it said his first generations of children lived for hundreds of years. If Adam and Lucifer are the same then he could be still alive, the evil one who was given rule of the earth by God.'

Things were becoming more bizarre but at least they were interesting.

'We,' (We? Not me mate) 'think that evil is controlled by his acolytes who are given huge powers, they are the ones who control the wealth and the banks and the big corporations. Whenever a force arises that is outside their control they destroy it.'

I began to lose interest.

'Look at the way they are destroying democratic socialism.'

'Yes, interesting. You may be right, my glass needs a refill.' 'By the way,' I turned back, 'God did give us love to counter evil, I mean caring about our fellow men.'

As I headed for the drink it struck me that there are evil forces and that they work hard to destroy any culture that empowers ordinary people. The same forces work hard to confuse love and sex, two separate things but fantastic when linked. It's interesting that in the fifties and sixties women were steadily gaining power by using the moral codes that empowered them but by the eighties feminism had turned them either into amoral tarts or female men and had righteously freed them from the moral constraints that helped them avoid exploitation,.

About two years after I had been lectured by the conspiracy theorist I met Adam at a 'kR party. Ok, I'm joking but I shook hands with a guy who would have made Adolf Hitler seem like your best mate. Certainly he was inhuman.

Poor Darling
Bless him, he would listen and be interested even if he thought people were wrong, not wrong in the wicked sense but not

correct. In our early days he had been cross and a little bit hurt when Mr Morris told him in a rude way 'to keep his ...to not say too much. He said 'So much for freedom of speech!' and he was right. There are a lot of people in the theatre who act out 'FREEDOM' in large letters but it is a fantasy freedom supported by wafer thin argument and unlikely scripts. Real freedom is about hard reality and self-sacrifice.

He was a terrible hypocrite in a lovable way; he loved theatre, books, films and happy endings but he once said 'in theatre you write the ending you want, the hero survives by coincidence, luck and chance otherwise he would be dead in the first five minutes.'

He was kind to everyone, and got on well with most people because his only real philosophy apart from Christianity was fairness and justice; 'freedom' he disliked because as he put it 'one man's freedom is another man's oppression, one man's gain is another's loss best go for fairness and justice that balances people's needs.'

He also hated the misuse of words. 'It is essential to discriminate between good and evil, between quality and rubbish, the trustworthy and the liar. Now because some discrimination is unfair, sensible choice is suppressed. It is amazing how stupid some highly intelligent people are, it means that dimbos like me have to find out the truth.'

It is hard to believe that we did so much and that we could cope with many kinds of problems then move on and quickly forget.

Two examples; Bruce's death, my first experience of death and it was awful, close up and personal yet by the time of his funeral it was part of the past, the event upsetting only as a funeral. Mum was more deeply affected and her concealed grief was a worry.

Another example was coping with Chris first marriage; it was never an acceptance in any sense of the word, how could it be, but it was an ability to live with the situation and when we became lovers again the world righted itself.

Only when the fool 'let me go' did the blackness descend and for a year I shut down and coasted emotionally, avoiding anything more than friendship.

My effort to maintain an emotional balance was damaged by a frightening assault then blown apart by the shock of Sue's death.

The two events led to a breakdown that left me feeling worthless and for a while life seemed pointless. I improved slowly thanks to the love and kindness of family and friends who rallied round and helped me.

When I was still fragile mum suggested that we should visit Chris. I was unsure and said 'perhaps' to which she said 'mending friendships' as if it was easy.

She immediately phoned him, made the arrangements and a few days later took me to the farm.

It was familiar yet strange and I panicked, was afraid that Chris would be a stranger who was no longer my soul-mate.

I stayed in the car while mum went in taking Sarah; a few minutes later she came out and fetched me while Chris waited by the door.

I walked to the house trying to look confident but totally empty with mum holding my elbow as if I was going to run away.

I could see Chris's face and was shocked how sad he looked.

We shook hands and he led me to the kitchen to make coffee. We were still holding hands and all my fears fell away; I intended to be strong and cool instead I was hopelessly emotional and found myself crying on his shoulder; he was holding my arms gently and saying he had missed me.

Magic happened, I felt a great rush of love and all the defences I had built up to protect myself against disappointment crumbled. When he whispered 'Can we be friends again?' I whispered 'I think we always have been.' 'Soul-mates?' he said and I just nodded, there was too much emotion for words.

Later, driving home I tried to reassure myself with words that the moment had happened but there were no words, only feelings. It was the most complete utterly romantic, happiest moment of my life.

Our first ever date and getting engaged after our US tour with 'kR came close but both incidents were 'lightness to brightness', that moment holding hands in our kitchen was blindness to sight.

When I had my time out from being the normal me I learned a lot about myself.

I had been happy in my marriage was surprised to discover that I could enjoy an affectionate short-term relationship and happy that I had no wish to repeat the experience.

CHAPTER 23

A Word with Sarah Phillips

When you are small the world is as you understand it and there are no hidden problems.

I remember living with my nan Diane and there was a sense of total love and protection.

Mum was away for long stretches of time and when she came home she would hug me and cry.

Nan would take me to visit Daddy and sometimes we would stay for a weekend. The adults were all very caring so I didn't mind who I was with and I never thought about relationships

Mum and dad were separate people and when they married the situation was strange for me.

I was nervous when I moved with them to the farm; they were both young and selfish and I missed living with nanny Di because she spoiled me and that was my home.

When you are five you like security and I had several tantrums when I was told that things were going to change but when the change happened it only took a few days and the new routine became normal.

Mum and dad were very loving and they quickly established a routine that created a safe new world where Simon and I felt at home.

We had each other and lots of adults who made us feel at home. There was Marilyn and Caren and Vickie and Auntie Liz and of course we had three grans and grandads to visit.

We also had each other: Mum told me that Simon was my brother but he had a different mummy and I had to be kind to him because his mummy had died and she was his new mummy. The intricacies of the relationship were lost on me but I felt that Simon was my brother and I cried because he was only little and he didn't have a proper mummy.

I suppose my first five years were unsettled with dad and mum being away a lot but I didn't notice it because all my references were happy. Spending part of the week with Frank and Granny P and part with Gramps and nanny Di made me socially adaptable in a wholly comfortable routine. Obviously I didn't see it like that at the time, it was just 'how things are'.

I can remember Dad taking me for rides on his motor bike and I felt as if we rode for miles but it was mostly around the yard and sometimes down the road and back across our field.

The main thing I remember was nan's house because I spent a lot of time there and nan and mum were almost interchangeable.

I like to remember life as mostly good in a middle-class way. (Dad always said we were working class "middle class is an attitude, not a class" he would say).

My first crisis came when I was eight.

Mum was away sometimes 'doing her acting' and I was used to that so when she told me that she had made a record and would be on TV I was excited.

We all watched together and I was horribly embarrassed because my mum was dressed like a pop singer and dancing and singing with a strange man.

I screamed and ran out of the room and mum came and asked what was wrong. I told her she was horrid and ran back to be hugged by dad.

I didn't want to go to school next day but dad took me (I had decided that mum didn't exist and shut her out of my life, refusing to speak to her).

When we arrived at the school I saw Carrie my best friend standing by the gate. When she saw me she came running over and the first thing she said was 'I saw your mum on TV last night'.

I went rigid and wished I had stayed at home.

I was going to say 'I don't have a mum' but before I could speak Carrie said 'Isn't she fantastic?' Several other friends came and joined us; they had all seen the programme and they thought mum was wonderful although one of the boys said 'My dad fancies your mum.' which spoilt things.

You don't think about parents having jobs and considering that they were both running businesses and a band they were very supportive, too supportive in one case.

Dad was one of our school governors and when I had my first end of term Ball the committee asked if his band would play.

As a governor he couldn't really refuse but the thought of your parents performing in front of your friends is horrific and it seemed as if they were determined to spoil my life?'

I knew that they had been professionals and that their band was a top band in the south west but having parents dancing about on stage in front of your friends is utterly humiliating.

I decided I couldn't go and was so miserable that I couldn't stop crying. Mum hugged me and made me tell her what was wrong and when I told her she spoke to dad who promised not to acknowledge that I was his daughter. A few days later Mum told my best friends that it would be embarrassing for me if they said she was my mum. 'Imagine it was your mum on stage singing?' she told them.

They could, Carrie giggled and Helen blushed. They knew how I felt.

I was friendly with an extended group of girls and some boys one of which I knew quite well though he wasn't really a boyfriend in the seriously sense.

Parents don't realise the complexity of peer group relationships; your first Ball is a huge social leap in the dark, mired with anxieties. The added horror of your parents singing and performing in front of everyone is unimaginable.

Mum suggested that I went with Carrie to Helen's house and Helen's father could take us so that there was no obvious connection. I didn't want any sort of connection.

I was snappy all day until Carrie came and Mum took us to Helen's house. We spent ages dressing and getting made up and Helen's dad said we all looked gorgeous. Yuk!

When we got to the school I saw their van was already there and so was Aunt Liz' car.

We waited to see who was arriving and when we saw Barry and Chee go in we followed them. The stage was set up as I had seen too many times before.

I won't go into the activities of the first half hour, mostly chatting, a couple of the boys with beer and some smoking. It was, with hindsight a hive of anxiety, showing off, shyness and exploration.

Then Mr Beevis went up onto the stage and switched on a microphone. When he had got our attention he said 'Tonight we...well you are lucky to have a band that is very special. Two of our guests have topped the charts and have appeared on top of the pops.' (They hadn't though they had been on TV)

'So let's welcome Chris and Alison from the band 'king Rock with their band KR.'

He clapped and the band came on. I didn't notice dad but felt a small degree of relief as mum came on. She had dressed sensibly; like not glam but attractive, jeans and a sparkly dark green top that was perfect with her hair; attention grabbing without being O.T.T.

Carrie leaned over and said 'Wow, your mum looks great' and I shushed her. 'Sorry' she said and giggled.

Dad picked up his guitar and came to the mic and waited until he had the attention of part of the room then he said a few words, turned away then turned back and said something that made some of the people at the front laugh. '

He pointed at the keyboard player who started to play an intro, mum came in on guitar then the drums and Auntie Liz on bass and after an a few bars Mum began to sing.

I felt myself blushing and went with Carrie to the back to be as far away as possible. We got some lemonade and after a while Barry found us and said the band was really good. When we went back in Mum was talking and there were a little group up at the front talking back and laughing.

The band started to play and some of the girls began to dance; I felt more relaxed because I had been terrified my parents would look stupid. Their next song was a current hit and the atmosphere suddenly changed and every-one seemed to be dancing and enjoying themselves. It was one of those songs that make you dance; I even forgot it was Dad singing.

Barry grabbed my hand and said 'Ok Raych? and we started to dance at the back. 'While we were dancing Barry shouted 'Good band'. I nodded and he shouted 'Girl on the guitar's good.' I had to stop myself saying 'That's not a girl she's my mum.'

It seemed no time before Dad was talking and saying 'This is the last number before we take a break. Enjoy.'

It was an old one called 'Uptown girl' and some of the more precocious girls including Cass Shorland of course and Lindy were dancing in front of the band and showing off. I saw dad look across at mum and she laughed. At the end several jumped up and down and sort of screamed. Then they turned around and Cassie and her friend were laughing because they thought he was stupid.

I remembered something Mum had told me at one of their gigs; she had been performing quite wildly and I told her she looked stupid showing off.

She gave me a hug and said 'It's just an act darling, you have to connect with the audience. Sometimes they really like you which is lovely but sometimes they are rude and then you just ignore them.'

I went up to the stage and waved to Dad and he said 'Hi young lady.' I told him about Cass and her friend and he said 'The one in yellow and the girl with the blue dress?'

I nodded and he said 'Some girls of your age like to flirt and show off. I play along and let them have fun at my expense; sometimes they are quite fragile and they need to build their confidence.'

I was surprised that he knew things like that. 'I saw your friend Carrie watching.' then he paused 'I think she is just a tiny bit star struck, I expect you will put her right.'

We had a great evening because of course Dad's band is very good and professional.

At the end some of the boys shouted 'more, more'.

Dad looked at mum and she nodded 'Ok, we've had a great evening, one more dance then some Reeaal Rock.'

They played 'Kiss on my list' then they stopped, went silent. Dad said 'Dangerous', he played an intro then a huge chord and they went into this fast rock song that seemed louder than anything they had done. It was fantastic and the gig became wild. A lot of us were jumping up and down punching the air in time. In the middle, they stood back to back and mum leaned against dad as he did a solo and I heard Barry shout 'Wow'.

They got a huge ovation at the end but my emotions were all over the place; it was wonderful but it wasn't my mum and dad, I was watching two strangers.

Mrs Grainger went on stage and thanked them for a fantastic evening and dad said they had enjoyed it and kissed her. Everyone whistled and it almost spoiled things.

Next day Carrie phoned and asked if she could come round with Helen; I said of course she could because she is my best friend then I told her Barry had asked if he could come and he was cycling from Thornbury and staying for lunch so she could stay as well.

CHAPTER 24

Best Friends Talking

It would be true to say that most of my intimate conversations with Vickie were conducted in veiled terms; it is also true that most took place in the village café or one of the local pubs. I wasn't a drinker but gigs with Sextet took us to pub venues and sometimes my need to get out of the house was sufficient incentive.

Both of us probably said more than we wished when our tongues were loosened by a couple of G and T's.

    1. Vickie is lectured.

'Synergy' was a good band but we were too late for the folk-rock revival and we drifted into folk-pop. We were never part of 'the scene', Chris said that we were condemned equally by the rockers and the folkies. I loved what we were doing and didn't care as long as our audiences liked us.

When we turned professional we leapt to the bottom of the showbiz ladder knowing no-one and nothing and we were allowed to go on tour only when the management decided we were good enough.

I assumed we would tour with other bands but we found ourselves performing with all types of entertainers in all sorts of places.

Most of the people were ok but some had huge egos and limited talent. The successful ones tended to be talented and hard-working and though they were not always likable they were genuine rock'n roll..

I never understood the scene, it seemed to be controlled by money-chasers who used the talented, the professionals and even the loonies pretending to be avant-guard with equal indifference.

The 'Rock scene' was created by performers who grew up playing in youth clubs, pubs and small clubs. There was space for thousands of youngsters to make a few pounds gigging, most weren't very good but a few became local stars and a tiny number created original music.

Now the latest phenomenon seems to be the product of a cost benefit analysis and has a known shelf life.

I think there is just as much talent and more technical skill but less opportunities and the target audience seems to be 'as young as possible' because kids can't discriminate between fakery and fantasy.

2. Vickie being prurient.

'Was there a lot of sex available?'

'You know as well as I do; how much did you allow.'

'I meant when you were performing.'

'You mean when I was on stage?'

'You know what I mean.'

'Yes of course I do. The business attracts a lot of people who need the kick you get from audience approval. It's a business that is hard to break into, hard to get jobs and how people behave depends on the circumstances and what they...' I hesitated; second hand knowledge can be misinterpreted. '...what they wanted. Sarah got into 'kR by selling herself to Bruce.'

'Yes, Chris told me. Did you...'

'No I didn't, not in the sense you mean Mrs Mason.'

I quickly moved on.

'Synergy was a decent outfit but we had a hard time when we started; we had no spare money and it was a struggle to look good'

'We had a small core of fans and I used to get letters, some lovely, some sad. We were told to try and answer them but to be impersonal and we developed some standard replies which covered most situations.'

'The worst one I had was a scary; the writer was a pervert who saw me as a thing not a person. I was rather innocent and some of what was said I didn't understand.'

'What didn't you understand?' V always likes to know the details.

'Some of the words.'

'I was enjoying a novel recently and I had to guess what, the author had one of his characters doing.'

'I think a lot of authors make their characters do things they missed themselves. The biography of our early lives was mostly true but Justin often made me sound wicked.'

'Yes he did. Perhaps you should go back to telling me about the fans.'

'It was small time with Synergy and some of the fans were sweet. One I remember was good looking and he said I was so attractive that my niceness shone through my singing. He made me feel lovely when I was insecure and unsure of myself.'

'There was more fan input with 'kR and some of the girls were totally amoral.'

'If we had time and we weren't too tired we tried to meet fans and I remember talking to some young girls who were hoping to meet one of the band. One of them spotted Tony and chased after him.

Sarah had gone to search for Chris and she came back with him and Bep. We introduced the girls and after a few minutes it was clear that they were only interested n the boys so the two of us went back to our dressing room to collect some things. When we

got there we found Tony with the girl doing...'
'Doing what?' V giggled.
'He said 'Line up over there girls' and Sarah said "You're joking? My cat's better hung than you." It was a real put down and I quite liked her for a moment.'
Between giggles V managed to say 'Disgusting'.
'Have you ever seen anyone actually...you know?'
'No!'
'It wasn't disgusting but it was offensive...sort of ridiculous, violent and comical at the same time.

3. Vickie to Al
'You were lucky to have someone who was so mature.'
I asked her why she thought Chris was mature.
'He always behaved so sensibly; when we first met he seemed overpowering but really he was kind and understanding.'
'He was in his late twenties when you met him and he had grown up a lot in 'king Rock.'
'He sounded mature in the book.'
'He thought he was mature but really he was a little boy struggling to be sophisticated. Sol said he had the management technique of a school prefect; It was unkind but there was some truth in it.'
'That is so disloyal.'
'Yes...no, it is disloyal but it was true. Chris was twenty-two when we started touring and he had to be a performer, a manager, lover, minder and songwriter when in fact he was an engineering graduate finding his way in the world. He did get a lot of things right, our legal status thanks to Arwyn and the band worked well because he took some abuse but got a lot of cooperation.
He really wanted to have fun but once he made the decision to be a performer the band came first.
When I was in the same position a couple of years later I had learned a lot and I had Sol and Terry on my side but it was very

difficult.

'Chris, always seemed confident.'

'He needed to show a confident face but he wasn't mature. You saw the film of 'kR years ago; part of Chris was the boy walking on his hands showing his willy, part of him was the stressed guitarist taking bennys just to hang in, another part was your friend who used to take you shopping and well concealed was my over-sensitive, easily hurt darling struggling to do the right thing.'

'That is the one I miss so much that sometimes even now I don't want to see the next day.'

'Al, darling, don't talk like that, you can't pass on your unhappiness to your family or your friends, it's wicked.'

'I know, it would devastate mum and some people would be upset.'

'Some? Hundreds would be upset; if you ever feel bad come around to us at once. If I felt really low I would come and see you and expect you to sort me out.'

'Would you?'

'Yes, I was close to unburdening myself when…you know, when I was rather foolish.'

'Let's leave it. Thank you for your offer.'

4. Vickie

'Did you know that Lester is unwell and has been in hospital.'

'That's a shame, he had an interesting life and it was always fun to chat with him but we didn't keep in touch when he moved.'

'Neither did we. I saw him at an art show not long after he moved but then he dropped out of circulation. Clive said he had probably run out of suitable ladies to proposition.'

'Did he ever ask you?'

'No. I think he was lining me up; we were talking about art at a village market, and I mentioned a well known painter who spoke a few words at one of our publicity events. He was known to ask interesting people to model and I told Lester that I would have refused if he has asked.'

'He did ask me and I was slightly tempted because he had a lovely way with him but Clive would have said no.'

'Yes, he was very personable even though he was twenty years older than us. He did most of his good work as a landscape painter but everyone remembers his nudes. Chris and I went to one of his exhibitions and I was very impressed, they may not have been high art but technically they were very good.'

'Yes they were.'

'Did you agree?'

'Lester said 'If no one recognised you, would that be ok?'

'I didn't answer but he said if I allowed him to paint me he would alter my face so that I was unrecognisable.'

'I said "show me". He did a brilliant sketch of my head that captured me then he did a few changes to my lips and nose and eyes, quite small changes and when he changed my hair and it was nothing like me.'

'So?'

V was grinning and looking pleased with herself.

'The sketches of my head but not the rest. Really Al, can you hear Clive saying 'Yes you can pose naked.' Chris would be more likely to let you.'

'No chance, but I know someone he did paint.'

'Who?'

'Gwynneth.' I whispered.

'Did she? That surprises me, she must have been over forty and she was a pillar of the church and very straight.'

'We were talking about holidays and I told her that we had been the south of France and spent a lot of time on the beaches. She said that she liked the beaches in the south. We sort of edged around to the nudity and she told me that she and her husband weren't naturists but they often went to the naturist beaches.'

"It's rather fun isn't it" she said "relaxed and not naughty." Then she burst into giggles and said "You do see some odd sights and some that make you wonder what you are missing.' I saw a different side of her, the same lady but with a giggly side.'

'I can't imagine her running around naked, I mean she's...what shall we say, slim.'

'I was surprised too and she asked me to keep it to myself?'

5. Sarah Lewis

Dave stayed in touch with Sarah and it was he who told her that Chris had died.

She was a star in her own field, had a completely new life so I was astonished when he told me that she wanted to come to the funeral.

I was even more surprised when she flew over and instead of staying in a big hotel she stayed with Dave.

He brought her to the service and though she had dressed down, habit and lifestyle gave her a hard glamour.

When I spoke to her and thanked her for coming she hugged me and said 'Poor darling'. Then, with more sensitivity than I would have believed she said 'It is a long time ago darling but he helped me at a critical point in my life and that made him special.'

Then she smiled. 'He did it out of kindness; in our profession you appreciate that.'

I was in a state but I managed to say 'thank-you, he could be kind.' 'You were a lucky girl.' She kissed my cheek and I saw there were tears in her eyes. 'I know he was no saint, what man is, but he knew that helping me through a bad time risked upsetting you.'

It was true. He owed her nothing and when I discovered he got her the gig with 'kR I was very angry. Much later I realised that her support took a lot of pressure off him.

'You need to be tough and selfish to have success,' she told me 'I never had the chance to be anything else but now I have some success I have the time and space to help and encourage others. You could say it's Chris' legacy.'

6. Thankyou Maurice.

When the band finished as professionals I did some session work.

I wasn't a proper session musician but my manager had contacts and I was lucky to get the chance to sing on several backing tracks.

On one session I met a girl who sang in a gospel choir and had a fabulous voice but she didn't do the squawky warbling that was fashionable so her voice was wasted doing backing vocals.

We hit it off and she asked me if I would like to join her that evening.

She still lived with her parents in a small terrace that was close to my Hotel.

I had no plans so I was delighted to join her. I caught a bus to the corner of her road, walked the hundred metres to the house and rang the bell. Her mother answered, smiled a welcome and asked me in. She seemed a bit reserved but was very friendly.

I had made an effort to look smart but when Nini came down she looked so glamourous that I felt like a country mouse. Her boyfriend arrived soon after with a friend (Oh yes?) who was rather good looking and I admit I thought 'hmmm' but that was all.

We went to a club; I really enjoyed the dancing, learnt something about cultures that weren't so different, felt very tired by the end of the evening and had just enough money to pay for a taxi.

7. Vickie

Vickie's phone call came at 9.30 in the evening. It was an unusual time for her to ring and the call left me feeling cross, partly because of the subject and also because V tried to shift the responsibility onto me. Since I have been widowed it is less easy to shrug off.

'Al, it's awful. I know it was a long time ago but you should have had more sense.'

This from my best friend who to my knowledge has sailed very close to the wind and has possibly made landfall and docked.
'What are you talking about?'
'Studland.'
'Studland? I haven't been there for twenty years, nearer thirty.'
'Neither have I but once was enough it seems.'
'Just explain.'
She did.
Clive had finished some work and had engaged in a little bit of surfing. V, with much hedging explained that he sometimes looked at the performances of Synergy and 'kR and a general search of Alison Smith had found my name on a site entitled Minor Celebs Unveiled.
As she said it I felt a twinge of irritation; my sole indiscretion in my film was common knowledge but for it to be displayed on a website probably with the shots that were clearly not me was annoying.
'So what is the problem?'
'Studland, I told you.'

I remembered that many years ago, we had gone to Studland.
It was a lovely day and a picnic on a beach was a great idea. Mum had come with us and had surprised me by saying 'Can I wear a bikini?' followed by 'I won't if you feel it is unsuitable.'
Vickie, *not me* said 'If you don't wear a bikini we won't.'
We took our tops off and when we went swimming there was a certain amount of giggling and V took her bikini bottoms off. I did the same but was surprised and embarrassed when Mum said "Could I join you?'
'Of course you can.'
Vickie is very naughty; she wouldn't say that to her mother.

The purpose of the call was to tell me that a pervert with a camera had recognised me and photographed us.
I could understand why she was annoyed but apart from being cross there was nothing I could do so I told V to ignore it.

'That's all very well but I'm not as blasé as you, you are used to that sort of thing.' (Nonsense.)

'I'll send you the link, then you'll see!!'

That evening when I dealt with the days emails I opened the link scrolled down through some garbage about nonentities and found a section entitled 'Beach fun with singer Al Smith and friends.'

I looked and realised why she was annoyed; as well as a still from my film there were several shots of us on the beach.

The first two had been taken from some distance; one an enlarged shot of a scarcely recognisable group, the second a fuzzy shot of three naked women walking back from the sea.

The single crisp shot must have been taken from a short distance.

It showed me standing with a towel around my waist combing my hair with mum facing me wearing bikini bottoms and drying her top. Vickie was between us facing the camera towelling her hair with everything on display.

No wonder she was cross. All the photos were unwelcome but V's was practically pornographic.

I had to smile.

CHAPTER 25

Random Jottings

Correcting a misleading article.

Justin had interviewed Gary when researching his article on our early lives. He showed me the illiterate scribble that resulted from his interview and allowed me to edit the cruder and more explicit original.

When we met I saw she was class; a bit on the skinny side but good-looking and clever. Some of my mates would have described her as a snotty tart but she was ok, looked you in the eye, didn't moan, cheat or score points.
She acted as if she was a virgin despite being screwed by the guy who ran the band; It didn't bother her he was married.
When the tosser dumped her I knew what she needed and it didn't take long to get her into bed.
She had a good body but when we got down to it she acted nervous though she must have done the business hundreds of times. Once she let go she loved it but afterwards the silly cow cried as if she had just lost her cherry. The sex got better when I taught her a few tricks and once she was randy she was happy to show off.
Pushing her up-market was a problem because she didn't realise that showing off her assets and giving the lads a treat was part of performance.
We made plans for a new band but she was a sodding tease; on, off, on, off so I decided to give her the business, either she would be

hooked or not. When it didn't work I dumped her.
I saw her later on television playing a tarty barmaid, I recognised the snotty tart but not the free and easy barmaid. I heard through the grapevine that she was considered to be a really nice girl. The grapevine hadn't heard her in action when she was randy.

To put the record straight, the beginning is correct; when my idiot soulmate broke with me I was shattered and I needed all the support I could get. Gary was a stranger, not unattractive and very supportive.

He began to install himself in my life and worked on my need to feel like an attractive woman.

His 'charm' was the sort that eases a girl into a corner and bullies her but I needed to punish Chris so I went along with it and we became lovers.

I'm not ashamed of the relationship, the sex was normal and I enjoyed it but suggestions that I did anything else are fantasy. Probably he was confusing me with one of his tarts.

Once when I was taking a shower he came into the bathroom with a camera partly concealed; I threw a towel over myself and told him to get out. I was sharp enough to realise that the results would be misused.

I did go along with his suggestion to try sexy clothes, partly to keep him on side, partly because I wanted to annoy Chris and I wasn't ready to go my own way. It was a limited concession; the so-called sexy undies were concealed under blouses and jeans and the see through tops and very short skirts were worn with all concealing bras and thick tights.

As to his other implications I can only say 'In your warped mind'. When he showed his real interest the worst of the hurt had gone and I was ready to go my own way.

If he had been civilised like Terry or Dave maybe something might have grown from the situation; he wasn't, it didn't and all I gained was a worthwhile life experience. We need to have experience of other men, even my virtuous friend V had a lover before Clive and possibly one since.

Gary was there at a time when Chris had behaved appallingly and the experience showed that I was missing very little sex-wise.

When, in tragic circumstances I was able to reunite with my soulmate everything I wanted came together and I was totally happy.

Perhaps middle class suited me. It isn't really a class, at least not at the lower end, just people with a philosophy that enables them to cope with life's problems.

Justin interviews Vince

Vince was still playing, still superficially hard, tattooed and unpleasant but it was a hardness gone to seed, an aggressiveness supported by a minder.

I wondered what he might have been without his Bass; a small time crook, an alcoholic? I didn't ask, there was a worrying unpredictability about him that implied drugs, a short fuse or both.

I asked what he remembered about Chris Phillips and was told 'Never #### heard of him.'

'king Rock?' Guitarist?' He thought insofar as he seemed capable of thought and after a measurable time the words 'Blonde wanker' came out.

'I'm writing an article...'

'Shouldn't take long, he was f### all.' Vince warmed to his theme. 'Middle class tosser pretending to be a rocker with a girlfriend who was a tight assed posher. Crew called her 'Dorothy'.

'What was he like musically?'

'Musically?? Yeah that sums him up, we were playing rock and he was playing the notes, I was living rock and he was drinking tea. There were girls around and he had a snotty tart with a zipper on her crack, well, one of them, the little blonde was alright, feisty, tough, knew what it was for.'

'You make him sound like a wimp.'

'He was a fu.... no, he wasn't a wimp, he wouldn't have lasted five minutes if he had been but he didn't have the edge, didn't live it. He was in because he could fake it, Christ, he even faked me for six months when I joined a better outfit.

'There must have been some ...'

Only good thing I remember is after a show Bruce had a video and caught him giving the blond one up against the wall, she was loving it and shouted 'piss off or get in line!!' That was before Dorothy arrived, if it had been Dorothy he'd have been looking for the key to the padlock on her zip.' Vince burst into loud guffaws at the thought then the craggy face collapsed.

'Nothing else to say...ang on, want a quote "Priss Phillips" he pursed his lips grotesquely "played tunes with a rock band". Ok? Right f### off.'

My respect for CP actually increased.

My older best friend.

My break up with Chris was brutal but even when I was most angry a small part of me knew I could never completely let go of him.

I had moments of panic because we were apart for a whole year and there was no sign that we would become friends again. During that time it was mum and Arwyn whose support and reassurance kept me going.

Arwyn told me 'You are a good person in a difficult place and unless you make the decision to let your problem go and move on you should try to regain your friendship.

I asked 'What is the point, there is no future, he is happily married?'.

Arwyn looked at me then in his silly way he held my ears and kissed my forehead.

'Susan' he said 'is a very pretty girl and she is still rather innocent. Her husband is away a lot and she will gain admirers.'

'I had admirers. Chris learned to cope.'

'You are speaking to one of your admirers. Susan is a fan of her husband; she likes the idea of the 'rockstar' but when he is away she will be lonely.'

'Yes, she told me that when Chris is away she often stays with her parents or her mum or a sister comes to stay with her.'

'But sometimes she is on her own, a lonely girl who will attract men and the more unscrupulous will try to charm her.'

'She did when we were touring but she never behaved badly except when she let a photo session get out of hand."

Arwen smiled again. 'Yes, David showed me the results. Listen now, I wish her no ill, she is a sweet girl who would be a happier girl if her circumstances were more ordinary and I suspect that she will begin to feel the same. Perhaps you might visit her on a day when you are not working. You are friends still?'

'Yes, it is a difficult friendship. I never blamed her...not completely. Part of it was my fault.'

He took me by the ears again and looked into my face.

'Nonsense, you were foolish; being over generous is a mistake.'

'The first time we met I felt that you were someone special. You were sensitive and kind, lovely and so innocent. I fell in love with a pretty girl on her best behaviour; thankfully I was wise enough to know that it could not be returned and settled for friendship.'

'The friendship isn't taken for granted. I don't really understand but it is very much appreciated. I make myself assume that you care like mum cares.'

'Not quite but I try to keep it well managed.'

I went to see Sue late on a Saturday morning; I pretended that I had a free day though I was gigging and staying near Solihull that evening. The visit was made more difficult for me because she was living in a house that was half mine.

Sue was pleased to see me and we settled into a chatty state that was almost like old times; old times but with a cancer of unhappiness festering somewhere in my unconscious.

We went to Thornbury for lunch taking Simon. The worst of

my discontent had been suppressed and we had a happy time (almost) talking about what I was doing on tour and how they were managing.

Since I left the band, Synergy had played only a few high-profile gigs and now, these had finished.

To earn some money Chris was standing in for the burnt-out lead guitarist of a 60's band that was still touring.

We finished our coffee and when we returned to the farm I was invited into *my* house and allowed to put Simon who was a darling down for his afternoon sleep.

The conversation had slowed, it was time to go and I was collecting my coat when the kitchen doorbell rang.

Sue hurried to the door and from the lobby I heard. 'Hello Graham, this is unexpected, two visitors on the same day.'

I heard a man's voice and when I entered the kitchen was introduced.

'Graham runs the Garden Centre, he sometimes brings plants and things that I have ordered' she said quickly. 'This is Alison, we used to be in a band together with Chris.'

'Hi Alison.'

'Hello.'

'I will get your plants Sue.' Graham went back out of the door and fetched a tray of tomato plants from his van giving a good impression of a man who came to deliver plants.

'Shall I leave them in the generator barn' he shouted.

'Yes please.'

He loaded the plants into the open end of the barn and returned to the van. He waved a small wave, got in, started the engine and drove off without giving any indication that he was expecting to stay.

I turned to Sue and explained that it was time to go. She was still looking at the van as it disappeared down the lane.

I was kissed. 'Yes of course, it's been lovely to see you.' She waved from the door as I drove out.

Probably it was what it appeared but she had called him Graham and Arwyn is a solicitor and good at predicting how people behave.

'Imagine' he told me 'that you are an unattached man. You meet a pretty married woman who is lonely; you check her out and your presence is appreciated because she needs company. If she is happily married or in love it is probable that nothing will happen; if she is unhappy, lonely or vulnerable, affection might grow and an affair might follow.'

Sue loved Chris, they had been married for less than 2 years; she was a little naïve but not stupid, she would know that in a village these things are soon common knowledge. You might get away with a one off but an affair would be suspected in a week and the details public property within two.

Four months later she died in a horrible and unnecessary accident and things like affairs seemed utterly trivial when faced with tragedy.

Alisons party (Chris' Story)

I had my moments of enthusiasm, sometimes I worked out the details of a new band to play exciting new music that I had dreamed the night before, sometimes it was completing a repair to our second-hand chicken shed, and sometimes I dreamed that I would be swept off my feet by someone gorgeous.

Alison's enthusiasms were usually of the chicken shed variety and more often reached fruition.

'I'm going to have a reunion' she told me 'with the girls.'

'Great, can I have some too.' I was in a hurry, not listening and offered a throw away remark.

'Don't be stupid.'

'Which ones?' This time my question made sense.

'The...my friends.'

'Youth club, school or band? If it's band it will be all men, you could do a survey, which one gave you the most stars.' I rose from the table quickly but she didn't bite.

'It will be mostly the girls from the youth club and some from school, especially Maggie and Claire and Dierdre, the twins. I'll ring Pauline and we can arrange it between us.'

'It's ten years since we were all together but I met a few at our fund-raising gig and I keep in touch with her and Jane and …'

'Is that the attractive one with the largish…'

'Yes…and Heather. Some of them will look older' she looked up 'not all of them will look as young and slim as me.'

Within two or three days the plans were in place, Al would hire a reception room in a pub on Saturday fortnight and put on a buffet.

'We can afford it Golden Phillocks; just the girls, not all my former lovers.'

'I forgot to say, Pauline rang yesterday. There are twenty-one confirmed and two more expected.'

The plans were thrown into some disarray because Al thought I was phoning the pub (why?) and when the call was finally made the pub the room was unavailable so it was decided to hold the event at home.

It wasn't a problem; caterers were supplying most of the buffet and my role was to provide hot drinks on arrival and to set up the food in the kitchen when it arrived.

I was unsure what other roles I had so I asked the question.

'Do you want me to go out after I have set up the food or am I needed to support you if you are asked to sing?'

The question caught her out and she began to stutter.

'I wasn't teasing. The answer is I will play if you want support.'

'I hadn't thought about it, I've been busy and anyway…don't be horrid.'

Five minutes later while I was checking the fridge she caught my arm. 'I don't want to be Al the singer, I want to be one of the girls.'

'I understand.'

'Should I do something? Would you mind?'

I thought for a moment. 'There is no obligation, if you are asked decide whether it is appropriate and if you need me, call me. I'll have the acoustics ready and we could do a couple of songs.
You'll only miss about 10 minutes of chat and you can say you didn't intend to sing…whatever.'
'Thanks. That will be lovely.'

I was in the kitchen when the girls arrived, mostly in ones or twos but one noisy group arrived in a minibus. It was left to me to welcome them and to interpret some glances.
'Are you Chris?'
'Yes, I'm Al's husband, come on in.'
'We saw you on TV.'
'Did you?'
One of the girls made a comment and her friend stifled laughter.
'Are you going to give a performance today?' More laughter, they had obviously seen the 'kR video.
'Maybe later.' I had a momentary urge to walk through the party naked but Al would never forgive me and I didn't have the nerve, not in that company.
Once they were installed, spread through the lounge with the door open to the dining room and straggling into the kitchen I left them and retired to the study.
It was about an hour later that Maggie was sent to fetch me. "Can you come, Al wants you."
'Chris' I was greeted, 'they want me to sing, could you set up something.'
'What do you want, just a couple of accoustics, a mic?'
'The minimum, it isn't a performance.'
'Ok, just the guitars and a couple of mics into the accoustic amp.?'
'Whatever.'
The guitars were in tune, I brought the mics and the amp into the room, and crawled around the floor to plug it in admiring several pairs of legs, a short skirt, and some splendid boosies that bent forward and asked if I needed help.

Al was waiting. 'Hurry up. They don't want to see you crawling around.'

'Any rudeness and you'll be playing without a star guitarist.'

She frowned.

'Don't be silly. He still has delusions of stardom.' She informed the room.

Huh; if anyone had delusions it wasn't me.

She played a chord. 'Soul friend?'

I played the intro and off we went.

The performance extended to three songs and some of the 'girls' were surprised to discover that we were good. All except the tone deaf enjoyed it. Al was happy and I imagined that a couple of her friends were showing an interest in me.

Al

Jane arrived late and stayed on after the others had left. There had been some coolness between us when we were teenagers but several years later we met again and discovered that we had a lot in common. Our conversation inevitably drifted back to youth club days and when we began to discuss some of the people who remained in the area, the subject turned to who had dated who and who had good and bad reputations.

I discovered that my reputation was 'skinny but probably a go-er'.

There were two older girls with steady boyfriends who we supposed were sexually active and a couple of girls who were thought to be available; these out of a core of twenty or so girls between fourteen and nineteen.

According to Jane almost half the girls were into sex (The list included me and Pauline of all people who was in a relationship with a local garage owner. It also included Susie, a pillar of the club who was engaged to one of it's leaders.

She, according to Jane, had been on a mission to eliminate virginity amongst the lads in the club. Oddly enough, the girl with the worst reputation for availability had been wrongly condemned because like me she went out with (and disappointed) a number of boys. I also discovered that one of my best friends preferred girls. At that age you are open-minded and discovering what suits you; bigotry is something for older people.

Chris could confirm that my reputation was undeserved which showed that the grapevine got it wrong.

CHAPTER 26

Epilogue

I keep busy during the day but the evenings can be lonely and I was glad when Mum came to live with me because I was alone in a house that was too big for me. I am often asked out by friends, I still see Phil occasionally and a friend from the folk band has taken me out several times; I still play tennis and there are the gigs and the folk music.

I had been dwelling on the past, remembering the good times when we were a family and the house was filled with children, their friends and ours. I had drifted into speculating on how my life might have been and how a few different words could have changed it completely.

When I left school I was intending to go to Uni and I had a place at Cardiff; I didn't go because I was in love with Chris and our band but

I was just a little bit envious because he had a degree. In fun I would call him Mr Know-all which was unkind because he never tried to be clever or superior but I suppose it was natural to be secretly pleased when he got things wrong.

When I told him about my offer of Cardiff he tried to be supportive but I could see that he was upset and later he admitted he was miserable because he knew he would lose me.
I told him he would never lose me but he was probably right, I

would have involved myself with people on the same path; with music and drama and the social scene.

I would have met someone I liked, become involved and the ongoing friendship would have become intimate.

Chris might have married Sue and they would have had a happy life, maybe they would have created a semi-pro band that was quite successful.

How tiny events and words can change your life.

What would have happened to me? I would have lost Chris and perhaps his memory would have stayed with me as my lost love. I would have had a great experience at Uni but then what?

A different me would have joined the generation who believed that sexual morals were outdated simply because science had made pregnancy unnecessary.

Perhaps I would have become a teacher who marries or lives with another teacher? Children would have arrived but with a dull marriage and a dull job would either have lasted?

I am being hard on myself but Mum told me that Chris was right for me because I wanted safe excitement. I denied it saying that Chris wasn't especially exciting; he wasn't most of the time but he could be fun and our early life together gave me all the excitement I could handle.

Synergy was an eye opener for a schoolgirl with a comfortable and protected homelife. And sometimes it was scary though the boys did their best to look after me.

My time with my own band and with 'kR were periods of stress but with the latter we enjoyed the status of minor (very) celebrity, we were looked after and the music was exciting.

The 'kR experience allowed us to create a really good professional band that gave us a lot of enjoyment and the exposure led to my acting career.

Would I have settled for a more ordinary life? I did, Synergy lasted three years, Cats Whiskers a stressful one, 'king Rock just over a year and KR eighteen months as a professional outfit. My acting career spanned three years but much of that was spent 'resting'.

Most of our exciting time was busy with the normal activities of life on the road; travel, washing, ironing, eating. Only the performance with its nervous excitement and audience approval was satisfying. The rest, if unexciting was mostly enjoyable and there were many happy moments.

I remember one of those moments with 'kR; the concert the previous night had been great and afterwards I drank too much which was very rare.
I had a headache next morning and was feeling bad tempered.
I showered and dressed and was washing out a couple of pairs of knicks when Chris knocked.
I let him in and said 'What do you want? Make yourself useful, make me a cuppa!'
He said 'Good Morning Treasure' and I went back to the bathroom.
I had finished the washing, wrung out the nicks and was hanging them on the showerhead when a cup of tea was placed beside me. Chris put his hands on my shoulders, kissed my cheek and said 'Isn't it great being a star.'
All the grumpies went and I just giggled and gave him a big hug.

He was wearing a T-shirt that said "How many Guitars does a man need?" and underneath was "Just One More."
I pointed to the shirt and said 'only one more?'
He smiled and said 'It's fun, it isn't true, nothing will ever match the joy of getting my first Strat and the same probably applies to partners, performances and all of life's activities. "One more" is marketing bullshit.'
Bless him, I agreed but I wish he wouldn't analyse things. It doesn't happen too often so I ignored it.

We suited one another and except when he had problems with the band or his business he was the guy I loved.

I wasn't the impossibly lovely person' that Phil joked about but I did my best and our marriage worked.

I have had more happiness than I deserve and my 'just one more' would have been another ten years with Chrissie. He let me be me, let me develop in my own way and only asked for fairness.

Turning sixty was waypoint and I finally accepted that I was old. Hard to believe that I was so much older than 'old' people were when I was young.

When I met Chris, people in their twenties were 'older', those in their forties were old and people over fifty didn't exist.

I don't feel old and I still feel part of life even though I realise that my world and my references are slowly disappearing.

It is hard to accept that the new is better, so many real freedoms have been exchanged for fantasy freedoms, so much empowerment for legal rights.

Philips darling, the legacy you have passed on to me is your tendency to analyse.

Mum came to live with me. After her heart scare several years ago. I felt that she should not be on her own and I made the offer but I know she has a life so I left her to make her own decision. She is quite fit and has made friends with people in the community including the most eligible widower.

She was disappointed and a little upset when Colin stayed in Canada. He went to support his ex-wife who was seriously ill; she recovered, but remained fragile; his support role became a habit and the move permanent.

Mum was comfortable in her modern flat but had reached the age when having someone close as a companion was desirable. She was reluctant to move but once the deed was done, settled in quickly telling me that the house brought wonderful memories. Lisa lives just down the road and Sarah is only a few miles away so my grandchildren often visit.

My young sister provided me with two nieces and is firmly settled with her partner, a second-generation migrant who is best described as English of Iranian origin.

Phil and I retain our friendship and we go out together sometimes but we never became an item.

I value my independence and the brief period when I enjoyed the excitement of an uncommitted relationship seems to have got the need out of my system. If Stuart had been fifty, keen and committed a serious relationship might have developed but he wasn't and it didn't. My few months of uncomplicated fun were a watershed, largely forgotten, sometimes revisited with a thrill and a blush.

There has only been one disaster though it was an accident waiting to happen. As a widow the only constraints on my behaviour are those I impose on myself; my sole affair was brief and discreet and my other activities have been ordinary fun like my holiday with Vick and the folk music.

Several years ago Vickie met a younger man, Clive had been concerned but she had assured him that it was no more than friendship and she hadn't realised how foolish she looked. The situation was forgotten but visits to clubs were curtailed.

We missed the dancing and we joined a 'le roc' club where most people were friendly but a few saw us as 'fresh meat' or rivals.

It was here that Vickie attracted someone not unlike Stuart. My judgement was that he was fine as a dance partner on a casual date but was untrustworthy and best kept at a distance.

This time she behaved stupidly once too often.

Clive, away on business for several days had left early after a meeting was cancelled. Arriving home late he had quietly crept into the house to find his wife in bed with her new friend. I didn't know or want to know the whole of the angry and apparently violent situation except that the following day Clive walked out.

I was as upset as Vickie and spent much of the next week consoling her. She put on her sensible head, conceded that she had behaved appallingly, was ashamed and determined to build bridges.

Her determination lasted until she realised that the break was permanent. Clive, deciding that 'two can play that game' had taken comfort with a divorcee ten years his junior.

I visited him prepared to mediate assuming that his new love would be temporary, would have baggage and was making use of him.

It didn't happen; she turned out to be a quiet lady, the injured party in a highly unsatisfactory marriage and there had been a token romance at work for several years. Well well!

Clive was happy with his change of life.

Vickie on the other hand was devastated; the break was less destructive than it would have been ten years earlier but was socially and emotionally hard on her. It was several months before she recovered sufficiently to be able to put on a 'see if I care' face.

At 57 she remained trim and attractive by the standards of her contemporaries and was essentially a kind and relatively unspoiled person. After a few months of virtuous grief she felt able to demonstrate to Clive what he had lost.

With my support she investigated the singles market discovering that she was just one of the cattle in the market and that many buyers wanted a full inspection and probably a trial run before failing to commit.

She had several introductory dates and reported back that what was promised was not what you got. The fifty-two-year-old Building Contractor was a sixty year old plasterer. 'He did try hard and was rather nice' I was told 'but not remotely interesting.'

Her third date she told me was 'not too bad', had shown serious interest and they were to meet again.

It was the second encounter that brought her down to earth. Her report spared me most of the details but confirmed that she was unprepared for a partner who supposed that 'dating' meant an evening of dubious self-promotion followed by loveless sex.

'It wasn't that bad; he was fairly smart and I enjoyed the interest but I didn't have any feeling for him. I suppose if he had been interesting I might have considered sex eventually, but he seemed to assume I was available.'

'Really?' I shook my head.

'Are we the odd ones? He supposed it was normal.'

'I suppose that media propaganda has finally convinced people that loveless sex is normal which it is amongst the people in the media.'

'Which means?'

'Chris said it was about fragmenting...never mind.'

'I can't see why any sensible woman would accept ten minutes of sexual pleasure as a substitute for love.'

'I think Al' she gave me a look 'that we fool ourselves into believing it is love. As you know well.'

'I never......I took a deep breath. 'Yes, getting involved with Tony of all people so soon after Chris died was an act of desperation. I did learn a lesson. There are a lot of decent men around.'

She couldn't resist saying 'Yes, I've been out with him but he is still keen on you. If you aren't serious I might see him more often.'

'Feel free.'

I am so stupid.

She decided to be more cautious and my separated best friend began to date my best man friend.

Thank goodness for the stability of my beliefs and the family. Lisa has begun to attend church using the grandchildren as an excuse because she is worried that they are being formed by a godless society that promises everything and delivers nothing. These days it seems that the only purpose of life is 'not to die.' *Shut up Phillips!!!*

There have been a few more surprises; mostly sad old 'sex'.

It is strange how when you are older you can talk about things that would once have been impossible.

I was talking with mum about morality and saying that Chris

was my only one and mum said 'I seem to remember Gary and Tony, I don't know about any others?'

I told her that I never treated sex as a five-minute pleasure and that she knew that Gary was forced on me by a bad situation.

I always considered sex as part of a loving relationship, not a brief thrill forgotten ten minutes later; if that was all the excitement people got out of it I felt sad for them.

'I suppose the older generation, the holier than thou older generation' I added 'was never tempted.'

'Of course I was tempted, it seems strange to you but I was thought to be attractive.'

'It doesn't seem strange, Chris thought the world of you, several of our friends said how young you looked and Dave...well the less said the better. Was the temptation ever too much?'

'Your father was my only one really' and after a minute 'just once, well, I had a.... it was a few wonderful weeks I had a passionate affair'.

My mouth fell open. 'Bruce?'

'No that was friendship.'

Mum of all people was admitting that she had an affair.

Her voice changed as she remembered. 'I admired Bruce and I think he genuinely liked me but I was afraid that if I became involved I would let go completely and my marriage and friendships and everything would be sacrificed.'

'Oh mum, I never knew it was that serious.'

'It wasn't. I liked him but if I had taken the job he offered we would have worked closely together and I might have capitulated.'

'So it was serious.'

'I made my decision before your big party. I would accept the job only if it was part time so that I was home most of the time.'

'I remember the party, Chris hit someone who was getting too friendly with me and if I remember correctly you were wearing a dress that showed rather a lot of what Bruce was interested in.'

'Don't be silly.'

'Chris was impressed and' I continued giving her a meaningful look 'when we all went to our rooms at the end of the evening you were tiddly and when we got out of the lift you fell against him and revealed precisely what was on offer. I was very embarrassed.'

'I do remember that I felt quite glamorous, it was probably the most exciting night of my life; several men showed an interest, and there was the possibility of a job with the band though I felt a little guilty about being disingenuous.'

'No guilt about your other failing.'

'What other failings?'

'I think a few others have admired my virtuous parent?'

'I would rather not continue this conversation, we have both said too much. When you are older and a widow the situation is different. Apart from your dad there were only my few weeks of passion.'

I was surprised that we were so alike with only one serious lover throughout our life but I was a little shaken that my mum had an affair even though she claimed it was brief.

It isn't the sort of conversation we had so I took the opportunity to ask about the photo I had found with Chris things.

She blushed and after a lot of self-justfication told me that it happened when she came with Sarah to help my darling husband.

She had been talking about me and he had said that we were alike in looks and character and that a photo similar to one of me would prove the point.

That evening they both had a few drinks and when they said goodnight she had gone upstairs, showered and changed for bed. Chris was still clearing up and feeling bold she had gone downstairs in her nightie and said 'Is this suitable for your photo?'

He told her that she looked lovely but he only wanted a portrait like the one of me.'

He fetched the camera and took a photo, just head and shoulders, and said that when it was developed they could compare the two.

'I was feeling naughty and posed in a sort of silly glamourous way saying 'Would this be better?'

He gave me a disapproving look and said 'Go on then' and took another photo then shook his head and said 'Off you go, photographing lovely ladies wearing nighties is bad for me.'

'I was feeling silly, so I deliberately misunderstood his comment and as he turned away, I took off the nightie and posed again saying 'Is this better?'

'I can't tell you what he said, but he took a photo of me and then he told me to dress quickly because 'he was only human'.

'I strolled out pretending to be casual then ran upstairs.'

We laughed about the situation next day and when I saw the prints I was pleased that I looked rather good (she looked wonderful) and very embarrassed.

In a way I was pleased. Mum had holidayed with us a couple of times and had been shy about wearing bikinis; my husband had been reassuring and told her to decide for herself.

In the same situation the photo would have been fun, not sordid. Thinking about it later I did feel a little deceived but it didn't make me anxious.

Endings:

I suppose that life does end very simply, petering out with a slow diminution of activity.

The decline happens partly through loss of physical energy but also because of cultural change and the loss of the friends that gave shape and substance to your life.

Bruce's death and the trauma that went with it was stressful but youthful resilience allowed it to be quickly forgotten.

Terry dying was the first time I became really conscious of mortality; we were close friends like brother and sister and my small involvement at the end was heartbreaking. His death left me feeling helpless and no longer in control.

The next to really affect me was Arwen. Dave phoned Chris who broke it to me.

"I'm afraid I've got some bad news luv, Dave rang, it's Arwen…he has been ill for a while…I'm afraid he has died."

I wasn't listening, Arwen had been my rock in my bad time and it didn't seem possible; I cried on and off for a week.

Perhaps it was a rehearsal because dad died two years later; Knowing he was ill helped in coping with the grief but the death was a horrible shock. I was devastated and it took a long time to recover.

I think about endings. I probably have 20 maybe 25 years of life but I will slowly lose friends and family and my world will change. I have thought about faith and how it is easy and comfortable when you have youth, a future and a comfortable God in the background.

I believe I have reconciled God with the reality of age and inevitably death. I hope so, the God I now recognise is more than invisible father figure, God is the power that makes everything work in the way it does.

It is a harder concept, less personal but more realistic. You could say that God is the name we give to 'The power behind the working of the universe' personal because we can communicate with God through the holy spirit.

Do I get anxious or embarrassed about the past? Not really, there were embarrassing moments but we dealt with them.

My topless moment in a film was annoying because I felt pressured and because it affected the family and relationships. Mostly I avoided exploitation and my reputation was based on the person I was.

There were times when I had to fight my corner, be assertive and push myself but I treated other people with respect and didn't misbehave.

I could lose my temper when pressurised or assaulted (which doesn't mean a friendly fondle). The real thing didn't happen often; the first when a frightened seventeen year old had to fight her way out of a car, the worst when my best right cross gave a druggy rocker a nose bleed to emphasise 'No!'

No-one is perfect and my failings which could have been numerous were minimal: one relationship to hurt Chris because I was angry, another after he died when I was emotionally unbalanced, and one as a widow that helped me to turn a corner in my life.

I am still fit and trim and my only concession to age is intermittent back pain, some greying (easily dealt with) and the tinted varifocals. I used contacts for ten years but finally got fed up with the discomfort when removing them.

That's it, I have a future but it is mostly the same as the past, my business, music, church, exercise and family and friends.

There was one other false start; a new man at the folk session. He was about my age, played mandolin and sat next to Caitlin who monopolised him.

I didn't really talk to him until our paths crossed at a pub session. We met at the bar where he gave a shy smile and said hello.

I said 'Hi we haven't met but I have seen you around.'

'Mm, yes.'

'I'm Alison.'

'Yes. Caitlin told me your name when I first came. I'm Chris.'

'Something went thump 'Hi Chris. My husband's name was Chris, he died several years ago, I haven't really got over it, I mean I have but things can still upset me.'

He backed away slightly from the stranger who was babbling.

'I'm sorry, I don't know why I said that.'

'It's ok, my wife died and I felt all sorts of things. I'm not very good at dealing with emotions, you know how it is.'

'I should know but knowing doesn't always help. I mean, when I was young our lifestyle should have made me strong but I faked most of it, I still do.'

'I always have, I am cursed by shyness but it gets easier to overcome when you are older.'

'Yes,' I smiled. 'Sorry, what a strange first meeting.'

He was looking at me, a serious but kind face, nervous perhaps? He had lost his wife and I hadn't even acknowledged.

'I'm sorry to hear you lost someone close, we have a common sorrow.'

'Yes.' He bit his lip and reminded me of my Chris.

I picked up my drink. 'Shall we sit, I bought a drink for Marion, I must take it to her.' I rushed the drink to her and saw that he was handing one to Catlin. He turned, looked uncertain and I dived into the nearest seat and indicated that he should join me. He hesitated then sat down.

He was a little shy but as we talked I discovered someone with a delightful oblique view on the world, caring supportive and broad without being fooled by cant or righteousness.

We only talked for fifteen minutes but when we stood up to return to our seats he looked into my eyes and smiled and I tapped his arm and said 'See you again?'

It was when I was walking home that I realised that something that I knew was never going to happen had happened. Phillip was a good friend, Stu was a rite of passage. I didn't know Chris full name but I was in love and I had no idea what to do.

I decided to be positive and when at our next meeting we engaged in a friendly conversation I asked him to dinner. He looked a little puzzled then said 'thank-you, that would be fine.'

We consulted our phones and the following Saturday was agreed. After a fraught shop I summoned up my best cooking skills to prepare one of my more successful recipes.

I am rushing my diary; normally I try to be measured and selective but I was being swept along on an exhilarating flood of confusion.

On Saturday when the food was prepared and ready for cooking I went upstairs to choose my most suitable clothes. I had showered, admired the trim, quite firm hmmphty-year old self and was deciding on make-up when the phone rang.

I threw on a dressing gown and picked up the bedside receiver. It was Chris and a small thrill of excitement ran through me.

We exchanged pleasantries and he got to the point. 'I didn't ask, I assumed the invite included a partner, is that alright?'
The little thump under the heart, a huge blush, thankfully invisible to Chris and in as casual voice as I can manage 'Yes, of course, I look forward to seeing you. Seven for seven thirty?'
'Yes, that will be good.'
The excitement has gone from my evening and I am empty but I recover, the tears will come later with the anger that I could be so foolish; probably I will feel old and ridiculous.
I look at the too short skirt and the pretty blouse hanging on the chairback, snatch at them, hurl them into the corner and sit there miserable and humiliated.
Five minutes and I realise that I have only humiliated myself. Think, think, damn, Phillip is out with Vickie tonight. Clive?
I ring him and he answers. 'Clive, I have a problem.' I explain, he is free he understands. 'On my own tonight, can't think of anything nicer than joining my favourite girl.'
'Thank-you so much Clive, I feel very stupid.'
'No need love, wear your glam and make sure that photo of you performing with 'kR is prominent.'

Sandra, his partner was a few years younger than me pleasant but nothing special otherwise the evening could have been an awful downer.
Clive was wonderful, welcomed them as the expected couple and treated me as his glamorous partner for the whole evening.
Upset became contentment especially when I casually explained the photo.
Chris was surprised 'I had no idea you were a professional.
My modest reply 'A singer most of the time with Synergy and then 'king Rock; you may have heard of them.'
He runs through the frown, think, remember and look surprised process.
'Yes. You were..?'
'A backing singer, but in my band Cats Whiskers and in Sextet I am the singer guitarist.

'Perhaps Chris would like to see one of your performances.' Clive times it perfectly.

'No, no, it's a long time ago.'

I was persuaded, the appropriate SD card found, the best ten minutes of the 'kR concert shown and I watched again my moment of greatest happiness fighting back sadness.

Chris looked uncertain, said 'I didn't realise' and became almost respectful. His partner looked a little uncomfortable.

Contentment was restored.

Before he left Clive thanked me for the meal, hugged me, said I looked as lovely as ever and that he wished he was staying the night.

Being appreciated is important and momentarily I wish .....but if I did so many links would become difficult.

Chris phoned next day to thank me for the meal. The conversation was extended and during it I discovered that the lady friend wasn't actually his partner, they didn't live together, she was a friend that he sometimes asked out.

'I thought you were just inviting me then I realised that you would surely have a partner so I decided to ask Sandra then I had to ring you at the last minute in case it caused a problem.

'No problem' I told him 'Clive is a good friend who helps me make up numbers if he is free. He does have a partner' I added. 'See you at the folk club.'

'Yes, great. I look forward to it.'

I feel that little flutter. No...I wonder...no, no.

End of book 4

Printed in Dunstable, United Kingdom